HOW WE PLAY THE GAME IN SALT LAKE

and

Other Stories

How We Play the Game in Salt Lake

and

Other Stories

M. Shayne Bell

Copyright information continued on page 299.

For information address iPublish.com, 135 West 50th Street, New York, NY 10020.

🅦 A Time Warner Company

ISBN 0-7595-5006-9

First edition: May 2001

Visit our website at www.iPublish.com

To my brother Bryant
For all the years gone by, for all the years to come

CONTENTS

CONTENTS

MRS. LINCOLN'S CHINA

So I stayed in the crowd across the street from the east gates to the White House. My son Cyril, he'd said to me, "Mama, I know how bad you want a cup of Mrs. Lincoln's to drink your coffee from, but stay back from those gates. If you're pressed up next to them, you're liable to get crushed before they give way. You don't have to be the first one in the White House to get a cup. You just come along when you can."

I figured there was some truth to his words. Three years before, my daughter Lydia Ann, who was just sixteen years old at the time, went early to some rock concert because the seating was open and she wanted to sit up close. She liked the drummer, and if you sit up close and take binoculars you can see everything there is to see about a man sitting onstage in front of you, down to the kind of socks he's wearing, but a crowd formed up behind her and started shoving forward and

I

my Lydia Ann thought she was going to suffocate in the press of people before security opened the gates, and even then six people got trampled to death when everybody rushed forward, so I looked at the crowd outside the White House gates and thought to myself, Georgia May, you want a cup of Mrs. Lincoln's because you love her husband and a cup of theirs would make you remember all the good he did, but there's no sense in risking your life, even for a cup President Lincoln might have drank coffee out of, so I took my Cyril's advice and hung back.

Besides, I figured I had the advantage over most folks in that crowd: Most of them had come just to take whatever they could get because they'd gone without for so long, and to maybe in the process scare the folks in power into running this country like it was meant to be a place where people could live a decent life. But me, I was going in with a plan. I knew just what I wanted to take from the White House. I'd toured the White House two years before and seen the China Room, and I'd looked and looked at Mrs. Lincoln's china and thought how she and the president I loved had eaten off those dishes, and when I started to see how things were going to go in this city and what was likely to take place with or without my blessing, I made up my mind to be in the crowd that would sweep into the White House and pick it clean, but I'd go there looking for one thing: a cup from Mrs. Lincoln's china—oh that, and maybe the saucer to go with it and a plate or two if I could get them, which explains the two sacks I'd brought along to carry the dishes in and the old dish towels I'd brought to wrap them in to keep them from chipping, but I would have truly settled for just one coffee cup.

It was a hot late-August day, and about noon the crowd quieted down. It was hard to keep up the yelling and screaming when you were so hot you could hardly stand it and sweat was making wet tracks down the front and back of your blouse and all you could think of was how you wanted a cold drink of some kind, maybe a Coke with lots of ice.

Some people tried to keep up the screaming and meant to rouse the rest of us to it, but it wasn't working. Only a few people yelled along with them, and I certainly didn't, not then. I started to wonder if we'd get in the White House at all or if we'd give up in that heat and go home, then try again in the evening or later at night, but I hoped we wouldn't have to rush the White House at night, because I didn't want to rush it in the dark. Storming a place like the White House seemed scary enough without adding darkness on top of it, when suddenly the marines guarding the gates just walked away and disappeared inside the East Wing. Everybody in the crowd was trying to see what was happening, standing on tiptoes and looking, and suddenly it made sense to me: they were giving up. They were opening the place up to us without bloodshed. We were going to get in the White House after all, and in the broad daylight. The president and everybody inside were probably gone already, out tunnels in the basement, whisked off to Camp David or who cares where.

The gates were locked, so people started climbing over the gates and the fence and walking a little warily up to the White House, almost like they were going to buy tickets and take a tour. Two nice young girls gave me a hand up to the top of the fence, and we all three jumped down together onto the grass on the other side and made our way up the lawn toward the doors of the East Wing lobby. The doors were swung wide when I got to them and shoved my way inside, but some folks were already trying to shove their way outside, their arms full of figurines and paintings and the like, no dishes yet. I saw a lot of people just standing around looking at the rooms and the things in them and at each other, amazed that we were inside like this and that nobody was trying to stop us.

For a minute, it seemed as if the spirit of the place settled over us: here we were in the mansion where the great and powerful presidents of this land had lived, some of them good people, and it didn't seem right, somehow, to just tear into the place and start taking things or breaking them right away. But somebody outside threw a rock and busted out one of the front windows, and somebody inside started yanking down the drapes, and I knew the craziness was starting. I made a beeline for the China Room.

And who should I find standing in the doorway but my own son Cyril.

"What kept you, Mama?" he asked.

I was about to explain the fence I'd climbed, which I didn't find as easy a thing to do as I used to, when he grinned at me and held up a cup of Mrs. Lincoln's white china with a gold edge around the top and a purple border below and the eagle that represented this country. The cup looked so regal, yet fragile, in Cyril's hand, while the breaking and the shouting grew and grew all around us. Cyril put the cup in my hands. It felt cool and clean. It wasn't dusty at all. Someone had taken good care of this cup.

"I want a saucer, too," I said, while I wrapped the cup in a dish towel and put it in my sack. "Wasn't there one with it?"

Cyril stepped back so I could walk past him into the room, which was empty of people. Cyril's friends, Randy Lewis and Vincent Henry, were standing in the other doorway, and they grinned at me—they were holding back all the people to give me first chance at what I wanted.

"We can't hold back these people long, Mama," Cyril said. "You've got to hurry."

So hurry I did. I went straight to the Lincoln china on display in its china cabinet. I knew right where it was. All the china was displayed in order of the presidents, starting at the right of the fireplace with pieces from the Washingtons' personal china and stretching around the room to a place setting from the present president's set. In the spot for the Lincolns' china was a display of just eleven pieces from Mrs. Lincoln's first set, including the saucer that went with my cup. Most of the 175 pieces of Lincoln china left were kept up in the president's private quarters or down in a basement storage area which I wouldn't have time to find. I opened the cabinet door, took out the saucer, wrapped it quick, and put it in my sack.

That's when the lights went out. It being the middle of the day, plenty of light still came in from the windows, but the riot was clearly getting worse. I started wrapping and packing as quick as I could: a dinner plate, an ice cream plate, a teacup and saucer. I'd pretty well finished wrapping the Lincoln display— water mug, three fruit baskets, custard cup and everything— when the shooting started, away off by the East Wing lobby. Cyril ran up and took my arm. "You've got to go, Mama," he said.

People had rushed into the China Room once Cyril left the doorway, and they started smashing the dishes in the cabinets and tearing at the paintings on the walls and breaking out the windows. I grabbed up a few more dishes and shoved them in my sack. I decided to chance the chipping, since I didn't have time to wrap them. It wasn't safe to stay here any longer. Cyril took my other sack and ran around the room shoving dishes into it, I didn't know then from what services, and he came back and pulled me toward the door. I kicked the cabinet door shut behind me on the off chance of saving what we left behind.

The crowd was going wild, breaking and tearing at anything they could. "Stop it!" I wanted to shout. "These are good dishes—take them home and use them." But nobody would have listened—nobody could have heard me in that noise. Some fat man tried to kick my sack of china, but I swung it out of the way, and Cyril punched the man's face.

"Come on, Mama!" Cyril shouted.

"I'm coming!" I shouted back.

But I couldn't help it. On the way out of the China Room I picked up an unbroken bowl thrown down on the rug and two wine goblets from I didn't know which services and stuffed them in my sack. Cyril helped me out of the White House through a back door and across the lawn to the fence, which surprised me. I thought he'd spend all his time in the White House having the fun he'd come to have with his friends. But he helped me over the fence, then handed me my sack of Lincoln china and his sack of odds and ends. I ran off down the street toward my apartment, and he ran off back toward the White House. I didn't see Cyril again for three days.

• • •

I lugged my china home and got it up the dark stairs to my door. The lights were out in the stairwell. I still managed to get my key out of my pocket in the front of my skirt and open the door by feel without having to set down the china and chance chipping it anymore. I carried the sacks into the bedroom and carefully set them down on the bed. Then I opened the drapes to let in the sunlight and looked out the window.

There were fires everywhere in the city, and smoke rising up from one point of the horizon to the other, not to mention the shooting and the deeper sound of what must have been cannons over by Annapolis. Seeing and hearing all that made me sick at heart. I started to wonder, what if they come to burn the building I live in? I thought maybe I shouldn't unpack the china in my sacks. If I had to run, I could pick up those sacks and run with them.

So I spent the evening getting ready to run. I locked the doors to keep people out till I was ready to go. Then I tried to call Lydia Ann, but the phones were dead. So I wrapped the Lincoln china I hadn't had time to wrap, this time in my good dishtowels, and when I ran out of those in my good pillowcases, which I'd want to take if I had to abandon everything else. I didn't bother with Cyril's sack of odds-and-ends china because I didn't even know what was in there and I wasn't sure I had time. Once I'd squared away the Lincoln china and packed up some food and an extra change of clothes and took out the money I'd hid behind the fridge and stuffed it into the box of Shredded Wheat cereal I planned to take, I sat by the window in the bedroom and watched and listened to the riot and worried about Lydia Ann and Cyril.

When night came, the city was lit up by fire. The shooting never stopped till three in the morning, when it stopped all of a sudden for about twenty minutes, all over the city. I stood by the window then, looking out and wondering if the craziness was over so soon, but of course it wasn't. It started up again. I sat by my bedroom window all the rest of that night and into the morning, watching.

• • •

By noon, since I hadn't had to run yet, I figured I might not have to. So I pulled all the drapes and dragged chairs in front of the door to block it and took a nap on the couch. I didn't want to move the china unless I had to, considering the pieces I hadn't wrapped in the second sack and the chipping I'd cause, so I left it all on the bed.

When I woke up, it was dark. I tried the lights, but the power was still off. I felt my way into the black kitchen and pulled matches out of a drawer and lit a candle. I tried the phone to call Lydia Ann again and Cyril, but the phone was still dead. I tried to cook some supper, but the water was off, so I just made sandwiches out of the cheese and tomatoes in the fridge before they spoiled and drank some of the water I had left in a pitcher. Then I carried my candle into the bedroom so I could take a look at the china in Cyril's sack of odds and ends and wrap it.

I reached in and pulled out a plate with a blue border and gold stems of wheat painted in that border. The American eagle was pictured in the white middle of the plate. I didn't know which president and his wife had had such a plate. I reached in and pulled out a dessert plate that had a pretty white flower in the middle. The back of the plate said "Syringa," and below that "Idaho." I figured the syringa must have been Idaho's state flower, but I didn't know which president's wife had ordered this plate either. I pulled out the two crystal wine goblets that were the last things I'd taken. They were simple in design, but lovely.

I took the candle and went after the Margaret Brown Klapthor book *Official White House China: 1789 to the Present* which I'd bought after the White House tour I'd taken two years before and carried the book into the bedroom. I put the candle on the nightstand and knelt by the bed and started leafing through the book looking for pictures of china that matched the china and goblets I had on my bed.

The plate with gold wheat and the blue border turned out to be President Harrison's. Mrs. Caroline Harrison had painted the wheat herself, the guidebook said, back in the days when women did that sort of thing. I picked up the plate and looked at it again. The wheat was beautifully painted, and I realized that Caroline Harrison had been a real artist. Her work looked professionally done to me.

The plate with the flower in the middle was the Johnsons'. The guidebook said Lady Bird had ordered a service of china that pictured wildflowers, not the state flowers, of all fifty states and D.C. People used to go on tours hoping to see the wildflower from their state on display in a place setting from Lady Bird's china. I pulled two more plates from that service out of Cyril's sack. They pictured the California poppy and the Oregon grape, which meant I'd ended up with plates of the western states. I wished Cyril had picked out the plate with D.C.'s flower on it. I didn't even know D.C. had an official flower, let alone a wildflower. Maybe they'd used the dandelion or some other weed that grew up between cracks in sidewalks.

I started looking to see if I could match a picture to the wine goblets, when there was a burst of gunfire just up the street from my building. I blew out the candle and didn't move in the sudden darkness. I heard shouting and more firing, then running in the alleyway below my window. I was glad I'd pulled the drapes so no one could have seen my light before it was gone altogether. I knelt there next to my bed and smelled the smoke from the candle and listened to the shouting and the shots and thought of my Cyril and Lydia Ann, wondering what was happening to them. When things had quieted down outside, I reached out and touched the smooth china of one of the Johnsons' dessert plates: the people who'd ordered these plates were the people who'd dreamed of a great society. It hadn't lasted long. It hadn't even been many years before the ugly billboards Mrs. Johnson had had torn down all over the country were put back up and you couldn't walk down a street or take a bus ride anywhere without having gaudy billboards scream at you to buy this or that bit of nonsense. It was all tacky and cheap. Tacky and cheap was what too many people tried to make all of our lives and the world around us. But Mrs. Johnson had tried to fight that trend, and she and her husband had dreamed dreams, and worked as if they could make a difference in the world, and ordered china with delicate wildflowers on them. It had been a time when grace and beauty stood a chance.

• • •

Over the next two days, I cataloged the china I'd taken: of the Lincoln china, 1 dinner plate, 1 custard cup, 1 fish platter, 1 regular platter, 1 water jug, 1 ice cream plate, 3 fruit baskets, a teacup and saucer, and a coffee cup and saucer; of the Johnson china, 1 plate, 3 dessert plates; of the Harrison china, 1 plate, one coffee cup and saucer; and in addition, 2 Kennedy wine goblets and 1 Hayes soup bowl with a crab painted on it. I wrapped everything in my best pillowcases and dishtowels and kept them in sacks at the foot of my bed, ready for me to pick up and run with if I had to. I also wrapped two green Depression-glass plates of my mother's and put them in the sacks. I'd want them, too, if I had to leave everything else.

• • •

Three days after we'd stormed the White House, Cyril came knocking on my door. I recognized his voice, of course, so I dared drag away the chairs and unlock the door, and there stood Cyril with sacks of food in his arms.

"I thought you might be needing a few things, Mama," he said.

I hugged him and cried a little, and asked him if he'd seen or heard from Lydia Ann, which he hadn't. I'd already decided I had to go and find her and help her if she needed it, but I decided to tell Cyril about that decision a little later. I asked him to tell me where he'd gotten the food, but he wouldn't say much about that. I made him stay while I cooked supper for us both. The gas was still on, and I'd dipped out all the clean water from the toilet reservoir, so I had water to boil with and drink. Cyril had brought me potatoes and a canned ham and all kinds of other canned things, soups and green peas, and even a jar of instant Taster's Choice coffee. I put the ham in the oven to heat through and set the potatoes to boil and decided to set the table with the Lincoln china.

I brought out my nicest white tablecloth and spread it over the table. The tablecloth had been my mama's, and it was way too big for any table I'd ever had, but I thought it was the tablecloth I should use with the Lincoln china. It hung down low, nearly to the floor, but it looked fine even so. I set the lit candle in the middle of the table. Then I unwrapped the Lincoln dinner plate for me and the fish platter for Cyril and set them out. They looked so pretty on my table, the dark purple of the border set off by my white tablecloth. The candlelight glistened off the china. I could imagine the president and Mrs. Lincoln hosting a state dinner, maybe for the ambassador from Japan who would have come dressed in a kimono for men or whatever it was men wore in Japan back then, and all of them eating in just the kind of light Cyril and I were going to eat in. I unwrapped and polished the coffee cup and the teacup and their saucers and set them out for the coffee. My shoddy old flatware looked sad beside all the presidential finery, but it would have to do.

Cyril stacked the furniture back in front of the door, then just sat at the table while I cooked, he was so tired. He told me he'd gone to talk to Randy Lewis, who had a shortwave radio and batteries to run it on, and that Randy had heard there was fighting and rioting all over the country. None of the networks were on, so we couldn't have gotten any news even if we'd had power to run a TV or radio.

The potatoes finished cooking, and I whipped them by hand with butter that hadn't quite spoiled yet and canned Sego milk, which works in potatoes when you don't have anything else. The whipping took a while, but Cyril and I both like our potatoes whipped, so I stuck with the whipping till it was done. I opened the canned peas and boiled them, then set water to boil for the coffee. When the ham was heated, I sliced it and made a gravy and we sat down to eat.

The food looked so good, and it smelled so good, and in the candlelight it seemed the shooting and the screams were far-off, somehow, though of course they really weren't. It struck me as a rare blessing that a mother and her son could sit down to a decent supper in times like these, and I was grateful to Cyril for his thoughtfulness to me.

I dished myself some potatoes and handed Cyril the bowl. "I'm going to walk over to Lydia Ann's apartment tomorrow when it's light and try to find her," I said.

Cyril looked up at me and took the potatoes.

"I'll go look for her after supper," he said. "Don't you go out yet, not even in the day. It will be safer for me to go in the dark."

I covered my potatoes with gravy and handed Cyril the gravy bowl. "If you go tonight to look for your sister, I'm going with you. I can't stand this not knowing about Lydia Ann."

He took the gravy and shook his head.

"Don't tell me no," I said, serving myself a slice of ham. "I'm her mama, and I have to know if she's all right. If you say the darkness is safer, I'll go tonight in the dark, and I'll go alone if I have to."

He took the ham and didn't say anything. I'd told him about my decision to search for Lydia Ann in the same tone of voice I always used with my children to tell them the discussion was over and that trying to convince me to change my mind was a waste of time. He still recognized that tone of mine. We dished up some green peas and started eating.

"Is the water ready for the coffee?" Cyril asked.

I'd left it boiling on the stove. Cyril got up to get it and the jar of coffee, but the shoelace hooks in his boots caught the tablecloth and Cyril stumbled and jerked the tablecloth forward and the candle fell over and went out and I heard Cyril hit the floor and dishes shattering around him.

I couldn't move. I just sat there in the dark till I heard Cyril start getting up. I went for the matches then and another candle and bumped into Cyril and told him to stand still and asked if he was hurt and got a match and struck it and lit the candle and held it up. Cyril and I looked at each other, then at the table.

"Oh, Cyril," I said, but he didn't say anything, not "I'm sorry" or even "Well, look at that." He seemed too stunned to say anything to me then. The fish platter was on the floor and busted, together with the teacup and saucer and my old bowl I'd put the peas in—all busted. But the ham and the potatoes and my plate of food and the coffee cup and saucer were still on the table. He hadn't pulled off the whole tablecloth. I got the broom and dustpan and started sweeping up the pieces, and the sound of that china tinkling into my dustpan sounded like a judgment on us all and I started to cry, and Cyril said he'd finish sweeping so I handed him the broom, but I got out rags and tried to wipe up the mess off the floor, which wasn't easy considering how little water I had, and all the while I was crying. Everything was just too much for me then. When the mess was cleaned up and the tablecloth straightened, I sat back in my chair and just looked at my food sitting on a Lincoln plate while Cyril dished himself some more food onto a regular melmac plate out of my cupboard.

"What have we done, Cyril?" I said.

"The dishes would have all been broken anyway, if we'd left them sitting in the White House, Mama."

But that was not the point.

"Eat, Mama, if you want to feel up to going for a walk with me to Lydia Ann's," he said.

"Don't patronize me," I said.

I stopped my crying and stood up and got myself a melmac plate out of the cupboard and scraped my food onto it off of the Lincoln plate. Then I ever so carefully washed the Lincoln plate and didn't begrudge it the water. I wrapped it up in a fine dishtowel and put it and the unbroken cup and saucer back with the other dishes in their sacks. Then I hid the sacks in the broom closet, where thieves wouldn't spend much time looking, I thought, if they came in here.

The china I'd taken was a duty I had assumed. I realized that now. It represented a heritage not mine alone. The day would come when other people besides me would want to take a look at Mrs. Lincoln's china, and Mrs. Johnson's and Mrs. Harrison's. They'd want to look and remember the dreams we'd once had in this country and the kind of lives folks had once led. Till that time, I had a duty to safeguard what had become my charge. Wouldn't the people in power someday be surprised when I walked up and handed them the china and said, "Look here at what I've saved for all of us."

And I got other ideas. I sat back down to eat my cold food and told Cyril what I was thinking. "The minute it starts to look safe," I said, "I want to walk back to the White House and take a look around. I'll bet there's a cup or two that didn't get busted and maybe a saucer thrown on the rug that didn't break or get trampled. There will be things here and there that I can pick up and bring back to save and take care of. Maybe I'm being called to do this, Cyril, or maybe I'm calling myself. It's folks like me, I guess, who will have to make ourselves responsible for saving some of our heritage through this time."

He looked at me for a while, then finally started eating again. "I'll go with you to the White House," he said. "I don't want you going up there alone."

"I'd be glad for your help," I said, and I thought how saving things like a president's china would give us a purpose to get us through the troubled days ahead.

While I cleared off the table, Cyril told me how Randy Lewis had heard on his shortwave that they were talking about setting up a temporary capital in either Denver or St. Paul. "I imagine they'll fight now over which one of those cities gets to be capital for a while," I said.

Meanwhile, we had the living to take care of, and a job to do after that. Little by little, we'd put the world back right.

I sent Cyril to pull the furniture away from the door again, while I dressed in my black dress so I'd look inconspicuous out on the streets. Then I set matches and a candle by the door for when I got back, blew out the candle, and locked the door behind me. Mrs. Lincoln's china was safe, for now, in my broom closet. I set out with Cyril to find my Lydia Ann.

THE SHINING DREAM
ROAD OUT

So I buckled myself into the Driving Simulation Unit and started connecting my head to Happy Pizza's central computer, which would connect up to Salt Lake County's virtual-reality road map of the valley, all the while looking around at the dump of a room I was in with its peeling paint on the walls and ceiling and the used pizza boxes thrown on the floor and the heat and the smell of garlic and onion in the air, but that box of a "car" I was getting into, that was beautiful to me, because I knew what it would soon turn into, and I was getting that hit-in-the-gut feeling of excitement I get just before I head out to drive and I wanted to laugh because I wasn't really going to leave the back room of Happy Pizza at all except through virtual reality in my mind, when the voice of Fat Joe, the owner of this particular franchise, came over the intercom:

"Ten-minute run coming up, Clayton. If you beat your last time of 8:23 you got your raise."

Yeah, I thought, all of fifteen cents more an hour. "So start the show," I said.

And a virtual-reality vision of southbound Interstate 15 settled over my mind: the section just past the 600 South on-ramp and the Salt Lake City skyscrapers east and the derelict houses west and a sunset shining red on rainclouds above and rain already spattering down on the windshield and I thought, great, I'm trying to get just fifteen cents more an hour out of a stupid pizza delivery job and they make it rain.

I turned on the wipers and thought how the box I was sitting in looked to me like a car now, a nice little Japanese fast car that motored along just fine, and I punched it up to eighty, even with the wet road: my tires had good traction and the road was rough enough in real-land to keep you from hydroplaning, though the city would never factor that into its VR road simulations no matter how many times I talked to them about it when they did their user surveys—it's like, did they really believe the state would ever get that road fixed? But they must have, because in every simulation I was ever in, I-15 was smooth, and we'd drive along on top of it like we were driving on a dream road, and you'd start to understand why Fat Joe wouldn't spring for new shocks in our real cars, not if all he ever drove was this simulation and he thought the roads out there in real-land were this nice.

I punched up the coordinates of my run, and they glowed red digital out of the dash in the dim car, dim thanks to the rain, and I turned on my lights and thought how easy can Fat Joe make this: I-15 south to the 53rd South exit, then west on 53 to the Reston Hotel, room 115? Easy run was right—it was too easy. I saw what was coming: there'd be cops along the way and stingy Fat Joe had known it, must have punched into the city files to see how many cops were on duty, maybe drove along a little on the road himself just to check it out, just to see if he could save fifteen cents an hour but happy that I'd learn more about the real-land roads and where the cops had their speed traps so I'd know exactly where to speed up and where to slow down when I was delivering pizza, and that hit-in-the-gut feeling of mine got tighter because I couldn't make 53 South doing eighty with cops on the road, so I braked my car down to seventy just to be safe, so I wouldn't get caught right away, and waited to pass the first speed trap coming up: 21st South, behind or in front of the railing along the merge lane—and sure enough, there he was, a cop just waiting for me to go by at eighty plus, but I was only doing seventy and nobody'd pull you over for that unless it was the end of the month and some cop hadn't met his quota yet.

Fat Joe must have been pissed: he'd thought a cop would get me right away, but now he'd have to sit in his VR getup, which he hated unless he was watching porn, and wait to see if one of the cops assigned to the net for a day could catch me on VR I-15, which I knew better than the back of my hand: once past the 21st South on-off ramps and speed trap I merged into the far right lane and shoved my car back up to eighty—roadblock ahead, some old grandpa trying to pass the city sight requirements and motoring along just under fifty in a blue "Senior Driver" practice car—merge into the middle lane, still at eighty, maybe plus—roadblock ahead, some trucker trying to get back a license after one too many speeding tickets—merge right again, back and forth, weaving in and out, always in the right two lanes, never in the far left, the fast lane, the lane cops looked in for speeders: if you weaved in and out in the slow lanes the cops would know somebody was going fast, but they wouldn't know who, the dots of the cars on their radar would all blend together if I merged in close, and sure they'd think it was probably the pizza delivery boy who'd been going a little fast when we passed them, not the old geezer trying to keep his car on the road and do minimum speed at the same time, but they wouldn't know it for sure, which meant they wouldn't come out—they'd wait for some sure prey—and you can bet I'd be a good little pizza delivery boy around all their traps.

And make my ten-minute delivery in under 8:23.

So I drove along, making good time, thinking there was a lot of traffic on VR I-15—was every trucker and school-bus driver and delivery boy out trying to pass some driving test or get a raise?—when this pretty lady in a green station wagon with peeling fake-wood side panels speeds by doing ninety who knows what—and there were these three little blond-haired kids waving at me out of the back window.

Weird, I thought. And thank goodness it was just VR—it was one thing for me to drive like a maniac in VR or real-land, it was another for a mother with her kids. I hoped she'd use VR to work out whatever was eating at her and keep it down out there on real I-15. The kids kept waving, so I waved back and changed lanes into theirs and sped up to keep them company from behind—no speed trap till around the 33rd on-ramp anyway, our only danger would be roving cops—and we hit ninety-three miles an hour.

I started thinking, who is the lady driving the station wagon in light rain at ninety-three mph and when would the wagon's engine blow, because it could, even in VR, just to teach you a lesson. Only somebody with nothing to lose or hot food to deliver would pull stunts like this, and when you looked at it that way her speed kind of made sense: I'd heard of people coming out to check the simulation to see how well it worked, and those types would certainly have nothing to lose. So I thought maybe the lady in the station wagon is the mayor checking up on her VR cops and taking her kids for a joyride and seeing what her car should be able to do in theory, all at the same time—I imagined that's what somebody like her with a decent income and a crappy car so you wouldn't look high-and-mighty to the voters would do on an afternoon: hold the appointments, I've got important work coming through on the net; then connect up, swing by the house in VR to pick up your VR kids who'd plug in when you told them to, and off you'd go—and fuck the city budget crisis.

We started coming up on 33, and she braked, and I braked, and I thought this is a smart lady, she knows where the traps are, which of course a mayor would, and I merged over into the right lane and pulled up alongside her and looked over, but she didn't look at me: she just watched the road and held the wheel so tight her knuckles were white. She wasn't the mayor. Whoever she was, I thought she must have some kind of bad trouble in her life.

I merged back behind a couple of Idaho Meat Packers' trucks because I'd been part of a fast blip with that wagon for too long and I didn't want to be near her when we passed 33, and sure enough, another cop was waiting there looking confused about which of us had done what and I was happy to complicate his life. He pulled out three cars behind me, and I didn't touch my brakes, just eased up on the gas a little, then a little more, not wanting to look the least bit guilty and thinking did he somehow figure out about me, and wondering how he could have done that, and hardly daring to breathe because we passed 45 and 53 was the next exit and I'd used up nearly 5:30 of my run and if I got a ticket I wouldn't get my raise for sure.

So I played the good little pizza delivery boy, and I watched 53 come up ahead of us and the green station wagon take the exit and drive down the hill and I followed her off and the cop stayed out on I-15.

But the wagon sped up down below me, and I thought what's the lady doing? Before the intersection, she suddenly slammed brakes, which locked at that speed, and she slid to a stop blocking the exit, in front of a red light. Real good, lady, I thought, like, did she forget this wasn't the highway anymore, then suddenly remember? Well, she'd stopped before the red light, but any cop driving by would think the position of her car a little strange and maybe worth investigating. I hoped one wouldn't happen by and stop to check her out because I'd lose time trying to get around them.

I braked to a stop behind her and waited for the light to change—she could just pull out and go when it changed—but she didn't pull out, and her head started banging around like she was being hit, though nothing I could see was hitting her in that car, and I honked to maybe bring her out of it, but she didn't even look at me.

What is she on? I wondered, and I watched her head jerk around for a minute. Then I saw that the kids were popping out of VR—they'd look at their mom, then just be gone, just not there, like they were maybe pulling out the connection and running in real-land to help her or something, and I thought: I have no choice. I have to screw this test and my raise. And I put the car in park, and unbuckled and got out and ran up to the lady's door and opened it.

That's when she looked at me for the first time, and her eyes were wide like she was scared, not of me but of something. And I said, "Lady, what can I do to help you? Can I call someone? What's going on?" And she said—

"My husband's beating me."

Then she was gone, like the kids, as if somebody'd pulled the connection out of her head. The car disappeared next, and I was left standing in the middle of the off-ramp with four other cars honking behind me.

I stood there for a second or two, thinking how I'd blown the test and there was no point in going on and what Fat Joe would say, then I ran for my car and took it across 53 and up the VR I-15 on-ramp and back out onto the VR interstate looking for the green station wagon. I knew it was stupid to look for that wagon if the lady driving it was getting beaten up somewhere in real-land and I didn't know where and I couldn't even remember her license plate to stop and call the stupid police, I'd just been watching the kids in the back of a wagon doing ninety-three mph, I hadn't been memorizing license-plate numbers, and I didn't know what to do, and I wanted to do something, something, something. Before long, but before the ten minutes of my test were up, I was past Draper and the prison and going up the Point of the Mountain doing 102 and when I hit the top, the VR blanked out and a screen came up that said, "You are not a driver authorized to enter the Utah County Driver Simulation Net," which meant I didn't have the right kind of access to make the Salt Lake County net network me over to the Utah County net, and then the screen went all black in my mind: But before the words had come up I'd gotten one quick glimpse of the Utah County net, and it was all color, not city: I saw the sun glinting off Utah Lake and the green spring wheatfields and orchards around Alpine and a tall mountain south with snow still on the top and I-15 heading south to that mountain, the road looking like it had been polished and looking like it ached for me to drive on it.

• • •

"So you blew that one, Clayton-boy. You blew that one—and you're supposed to be my best driver?"

I was unhooking my head and one of the wires had stuck in the back, so I kept working at it and looked at Fat Joe who seemed just a little too happy about my fifteen-cent-an-hour loss and said, "Yeah, so I want some practice time in VR."

And it wasn't just VR fun I was after, though Fat Joe wouldn't know that: I wanted to get back out on VR I-15 and look for that station wagon and write down the license-plate number if I saw it again.

"You can practice when you don't have runs to make in real-land, Clayton-boy. We've got one waiting for you now."

The wire came loose, and I hurried out of the car and into the kitchen: It was two pepperoni and mushroom pizzas on a Midvale run waiting for me, and the kitchen staff had already boxed up the pizzas, so I took them and ran, sat them in the backseat of my little Japanese fast car and buckled them down and slammed doors and buckled myself in and rolled down the windows while I pulled out onto 600 South heading west to the I-15 on-ramp: I never used the air conditioner because the drain on engine power would slow me down, and I was out there in real-land, which is weirder than VR: in VR you have people driving along trying to pass tests, most driving like they always meant to be good little boys and girls of the road and only a few like me driving like maniacs because we had different kinds of tests to pass—and it was only those people out there.

But not in real-land.

In real-land everybody had already passed their tests so they could all go nuts and all two million of them in Salt Lake Valley are out driving around all the time, usually heading for I-15, and you never know what to expect except lots of craziness and unpredictability and I loved it, I loved playing the game that went on in that traffic: Drive a fast car fast and you'll find one or two or three others doing the same thing, and an interstate highway can become your own little VR game in real-land: slow cars doing sixty or seventy to block the road ahead when you can't change lanes left or right and the other fast cars speed past and the drivers laugh at you, but you get your turn to laugh down the road when their lane is blocked and you can speed past, and you drive, weaving in and out, and nothing feels like it, nothing, with the wind whipping your hair and the hot summer air off the desert blowing over your skin and no music off the radio at all because you don't need it, not then, not during the game.

And I merged out onto I-15 and shoved my Japanese fast car up to eighty plus, close to ninety, because I wanted to play then, real bad, and the Happy Pizza clown head stuck on the hood of my car flapped around like you wouldn't believe, but nobody was out playing the game, just me, I was the only driver weaving in and out, getting blocked and slowing down and speeding up again and weaving in and out, and I couldn't help it: I kept looking around for the green station wagon with the peeling fake-wood side panels because a car like that existed somewhere in the valley and was probably registered to the lady or her husband and the lady was probably a hacker because how else could she get out onto VR I-15? A woman with a car like that didn't have the money to buy her way on to the net.

I wished I'd looked even once at the license plate on that car.

• • •

It was more of the predictable same-old family routine when I got home that night after work. My mother would ask "How was your day, Clayton?" just like she did every day, and I'd say "Fine, just a lot of driving," and I'd never be able to tell her or Dad just how I drove and the kind of fun it was and what I'd felt, and my father would look up from his paper and not say a word because he was pissed that I'd taken a pizza delivery job, not something at his bank to keep me busy through the summer till I hit the one year of college I'd get before my two-year mission preaching religion. I looked at them and wanted to try to tell them I had taken a VR driving test to maybe get a raise in the slow afternoon hours after the lunchtime rush and that I'd seen this woman getting beaten by her husband and that I didn't know how to find her to help her. But I didn't know how to tell such a story to my parents; there'd be too much to explain, so I didn't say a word about it.

"Supper's at seven," Mother said, and I just stood by the fridge getting a drink, and I looked at us and thought we all seemed like little robots going about doing what we were programmed to do, no matter what happened in our lives: Mother programmed to make supper, Dad programmed to read the paper and disapprove of me, me programmed to go up to my room and do who knows what till supper, my two little sisters programmed to wear expensive clothes and be little brats, and I thought, God, I'm going to break this programming, I hate it, so I said to Mom, "Let me help. I'll set the table and get the water—did you want us to drink water tonight?"

And she looked at me surprised and said water would be fine, and Dad looked at me and I knew what he was thinking: that's a woman's work you're doing, Clayton, you're a fucking man doing women's work, isn't that a great kind of son to have? He would hardly move his arms and the paper when I tried to spread the tablecloth on the table or put his plate down in front of him, but he didn't try to stop me either because I was after all just a son who might just as well do work to serve him and we all ate supper and didn't talk much; Dad had the TV on, and I stayed behind to help Mom clean up and she said, "Well, isn't this a surprise?" But I just wanted to be close to her, and I kept thinking about the lady I'd seen in the green station wagon and what had probably happened to her.

We finished rinsing the dishes and putting them into the dishwasher and I went up to my room and stood in front of the mirror in my bathroom and played one of the other games I played with myself: Clayton, the little Robot Boy. I twisted an imaginary knob on the upper-right-hand corner of the mirror to turn me on and left more fingerprints there and wondered what Mom or one of the housecleaners thought about that little circle of fingerprints that was always on that spot of my mirror waiting to be wiped off, and I said, "Hi. I'm Clayton. I'm programmed to comb my hair just like this, with every hair in place, and I'm programmed to eat at certain times and take showers at certain times and I always did all of my homework well when I was in high school so I could get good grades and get accepted into a Utah college that doesn't really care about grades, it just wants to know if you'll go to church every Sunday you're enrolled with them so you can sit and hear people talk about being a Christian, never asking 'What would a Christian's life actually be like?' while outside the air-conditioned church building decent women are getting beaten up by their own husbands and you even see it on VR I-15."

I'd seen it.

I sat down on the edge of the tub and looked at myself in the mirror. I hated Clayton the little robot church boy whose life was all programmed for him: college, mission, marriage, kids, college, career as a lawyer or banker, and numbers and money and deadlines all my life and maybe I could even die on schedule: write it in my day-planner sixty years down the road—Wednesday, June 16, 3 P.M.: Die. Contact funeral home beforehand. Prepare final will that morning.

I stood up and twisted the imaginary knob and changed the program: I became Clayton, the pizza delivery boy, and I remembered me the first day I'd played the game out on the highway on a pizza run, the day I'd caught on to what had always been going on around me but which I'd missed because I'd always driven so slow and predictably and couldn't see it through my slow-driving programming, but when I started driving fast I'd found a whole subculture of people who drove just that way, people who made driving to the grocery store an adventure, and driving south to Midvale an event, and if you got a ticket it was just the price of admission to the game which you wouldn't stop playing because it made you feel so alive.

That first day I'd hooked up with a blond-haired girl in a red Ferrari and a thirty-something guy in a Japanese fast car like mine and the three of us would weave in and out of the traffic and laugh at each other when one of us had to slow down and race to catch up to the others. Down by Draper, we all took the same exit and stopped at a Sinclair gas station and all of us laughed about the fun we'd had, and they pumped gas into their tanks, but I didn't need to, I'd just come in to talk to them, and I said, "I'm Clayton," after we'd talked for a while, and I held out my hand to the guy, and he and the girl looked at me like I was some kind of alien and wouldn't tell me their names—and they didn't care about mine. It didn't matter to them. All that mattered was that I'd had a fast car and that I was smart enough to learn how to drive it fast and that when I was out on the road I would play the game with them. So those were the rules and I learned them and I never again tried to follow anybody off the road to try to talk. It wasn't the point.

And I turned the knob and changed the program and I was Clayton, the Peace Corps volunteer of the future, though the future was fast coming up to meet me: I'd sent in my papers and was waiting to hear back and I hadn't told my parents and I didn't know how to. They wanted me to do one set of things with my life, and I wanted to join the Peace Corps then maybe do some of the things they wanted. So I just skipped that entire inevitable conversation and imagined I looked like Indiana Jones with a shovel, not a gun, black stubble on my face and me wearing a fedora, and I was saying, "Yes, sir. I'd be glad to go to Ethiopia and show them how to dig ditches and teach them to have fewer kids," and maybe I'd actually help the people there, and I imagined I was setting off with my Bible and Book of Mormon and the shovel—but I was mixing up my programs, the mission program and the Peace Corps program, and I sat back down on the edge of the tub and thought how all my programs were mixed up because I didn't have a central program to guide them: I'd just been programmed to do this or that so much I didn't know what Clayton really wanted or how to cut through the programs to ask the questions to even find out what Clayton would want to do with his life if he were ever asked, if he ever asked himself. I was so programmed to want what I was supposed to want I couldn't even ask myself questions I needed answers to because the old programs would all keep running in my head and block the answers and I wondered if any of us could ever break out of the programs that ran us?

And I looked at myself in the mirror and thought, I'm going to go tell Mom what happened today. It's not part of any of our programs. Seeing what I saw upset mine and it will upset hers and maybe we'll be able to talk to each other about more than the stuff we've been taught to think about and talk about.

So I went down and found Mom in the kitchen reading the paper; it was her turn to read it now. "Mom," I said. "We've got to talk."

And I told her what had happened, and she sat still for a minute, not looking at me, then she said, "Don't call the police if you see that lady out there again. Her husband would be a sweet angel while the police were there, but once they left he'd beat her for sure and maybe the kids. Just get her license-plate number and talk to her and see if we can help. Maybe we can send her somewhere—to her parents? Now tell me what that car looked like again and what the woman looked like." And I did and she hugged me after a while, and I thought this was a good program we were downloading into our systems. A different kind of program, because I'd made some decisions and taken some chances. When I went to sleep that night I didn't feel so much like Clayton the Robot Boy in the mirror, and I liked not feeling like Clayton the Robot Boy.

Fat Joe let me do some VR practice the very next afternoon, and he merged me out onto VR I-15 and let me loose, and who should I see driving along in her cute little red Mustang convertible but my mother, with the top down but her windows still up so she wouldn't get blown too much and her black Gucci sunglasses on and a scarf tied down around her hair. She waved and cut in front of me and took the 21st South exit and I followed her into the parking lot of some abandoned warehouse by the off-ramp. She stopped and I swung around and parked next to her with my driver's-side window facing hers so we wouldn't have to get out of our cars, just roll down the windows. Mom reached over to turn down her music: she was listening to a CD of some old-fashioned group, Def Leppard or Scorpions, and I didn't even care then because I was so surprised to see Mom.

"I've been looking for your green station wagon for two hours," she said. "No sign of it."

I thought, wow, Mom—we're calling out the cavalry for this one, you and me, and I said, "How have you been looking?" and she said, "Driving up and down the interstate—Bountiful to Draper, and back again."

"I think she'll come," I said. "I think this is a release for her—maybe a kind of escape. Maybe she's even planning to escape and she knows she'll have to do it in her old station wagon, so she's practicing in VR, learning where the speed traps are, seeing what her theoretical car can do."

Mom agreed. We went back out onto VR I-15. I went ahead fast, looking, while Mom came along behind at a slower pace, just in case the lady merged onto the interstate behind me.

I drove down to the Point of the Mountain just past Draper, right up to the Utah County net, then turned around and drove north to Bountiful, then headed back south again—when there it was, the green station wagon, merging onto VR I-15 from 21st South and going fast. She passed me, and I sped up to keep up with her, and the kids waved at me again, waving hard and laughing like they recognized me, which they probably did thanks to the Happy Pizza clown face stuck on the hood of the car, and I merged into the right lane so I could get up alongside her, but a Brink's armored car roadblocked me doing sixty-five, and I had to change lanes again, weaving in and out till I could get up alongside her. I honked and waved and motioned for the lady to pull over and she looked at me but then wouldn't look back, just sped up.

Great, lady, I thought, I'm only trying to help you, and I followed her along till 45, and she took that exit and went down the hill, and I followed, thinking maybe we'd stop at the red light and talk, but suddenly she gunned the car again and sped through the red light, across 45, up the on-ramp, and back out onto VR I-15. I just stopped at the red light. It was obvious she didn't want to talk to me.

Mom pulled up alongside me and lowered the electric window on her passenger side. "She won't talk to you because you're a man," she said. "Let me go ahead and try. Don't follow us for a while." Then Mom sped through the red light and out onto VR I-15, and I just pulled off to the side of the road.

A cop car stopped behind me five minutes later, and the cop got out and asked me what I was doing.

"I'm just thinking," I said.

"Well, it's costing your company money for you to come think in here," he said, and I told him to write my company a

letter about it, which pissed him off, but since thinking wasn't
illegal yet, all he could do was tell me to get my car off the side
of the road and into a parking lot somewhere, so I took it out
onto VR I-15 instead. I motored along pretty slow—doing the
speed limit, actually, because I didn't want to come up on Mom
and the lady too soon, but I never did see them. I was down past
Draper and heading up the Point of the Mountain when Fat Joe
broke into the VR and told me I had a run to make. Before he
could pull me out, I raced my car up into the Utah County net
boundary and caught a glimpse, again, of the country that lay
beyond in VR and looking better than I ever remembered it in
real-land: all green in the valley and white snow on the blue
mountains and I-15 shining below me, and no sign of the big
cities down there, Provo and Orem. I wondered why I couldn't
see the cities.

• • •

When I got back from Fat Joe's run, which took me all the way
out to Sandy, he had another waiting for me in downtown SLC,
some banquet of ten pizzas, but my mother was sitting in the
front diner by a window, eating a pizza of her own. "What happened out there?" I asked her, and Fat Joe told me to get out on
my run, I could bother the customers on my own time, and
Mom said, "Send one of the other boys. This one's making a run
for me in about ten minutes," and Fat Joe looked at her as if to
say "When did you buy this place so you could order my help
around?" But he sent somebody else out on the run and didn't
say anything. Mom was, after all, a paying customer, and you
don't argue with those types when you're in the pizza business.

I pulled up a chair at Mom's table, and she said, "This lady
is in bad trouble: her husband beats her two or three times a

week and has put her in the hospital twice. She left him once before but went back to him, so I don't know what to think. You know how people in her situation are: they can't let go of the person killing them, and they leave them and then go back to them, and who knows what she'll actually do in the end, but I told her, 'Honey, you'd better get ahold of yourself and break this marriage apart before your husband kills you, so you can raise these three babies. If you don't want to think of yourself, think of them.' And she thought about it in those terms and told me she'd leave her husband again. She has a sister who just moved to Baker, Nevada, who will take her in, and the husband doesn't know the sister's gone to Baker, so the lady should be safe with her. I told her we'd drive her out there. The Nevada courts can get her a divorce by the weekend. So this is the plan: she's going to call in a pizza order anytime now. You'll take it to her in my car, which is faster than yours. When you get there, she and the kids will come out to pay for it, get in the car instead, and you'll drive her on to Provo. Your Dad and I will meet you at the courthouse, where she'll arrange for a restraining order on her husband. Then we'll all go on to Baker."

"Dad?" was all I could say.

"I told him this morning what we were doing," she said, "and he's been checking into the legalities of helping this woman, which is all legal, and taking your sisters to your Aunt Cheryl's and getting us a reservation at a campground in Great Basin National Park. He's home packing his van now. He and I agree this will be a great chance for the three of us to talk. Here are the keys to my car," and she handed me her car keys.

I gave Mom my car keys and realized I maybe had some rethinking to do about my dad. Maybe I'd been running the wrong programs about him and let a few I/O errors affect my brain and keep me from seeing things right. I guess I'd find out. Fat Joe walked over, and I looked up at him. "So what's going on?" he asked.

"This boy's your best driver," Mom said. "I need his services." And she pulled out a hundred-dollar bill from her purse and handed it to Fat Joe. "That should cover any inconvenience you'll incur from his absence this weekend."

Well, Fat Joe was all smiles then, and I knew my job was secure if I took off the next week, not just the weekend. The funny thing was, Fat Joe probably didn't even know that this was my own mother doing all this, and I sure didn't tell him. He came out to help me put a Happy Pizza clown face on the hood of Mom's Mustang, and it looked so stupid there, but then, it looked stupid on any car.

When we walked back in, Mom was pacing up and down, looking at her watch, and then the phone rang. We all just looked at it till it rang again, then we all dived for it, but Mom got it and it was the lady. "Yes, I've got your address right here in my purse," and she read it back to her. "Ten minutes," Mom said, and she hung up and handed me a paper with the address on it. "Go, Clayton," she said, and I started for the door, but Fat Joe said, "Don't you need a pizza?" and Mom said, "For heaven's sake, yes, but who cares what it is or if it's even cooked," so the kitchen help rushed a frozen Italian sausage and pineapple out in a box, and I ran for the car.

The address read Layton Avenue, which meant out to I-15, down to 21st South, east to West Temple, then north five blocks to Layton. I got there in seven minutes. The three kids were out sitting on the lawn, and the oldest, a girl maybe five years old, took the hands of the others and started walking them toward the car. I left the door open for them and left the car running, hoping the kids had sense enough not to touch anything, and I walked the frozen pizza up the steps to the door and rang the doorbell. The lady answered it, and I couldn't even talk for a minute when I saw her in real-land. Her eyes were both black, and her wrists were bandaged and there were bruises along her neck above her shirt collar, and her hair was a wreck. She looked at me with tears in her eyes, and I thought, Lady, don't back out now, your kids just climbed into my car. She handed me a ten, and I gave her the pizza and said I'd have to go get change from the car, could she come out for it? She nodded and set the pizza on the TV. Some man I could barely see on the couch growled, "This doesn't even smell like a pizza. Where did you order it from?" But the lady just walked out of the house and followed me down the steps. She stopped and pulled a suitcase out of the bushes by the front door and hurried to put it on the floor in the backseat. The kids were in the back. We climbed in, and I started backing out and I looked at the lady again and thought how I'd known that people look better in VR because you can touch yourself up after you're in, so I should have known a woman would take away black eyes and bruises. I should have looked ahead and been prepared for seeing her in real-land, but I hadn't and it was hard to look at her now. That's when the husband ran out of the house. He must have looked in the pizza box and seen that the pizza was frozen, then looked out the window to see that his family was making an escape. I could easily outdistance him in a Mustang, and he turned and ran back to the house.

"He'll follow," the lady said. "Can you drive this thing?"

I didn't even answer her. I just took us out onto I-15 and

started the game. It was all the answer she needed. She turned around and buckled the kids in, then buckled herself in.

We weren't going to have an easy time of blending into the traffic in Mom's red Mustang with a Happy Pizza clown face flapping on the hood, and I just hoped her husband was way behind us somewhere, which was too much to hope for. The lady was watching behind. "Here he comes," she said. "White Bronco, center lane. He'll want to kill you, because he'll think I've been stepping out with you."

I thought about that for a minute. "What about you and the kids?" I asked the lady, finally. "What will he do to all of you?"

"He'll just want to hurt me. The kids don't matter to him yet."

So play the game, I thought. Play it better than you ever have. He was right behind us and gaining, doing ninety plus. I sped up to over ninety and thought that this is what I would do: come up fast on the speed trap at 33rd South, get in the inside lane, then slow down fast, send the Bronco speeding past, the sure prey of any cop waiting there. We came up fast onto 33rd South, I took the inside lane and braked. The Bronco sped past in the middle lane.

But there was no cop.

"Now he's in front of us," was all the lady said.

He slowed right down in the middle lane, so I got in the fast lane and punched it. When we were alongside each other, doing eighty plus, he tried to shout something out his window. The lady wouldn't look at him. The five-year-old girl climbed out of her buckle and over the seat into her mother's arms. She looked at her dad, but didn't wave. The other two kids started crying because they wanted to come up into the front seat, too, but the lady just ignored them. I punched it

again to get past her husband, and he swerved in behind us—
I didn't know if he'd meant to hit the back of the car or what,
but he was right on our tail, and speeding up behind us to
maybe ram us. I shoved the Mustang up to ninety plus, and he
was still gaining.

I merged right, and he followed us. We passed a Smith's grocery store semi in the middle lane and just ahead a white
Lincoln was going to roadblock us doing seventy. I got an idea
and slowed down while the semi closed up the space between
us. The lady's husband slowed down, too, though he stayed
right on our tail. He didn't ram us after all. I waited till there
was room for just us to merge into the middle lane between the
semi and the Lincoln and did it. The semi let out a blat of horn
and I sped ahead. The Bronco was sandwiched back behind the
Lincoln and the semi.

We'd passed the 45th South exit and were coming up on
53rd South and one mile later the I-215 turnoff. The white
Bronco reappeared behind us. He'd slowed down, gotten
around the semi, and was speeding up toward us again. "I know
where I can get some cops," I said.

At least I hoped I did. They were always there when you
didn't want them: just off the I-15 merge lanes onto I-215
heading west toward Redwood Road. I'd gotten my first ticket
there after starting work for Fat Joe and Happy Pizza. Be there
today, cops, I thought. Just be there. I didn't care if they pulled
us all over and helped us sort out the mess. The husband
couldn't make his wife stay with him, and he couldn't kill me
if there were cops around.

So I got in the inside lane, passed 53rd South, and headed
for the I-215 exit. The Bronco followed. I dropped down onto
I-215, doing eighty plus, and braked. The Bronco changed lanes

and sped past to get ahead of us, and a cop pulled out after him, lights flashing and then the siren started up.

We stayed well behind the chase, and eventually the Bronco pulled over. We drove past them, turned around at Redwood Road, and headed back east for I-15. The police still had the Bronco and the lady's husband pulled over when we went past.

"He's probably telling them that you kidnapped us," the lady said.

"You can straighten things out at the courthouse in Provo," I said.

We got onto I-15 and headed south past 72nd South. I realized I was breathing hard and tried to slow it down. I also slowed down the car. After all, I had a mother and her three kids in the car with me and no reason to race anymore. I dropped us down to seventy and kept it there. The lady turned around and unstrapped her crying kids and took them all into the front seat with her and held them, quieted them down. "Thank you," the lady said to me, almost in a whisper, looking straight ahead.

"My name is Clayton," I said, suddenly thinking it was important for her to know that.

She looked at me, then, but didn't smile. "I'm Elizabeth. The oldest one here is Jane. This is Amy; and my youngest is Clayton, like you."

There wasn't much else for us to say. Not then. We drove past Draper and the prison, then started up the Point of the Mountain. When we drove over the top, we could see Utah Valley. There were the green wheatfields and the orchards around Alpine, the snow on the blue mountains. I-15 stretched out below us and ahead, to the south. It all looked nearly as good as it looked in VR, though I could see the cities from the

Point if I looked hard, so I stopped looking and we dropped down into the valley and I couldn't see them anymore. We'd be in Provo in thirty minutes anyway, and then my parents would come.

I thought about that and decided to tell them about the Peace Corps later that night around the campfire when it was just the three of us, after we'd dropped Elizabeth off at her sister's, the three of us without TV so we could talk, away from the things that reminded us of all the programs in our lives, out under stars in the cold mountain air and the only sounds the sounds of our crackling fire and the wind in the trees and our voices. Our lives would all seem short and valuable out there, and our dreams worth dreaming. I got that hit-in-the-gut feeling of excitement again, and it was strong because it came from being excited about talking to my parents and from being able to drive my mother's red Mustang down the road I'd wanted to take in the net, where the road out looked so achingly beautiful.

Lock Down

As soon as the last member of Night Team A hauls his tired ass up the ladder, you lead your team down it, into the time bubble. The bubble smells like sweat, and Megan hits on the fan first thing, like always, though you all know it won't chase out the smell: you don't give the fan time to make the bubble smell decent.

You don't have the time to give it.

"Secure hatch," you call back to Megan, your operations expert, and you know she's already started, you can hear the bolts slamming into place. You don't even bother to order Paulo to replace the battery and check the cabling in the time stabilizer because you've heard him snap open the case and tear into it, and while you check that the time stabilizer is synchronized with Mission Control/Greenwich/Tokyo you think: this is a good team. These people know their jobs, and you know

41

yours, and you can do your jobs. The three of you are Deep Night Team B, and you want to be promoted to Deep Night Team A before the break in time is locked down, which means you've got to break some records—which means you'll work to maybe lock down a whole day on this shift.

"Hatch sealed," Megan calls out.

You flip switches that start the pressurization, and the constant hiss you hear behind all your work starts up again.

"Batteries replaced, full charge, ready to go," Paulo calls out. You'll work till the batteries are within 4 or 5 percent of 10. You won't come back sooner no matter how much actual time you've worked. "Cables check out 100 percent."

"Hatch double check, Paulo," you tell him. "Megan, battery and cable double check."

You double-, then triple-check everybody's work because you don't ever want to be in fractured time with a bad seal or bad batteries. You don't know exactly what happens to teams lost, for a time, like that—it's classified info—but the rumors aren't good, and you don't want to find out which are true and which are stupid stories like the ones older guys told you when you started training for this job. Besides, you know without being told the two choices a lost team has: suffocate, or depressurize to take on air—and expose yourselves to a timeline on which maybe nothing adds up to you and you are sundered from existence. You check the backup batteries yourself. You check the seals on the hatch and the main batteries yourself after Megan and Paulo have checked them. You all check the time stabilizer, its cables, its synchronization, the air tanks, and the virtual tether that hooks you back to real time and snakes out silver behind your bubble through the fractured mess you're heading into.

A green light flashes above the main computer: Mission

Control's info dump is finished. You've got the data hundreds of research teams brought back since the last shift went out, true time data on everything and everyone surrounding the point in time you're going to. You strap yourselves in. Out of all the chronometers in front of you, you look first at the one in the upper-left-hand corner of your console, the one that records the total amount of time the last team managed to lock down: 2 hours, 13 minutes, 17.56.24 seconds—what were they doing? You think: a whole shift for only two hours and thirteen minutes.

"Move us out," you radio to Mission Control.

And they move you out into fractured time.

• • •

The radio is instantly dead. You know you're there. You follow back the break, which occurred between 12:11:32:46:22 P.M. on July 14, 1864, and a time you remember, not too far back, that you don't like to think about. Teams are working from both ends of the break, and yours is working up from the bottom: you're at March 19, 1948, following Marian Anderson, the opera singer, because the break centers on one life and the events in it, and for now it's centered on Marian Anderson— and from each breath she takes, from each turn of her head so that she sees something new, from each word she speaks to another person, uncountable futures shatter off, and all the possible actions of all the people she meets or passes or speaks to become possible again, all the evil in their hearts and all the good, and it's your job to lock down what actually happened, no matter what that is, no matter what you watch, because no one knows if the world can persist if you don't get it right.

And no one knows how much time you've got to get time right.

43

"Night Team locked down at 6:45:10:59:36 P.M., March 19, 1948," Paulo calls out behind you, to your left. "That's where we start."

"Hold us there, Megan," you say, while you check the probability calculations on record at the end of Night Team A's shift. Computer checks them out at 100 percent. Hand calcs say the same. "Move us forward," you say.

And time starts running.

You watch Marian Anderson try to hold the train of her burgundy satin concert gown out of wet snow as Franz Rupp, her accompanist, helps her climb out the window of her room in Hotel Utah and start down the fire escape. Franz follows her out. Bessie George, Marian's servant and friend, closes and latches the window behind them, then takes the stairs down and exits through the hotel's main doors.

You'd already followed them as they'd boarded the Great Northern in Vancouver for Salt Lake City the day after Marian's concert on March 15, and you'd locked that down, and you'd been the team that locked down their arrival in Salt Lake on March 18, at 9:45 A.M. on the dot—trains had prided themselves on being on time like that back then, utterly dependable—and you'd followed her in the taxi through heavy snow and almost impassable streets to Hotel Utah, where the doorman had stopped Marian from entering through the main doors under the canopy that sheltered them from the blizzard. When Franz had protested, the manager had come out to stop Marian from entering, and finally Franz had gone in to check them all in to the hotel. They hadn't known where else to go in a blizzard or if anywhere in Salt Lake would treat them any better. Marian had stood outside on the sidewalk with Bessie and all their luggage. After a time, Franz had walked out with keys to their rooms. He'd looked embarrassed, but Marian hadn't seemed at all embarrassed or surprised when he'd led her around to the servants' entrance to the kitchens and an icy fire escape above the first two floors. Bessie had taken the keys, helped a bellboy collect all the luggage, went through the main doors and up to their rooms on the sixth floor to open the windows to Franz and Marian.

"Marian's better than all those people who don't want her in their hotel," Megan had said.

It disgusts you to see the meanness thrown at Marian in places like New York, Los Angeles, Chicago, Philadelphia, and now this place. It disgusts you to have to lock it down—to realize that no place in America treated her better.

"She sings Brahms and makes people weep," Paulo had said.

And Marian was black. In America in 1948, that meant you couldn't go through the front doors of a hotel.

You'd already locked that into true time on your last shift, and on this shift it is now time for Marian's concert in the Mormon Tabernacle on Temple Square. You watch her climb down the icy fire escape, trying to hold her concert gown out of the slush, and walk the half block to the Tabernacle to warm up—"literally," Megan says—for her concert. Franz goes to work immediately to make sure the piano is tuned—oh, the Tabernacle staff assures him it is, but he checks anyway, and he plunks away at a key he can't get right, tightening, then loosening the string, then tightening it again, while Marian runs through scales in the space under the choir seats—the Tabernacle equivalent of backstage—and Bessie makes Marian a lukewarm tea and squeezes a lemon into it. The Tabernacle fills to less than half capacity—exactly 2,347 people—though in that small audience the Democratic governor of Utah,

Herbert Brown Maw, and his wife Florence take good seats near the front.

You're watching the calcs, and they aren't good. "Probability's slipping," you say. The total measures out at only 75.467 percent now.

"What's gone wrong?" Megan says, and it's your job to find out.

"Weather: heavy snow—the blizzard out there—99.876 percent of all possible true time has that," Paulo calls out. "Storm holds true."

You start checking the probability of each person waiting for the concert to begin having actually attended the concert, even during a blizzard, and they all check out at over 90 percent, including the governor. Franz keeps plunking at the key in front of the small audience, and now the Tabernacle tuner on staff is out helping him get it right. You hear that key plunk and plunk—always just a little flat—while you frantically run the calcs.

"Mãe de deus—what key is that?" Paulo asks.

"C sharp over middle C," Megan says. "I'm checking that: comp's going over recordings of past tunings of this piano in the Tabernacle—that key might be our problem. It rates only 48.575 of possible true time."

"That's still high," you say. "Let it run." Sometimes the only way to find where time took a wrong turn is to let it play out to some completely illogical end and backtrack from that.

Franz and the staff tuner get the key in tune, the plunking stops, and Franz hurries down the steps and through curtains to the space under the choir seats to enter behind Marian when the time comes. A young girl stands poised to pull back the curtains. While Franz and Marian stand there waiting to go on, the girl looks up at Marian. "Are you frightened?" she asks.

Marian smiles. "A little," she says. "But when I start to sing I always forget my surroundings and, as you forget your surroundings, you also forget to be afraid."

Marian nods, and the girl pulls back the curtains. Marian and Franz walk out. Suddenly there is applause, though not much since the Tabernacle isn't full. The concert begins. Marian sings one selection from Handel, "*Serse*, Recitative and Aria": "To win one's true treasure one must be cunning," the words go. "Vivacious laugh, a quick glance can make one fall in love. Sometimes it is necessary to trick and fool—ah, I can do all these things!"

Marian's voice is clear, the register deep and low at first. She sings with such confidence the notes seem effortless. The audience applauds, louder this time, and Marian sings Brahms.

"The probability of this order of music is only 33.678 percent," you say.

"No other concert on the tour had this order so far," Megan confirms. "It's usually Handel, then a couple other Baroques, then Schubert."

But the Brahms is lovely, and you still can't put your finger on exactly where time took its wrong turn. "Let it keep playing," you say. After intermission Marian turns from Brahms to Tchaikovsky's "None but the Lonely Heart," and the applause is louder now, and the governor stands to applaud Marian. She sings more Tchaikovsky, then spirituals—to a standing ovation. Florence Maw is crying—trying to clap, then wipe her eyes, then clap some more—and the governor calls out "Ave Maria!" and the applause gets louder and louder. Marian sings five more spirituals as encores, and the small audience keeps calling her back. She sings an aria from Massenet's opera *Le Cid*, and the governor shouts "Ave Maria!" again. When Marian comes out for the seventh time, she sings it. She knows which "Ave Maria" the governor is asking for: the Gounod, based on the Bach prelude. At the end of that song not only Florence is weeping. Florence and the governor go backstage to find Marian, Franz, and Bessie bundling up to face the blizzard.

"You walked over!" the governor says to Marian, incredulous. "You'll ride back with us."

And they do. Franz and Bessie and Marian all look at each other when the limousine stops in front of the hotel's main doors, under the canopy, out of the storm. The governor and Florence sweep them out of the limousine and partway up the steps. "Let's get you something hot to drink," Florence says, and she starts inside through the revolving doors. The governor motions for Marian and the rest to follow. Marian hesitates, then suddenly pulls up the skirts of her gown and does follow.

The doorman stops her.

"What's this?" the governor demands.

"She can't come through here, sir," the doorman says.

Florence stands on the inside now. She looks back, confused.

"What do you mean she can't come through here?" the governor says. "Isn't she a guest at this hotel?"

"I am," Marian says.

"Well, then." The governor takes Marian's arm and leads her toward the door—but the doorman actually puts out his hand and holds Marian back.

"*You* can enter here," the doorman tells the governor. "But her kind enters around back."

"They're making Marian climb the fire escape to her room," Franz calls out from the bottom steps.

Florence pushes her way back out through the revolving doors, and the hotel's night manager follows her. When he sees who is standing with Marian Anderson—the governor of the state of Utah and the first lady—he looks troubled.

"Your doorman tells me," the governor says, "that some of your guests may not enter this hotel through the main doors—including this woman, who happens to be the greatest singer of our nation, perhaps of the entire world."

"She is a Negro," the night manager says, nothing more.

"She is to be my guest for hot chocolate in your coffee shop. Florence and I are walking there with her. So how do we go? By way of a fire escape around back?"

"Governor, you and the first lady may of course enter through these front doors. I'll escort Mrs. Anderson to the coffee shop myself. We won't be long."

"Through what entrance will you escort Mrs. Anderson?"

The night manager says nothing.

Florence steps forward then and takes Marian's arm. "Are your rooms here adequate?" she asks.

Marian nods.

"What floor have they put you on?"

"The sixth."

"And you climb fire escapes up and down to get to your room?"

"Part of the way is inside through the servants' entrance to the kitchens," Marian says.

"Would you be a guest in my home instead?" Florence asks. "We'll take you through the front doors of this state's governor's mansion and put all of you in our guest rooms, then make ourselves hot chocolate in the kitchen."

"We'd be honored," the governor says.

Marian accepts. Franz and Bessie hurriedly pack their and Marian's things, and they all drive with the governor and his wife to Utah's governor's mansion, where Marian stays as an honored guest.

"Fast-forward, Megan," you say. "Prepare for backtrack." And while you and your team prepare to take the bubble back to find out where time went wrong, you watch events on this timeline rush by. The story of Marian and the governor and his wife is in all the Utah papers the next day, and the day after that in all the papers in America, and after that, abroad. Utah is shamed by what happened: but more than that, the governor introduces legislation outlawing discrimination based on race in all public institutions in Utah, and—after months of hard lobbying, behind-the-scenes deals, and arm twisting—it passes. Utah becomes a bastion of civil rights in 1948. It shows America the way forward.

"Hold us there, Megan," you call out. You know this didn't happen. You wish you could lock it down, but you know this didn't happen.

"It could have happened like that," Megan says. "It was in their hearts."

• • •

But it didn't happen like that. You go back to 6:45:10:59:36 P.M., March 19, 1948, and you inch forward, checking every probability. You follow a different timeline. As you watch it, you think this must be what had happened. You see Marian climb out the window in her gold silk concert gown, the one with real pearls sewn on the cuffs and around the neck, and both Bessie and Franz go down the fire escape with her to help her keep the gown out of the slush. "Good probability on that gown," Megan says. "Marian hasn't worn it since San Francisco." You realize Megan isn't checking probability calcs to say that;

she's just watching and using common sense. Marian had worn the burgundy in Vancouver just days before. She would likely wear a different gown now.

"It's the C above middle C—not C sharp—they can't tune," Paulo says while you all listen to Franz plunk the C above middle C over and over.

"That C rates 86.277 of possible true time," Megan says.

"Close," you say, in the middle of figuring the probability of filling the Tabernacle on the night of a blizzard—5,667 people to be exact, which is how many attend on this timeline. But close isn't good enough. Something's wrong, again.

Marian begins with the same Handel, then turns to Schubert's "Suleika":

I envy you your humid wings, oh western wind
For you can tell him how long I suffer, now we are parted! . . .
Yet do not grieve him, but hide my sorrow.
Tell him modestly, that his love is my life,
That if I am with him, two will rejoice.

Then Marian sings Brahms; after intermission, Tchaikovsky and the spirituals, as before. Marian receives a standing ovation again. Florence is crying—trying to clap, then wipe her eyes, then clap some more—and the governor calls out "Ave Maria!" and the applause gets louder and louder. There are cheers this time from the audience. The concert ends after five encores— the last the Bach/Gounod "Ave Maria"—and the governor and Florence drive Marian, Bessie, and Franz to Hotel Utah and sweep them out of the limousine and partway up the steps. "Let's get you something hot to drink," Florence says. She starts inside through the revolving doors. The governor motions for

Marian and the rest to follow. Marian hesitates, then suddenly pulls up the skirts of her gown and does follow.

The doorman stops her.

"What's wrong?" the governor demands.

"She can't come through here, sir," the doorman says.

Florence stands on the inside now. She looks back, confused.

"What do you mean?" the governor says. "Isn't she a guest at this hotel?"

"I am," Marian says.

"Then you are mistaken," Governor Maw tells the doorman. The governor takes Marian's arm and leads her toward the door—but the doorman actually puts out his hand and holds Marian back.

"*You* can enter here," the doorman tells the governor. "But her kind enters around back."

"They're making Marian climb the fire escape to her room," Franz calls out from the bottom steps.

Florence pushes her way back out through the revolving doors, and the hotel's night manager follows her. When he sees who is standing with Marian, he looks troubled.

"Your doorman tells me," the governor says, "that some of your guests may not enter through the main doors—including this woman, who happens to be the greatest singer of our nation, perhaps of the entire world."

"She is a Negro," the night manager says, nothing more, as if that explained everything.

"She's to be my guest for hot chocolate in your coffee shop. Florence and I are walking there with her. So how do we go? By way of a fire escape around back?"

The night manager hesitates. "Of course not, sir," he says, finally. "Please, will all of you follow me." And to the astonishment of the doorman, the night manager leads everyone—including Marian Anderson—inside, through the main doors. Guests sitting in the lobby stare, but say nothing.

The calcs aren't good. "We're losing it," you say.

"I get only a 13.227 percent probability that the night manager would do what he just did," Megan says.

"But it was in his heart," Paulo says.

"Only 13.227 percent of it," Megan says.

"He just didn't act on that 13.227 percent," Paulo says.

But you know that what was in the night manager's heart doesn't matter. What matters is what he actually did. "Fast-forward, Megan," you say. "Prepare for backtrack." And while you and Megan and Paulo prepare to take the bubble back, you let time run forward. The papers do not mention the governor's intercession on Marian's behalf the next day. He himself is quiet about it. He's running for reelection that year and is not sure how his intercession would play with the voters. But he knows the general manager of Hotel Utah, and he suggests to him privately that he ought to change the hotel's ridiculous policy of not allowing someone like Marian Anderson to walk in through the front doors. "I'll change the policy at once," the general manager says, and he does write a new policy that same day, but he sets it aside to think about it overnight. The next day he looks at it on his desktop, then wads it up and throws it in the trash can under his desk.

"Take us back, Megan," you say.

• • •

And you are back at 6:45:10:59:36 P.M., March 19, 1948, and you inch forward, checking every probability. You watch Marian try to hold the train of her green satin concert gown out of the wet snow as Franz helps her climb out the window of her room in Hotel Utah and start down the fire escape. Franz follows her out. Bessie closes and latches the window behind them, then takes the stairs down and exits through the hotel's main doors. "99.678 percent probability on that gown," Megan says. She's talking from computer *and* hand calcs this time, not just common sense. Marian hasn't worn that gown since Philadelphia.

"It's the *B* above middle C they can't tune!" Paulo exclaims. "Nearly 100 percent on that, too."

"Lock it down," you say. Paulo hits the timelock switch, and the time bubble shudders, then stills. You look at the chronometer in the upper-left-hand corner of your console and see that you've added 1 hour, 13 minutes, and 29.52.17 seconds to true time.

This is not going to be a record shift.

But everything on this timeline checks out at nearly 100 percent for hours after that. The Tabernacle fills with 6,104 people—it's standing room only: the box office sells 138 standing-room tickets for $1.20, half price—and the fire marshal won't let anyone else in. The girl at the curtains does not speak to Marian on this timeline. Marian begins with a different Handel, *Floridante*:

> *Dear night, bring back my love.*
> *At times I fancy my beloved standing in the doorway*
> *but alas, 'tis only a dream—how long must I wait in vain?*

After that she sings another Handel, then Frescobaldi, Legranzi, four Schubert lieder, and the Massenet aria—all before intermission.

"No Brahms," Megan says. "We're at 98.662 percent on that."

After the intermission, Marian sings "None but the Lonely Heart," four other early-twentieth-century pieces, then the spirituals. Florence does not cry, though some in the audience do. Marian sings three encores: "Coming through the Rye," "Will o' the Wisp," and the Bach/Gounod "Ave Maria," then she, Franz, and Bessie bundle up and walk back to Hotel Utah. Marian and Franz enter through the servants' entrance and climb up the fire escape to their rooms, where Bessie has opened the windows.

All your calcs check out at 98 plus percent. "This is it, isn't it?" you say. You look back at Megan and Paulo. Their calcs match yours. You've got time right. You've seen what really happened the night of Marian Anderson's only concert in Salt Lake City. "We have to lock this down," you say, but after seeing what might have been you hesitate.

"Come on, guys," Megan says, finally. "We've got a job to do."

And you know she's right. You don't like it, but you know she's right. You wish you had a choice, but you don't. "Lock it down," you say.

Paulo does, and the time bubble shudders.

You look at the chronometer: 4 hours, 17 minutes, 22.36.08 seconds locked down. "We beat Night Team A," you announce. You look back at Megan and Paulo. Megan looks up from her calcs and grins, but that's it. It doesn't feel like the times when you've had a good shift, beat Night Team A, maybe locked down a day without indignities in Marian's life.

"Batteries at 48 percent," Megan says. "Air tanks at 60."

You can stay out a little longer. You let time run through the true-time night, checking the probabilities, locking down blocks of time as you go. At 7:30 A.M., Franz checks out for his party; Bessie and a bellboy load the luggage in a taxi; and

Marian hurries down the fire escape and out the servants' entrance to meet the train to Denver. You've locked down 12 hours, 9 minutes, 46.22.54 seconds—not your team's best, but a good shift's work.

"Batteries at 14 percent now," Megan announces, which is as close to the 10 percent edge as you come. "Air tanks, 33."

"Prepare for return," you say.

While the three of you make the necessary adjustments and check each other's work, you let time run. You are still stationed above Hotel Utah. At 7:46 A.M.—you notice the time because you're setting comp's main chronometer for the return just then—two maids hurry out the back of the hotel with blankets, sheets, pillowcases, towels, and a bedspread in their arms. "Those were in Marian's room," Megan says. "She had the cream bedspread." And for a short time, while you strap yourselves into your seats, you all watch to see what these women are doing with the bedding and towels from Marian's room. They hurry through the slush and cold to the incinerator, where refuse from the kitchen's breakfast is burning, and they throw everything on the flames and stand there to watch it burn.

"Take us home, Megan," you say.

And she does. You follow the silver virtual tether across all the fractured time left between 1948 and your own time. You leave Marian in 1948, with its unacted good locked in people's hearts where it never mattered. The radio comes to life. You turn Mission Control over to Paulo while Megan depressurizes the bubble. You download your reports. Then you follow your team up the ladder.

INUIT

My sister Thule was frightened. She had said nothing all morning, and she had been awake before Mother lit the whale oil in the stone lamp and sang us out of our furs. I tried to joke with Thule—she was nine, and I was twelve and her brother who had gone to school before—but she would not laugh.

Without a word, she dressed in the new trousers and parka Mother had sewn for her. Mother knew the teachers would take our clothes and dress us in things that would let the cold kill us if we went outside, yet she made Father trade two good harpoons for the parka's white seal pelts. Father traded them without complaint, even took the pelts to Unalakleet, the shaman, who pulled the mask from his face and touched the mask to the pelts. When the parka was sewn, Father sang his magic songs over it as if it were a kayak, harpoon, or lance, as if my sister were going on a whale hunt, not to school.

Mother gave Thule and me a handful of dried berries she had saved through the winter. Thule ate hers quickly and would not look up. I thought, then, that she would try not to go, that she would cry, and when she looked up her eyes had water in them, but she did not cry. She followed me outside.

I held Thule's hand as we walked along the seashore to the school. The sea was gray, and still, and free of ice. The bowl of the world sloped up from us, and we could see Atka, just above our heads, the island where we had spent the spring, where Nulato, our cousin, had died hunting caribou.

Thule said nothing as we left the beach and walked up into the valley of the school, following the twistings of a sluggish stream, low now after the rush of spring melt. Rabbit and lemming tracks notched mud at the stream's edge. Thule would not look back or at the tracks or at me. I held her hand till we saw the stone buildings, and then I made her walk behind me and follow me inside, and I would not look at her.

· · ·

A teacher took Thule to the rooms for first-year students. I did not see her again for three months. She learned to read and write—things she could forget quickly—but my schooling was different, that year.

My class had two teachers. One was an old Inuit woman, angry, wearing furs though the school was hot. She folded her arms and sat frowning by the door. No one dared speak to her. The other looked Inuit, at first, but he wore a student's white shirt and blue pants, and when he spoke I knew he was not Inuit, not part of the people. I stared at him; we all stared at him, tried to understand him when he talked, laughed when he mispronounced words—and he laughed with us.

• • •

I had seen, six years before, men not Inuit. I was sitting in the prow of my family's umiak while we rowed from Atka to the mainland, and whales were in the sea. We meant the whales no harm—we had plenty of dried meat—and Father had sung his songs over our umiak, so he and Anvik, my older brother, rowed with confidence through the whales. The whales were spouting and taking fresh air, but suddenly the ones farthest out began to sound.

We saw, then, the men not Inuit. They came in a great umiak larger than ten the size of my family's, and they were hunting; they held harpoons ready to throw.

"The fools!" Mother said. She sat Thule down, threw me a paddle, took one herself, and helped row us away from the whales. I wondered who could be stupid enough to start a hunt when among the whales was an umiak loaded with tents, dogs, and people. Thule was little, and she cried. The dogs barked. I rowed hard.

But the men not Inuit held their harpoons. They stopped near us, among whales larger than even their umiak. The men not Inuit looked at us and at the whales, and we looked at the men. They shouted words to us I could not understand, and we rowed away quickly without answering.

• • •

"Where are you from?" I asked the teacher not Inuit.

He smiled. "Before I answer that, you need to know what to call me. My name is Joseph."

We laughed—who had heard anything like his name? Nenana could not even say Joseph, at first.

"Where I come from, people use names stranger than Joseph," he said. "Jane and Elizabeth for girls; Michael and Carlos for boys."

"But where do they use such names?" I asked.

"You do not forget your questions," he said. He paused and looked at Kwiguk, the Inuit teacher. "I am from the world," he said, finally. "They use names like Joseph there."

We stared at him. Of course he was from the world—we all were.

"I am not from this world," he said.

When he said that, Kwiguk stood up and stopped the class. She made us go to the cafeteria for supper though it was not time for supper, and we sat at tables for an hour till food came.

• • •

"What is the world?" Joseph asked us the next day. He asked many questions and said silly things: that men had made the world; that a building behind the school had a room called elevator that moved down into the rock; that the world had two levels—the one where I lived, and one below mine where men like Joseph lived. "Sanak-of-the-persistent-questions," Joseph said, smiling at me, "can you tell us what the world is?"

I stood up and cleared my throat. Nenana and Talkeetna giggled. I would have pulled their hair if we had not been in school. "The world is two stone bowls spit out from the Raven's craw," I said, looking straight ahead at Joseph, not looking at Nenana or Talkeetna. "The Raven placed the bowls one on top of the other, and we live on the inside surface. The seas are the Raven's spit."

"Or his piss," Kendi whispered, and we laughed.

"Wrong," the teacher said.

60

We looked at him.

"I will show you the world," he said.

• • •

He called the world "satellite" and showed us a picture of it: narrow, white, tubed like a marsh reed but tapered at the ends. "We live on the inside surface, like in Sanak's story," he said. "But what is on the other side?"

"The Raven?" Nenana asked.

Joseph laughed. "The true world is on the other side, the Earth."

He showed us a picture of Earth: round, covered with white clouds, blue where we could see through the clouds to the sea. Joseph put the two pictures side by side. "Our satellite circles the Earth like a mosquito circles your face, waiting for you to go to sleep," he said.

"It's moving?" Kendi asked.

"In different ways," Joseph told us: circling the Earth; rotating fast enough to make fake gravity to give our bodies weight. Weight fooled our bodies, made them think weight was gravity so they would stay healthy. At the ends of the satellite, north and south, we felt less weight, which made jumping easier.

Joseph took us onto the roof of the school to look through a telescope at the side of the world above us. We laughed to see Inuit walking around upside down. "Which way is up?" Joseph asked.

• • •

I looked away and thought of Anvik, my brother, and his scrimshaw. He could carve anything from the ivory tooth of a sperm whale or the tusk of a walrus. Father would give Anvik the best ivory, and on long winter nights when we could do nothing but stay in our igloo and laugh at each other's stories I would sit in front of Anvik and watch him carve. Anvik never minded. "I will teach you to carve when your hands can hold the knives," he would say, and he did, though I could never carve like him—we never traded my scrimshaw for good harpoons or even a dog. Anvik once traded a set of ivory combs for two whale ribs we used as poles in our spring tent.

One night, Anvik handed me a mask he had carved and put together from different pieces of ivory. "Which way is up?" he asked. I held the mask in front of me and saw the face of an angry man with narrow eyes and a thin nose, but when I turned the mask upside down it became the face of a happy man. I helped Anvik rub charcoal in the lines of the mask and then scared Thule with the angry face, but Anvik took it, turned it, put on the happy face and made us all laugh. I wished that Anvik were with me, that he would ask which way was up and make me laugh when I did not know.

• • •

Before morning, in the dark, Joseph gave us our parkas and took us to a room in another building. "This is the room that moves," Joseph said. "It will carry us to the rim of our satellite."

But I did not want to go. I stepped back by Kendi.

"Don't be afraid," Kwiguk said. "You will not fall off the world. You will see what few of your parents and none of your brothers and sisters have seen. New—realities—make us show you these things."

Her tone of voice and her stiff posture told us to remember that we were Inuit, the people, that Joseph was not.

"Believe what you will see," Joseph said. "Even Kwiguk knows you will see the truth."

He looked at Kwiguk, and, finally, she nodded. "Believe it," she said.

I remembered Joseph's stories I had not believed: that the Earth was larger than my world; that men traveled between the worlds in umiaks larger than whales; that on Earth men talked to whales and never hunted them. I was afraid, afraid to believe such stories, afraid to find out if the stories were true, but the door closed and the room dropped.

· · ·

Nenana threw up. When the room stopped moving, Kwiguk cleaned the floor and Nenana's hands. "That wasn't so bad, was it?" Joseph asked. He led us to a room filled with silver chairs that tilted back. The ceiling there was a telescope that let us see past the rim. The ceiling disappeared. We could see more lights in the sky than I had ever seen at night. "The lights are stars, not campfires," Joseph said.

And then the lights moved, and we saw the Earth.

The Earth shone: blue, white, green. The blue was water, Joseph said, the seas. The white not clouds was snow on lands the Inuit had come from. Joseph said more Inuit lived there still than lived on both levels of our satellite. He pointed to an island he called Ellesmere, said it was not quite as large as the world we had made.

And Ellesmere was small on the Earth.

I could only think that there was no Raven, that the Raven had made no world.

· · ·

When the doors opened that night, it smelled like spring. Joseph led us down a gravel path among trees taller than the willows on Atka. The flowers there smelled so good Kendi and I ate a red one, but it did not taste good.

Rock hung above our heads. The air was hot. Joseph and Kwiguk took us into another building, helped pull off our parkas, and gave us cooler clothes to wear. It was still hot. I never thought I liked the cold, but I learned the Inuit were made for it. Joseph and Kwiguk talked to us while we changed.

"The legends got mixed up when the people flew to this satellite," Kwiguk said. "That's all. And the Inuit came here for good reasons. On Earth, the old ways were dying. Men not as Inuit as Joseph came to teach us new ways of believing and living; when we did not accept them they tried to force us, and they took our good lands. But our bad lands were rich with treasures under the rock that made us strong with money, which is what men trade on Earth, what men not Inuit want most, and we traded them money for this world."

"Your ancestors chose to come to this satellite, take the inner level, make it a place where they could keep the old ways," Joseph said. "Mine left the old ways; kept our bad lands on Earth; were called Eskimo, not Inuit; took the outer level of this satellite where we make things and do things our ancestors never imagined. But my ancestors were Inuit; I am Inuit."

Kendi yawned, and Nenana and Talkeetna. Joseph and Kwiguk stopped talking, stopped trying to explain, and sent us to the same room to separate beds. None of us could sleep. I kept expecting our beds to slide away since we were next to the rim past which there was no gravity. So I lay awake holding the sides of my bed and thinking about what Joseph and Kwiguk had said, about what I had seen, and, finally, about home. Mother had told me the Raven made the world for a joke, that

that was why the Inuit were a happy people: we were made to laugh. I thought the Raven would have laughed to hear the things Joseph and Kwiguk said. I did not think my mother would laugh.

• • •

Kendi fell and cut his hand when he and I went running through the halls before breakfast. Joseph and Kwiguk took him to a doctor. I followed to watch. The doctor had hung a shaman's mask in each of his rooms. I kept expecting him to pull down a mask and touch it to Kendi's hand; instead, he smeared white cream over the cut and bandaged it. "All of you will soon have to use medicine: take your children to doctors, give your old people to us rather than leave them in the snow to die," Joseph said.

Kendi's hand healed overnight. A thin, red line marked where the cut had been, but no scab. I thought of cuts I got carving scrimshaw with Anvik, cuts that took weeks to heal. "Doctors can mend broken bones in days," Joseph said. "Grow back arms and legs. Medicine is not evil."

Kwiguk would not look at Kendi's hand. "Why extend life when the reasons for living have been taken away and your world destroyed?" she asked. But a quick healing did not seem bad to me—a man could not hunt when he was hurt; a woman could not cure hides or put up tents when she was in pain. I wanted to ask Kwiguk why it was good to live without medicine, but I did not dare.

"Have you seen anyone die?" Joseph asked. "Someone who, if taken to a warm place or given more help than a shaman's chants, might have lived? Would saving him have destroyed your world?"

• • •

A doctor might have saved Nulato, my cousin, who died hunting caribou on Atka. During the winter, herds of caribou walked across the frozen channel between Atka and the mainland to eat in the willows along the rivers and streams, to eat grass below the snow and lichens on the rocks by the seashore. When the channel ice melted, the caribou stayed on Atka for a time, confused, looking at the mainland. After the grass was gone, most swam across the channel and scattered in small herds in the hills. We always went to Atka in the spring to hunt caribou, and our camps were smoky with fires that dried meat and kept away wolves.

The hunting was easy. The hard part no one liked was dragging carcasses to camp. One day Anvik and Nulato came to me, smiling. "Come hunting with us," Anvik said, and he handed me a spear and my knives. We jogged up the riverbank and lost sight of camp. After we waded through six streams that fed the river, Nulato jumped down the bank and uncovered his and Anvik's kayaks hidden under willow branches. Nulato climbed in his kayak, tucked his spear at his side, rowed upstream across the river, and hid in the willows. Anvik took me around a riverbend to a watering place where caribou had worn down the bank. "You and I will drive the caribou into the water here," Anvik said. "Nulato will spear the stragglers as they swim across the river, and he and I will simply float the carcasses to camp. No more dragging them up hills."

He smiled. I thought of everyone's surprise—men often speared seals from kayaks, but I seldom heard of anyone spearing swimming caribou. A game trail led up from the watering hole to the grassy hills above the willows. Anvik and I ran upwind from the trail, circled back, and came out through the hills above one of the largest caribou herds either of us had seen. Eight or nine hundred caribou were grazing in the valley. At sight of us, they bunched together nervously. Anvik smiled. "We should have had all the men here," he said. "We could have finished our hunt with this herd." He tousled my hair, jumped up, and ran shouting down the hill. I ran, shouting, after him. The caribou bolted up the trail and plunged in the river. Hundreds of caribou were in the river.

But Nulato did not wait for the stragglers. He rowed out in front of the caribou. I thought the caribou would try to swim around him, but they swam straight on, too afraid of Anvik and me, in too much of a hurry to get out of the cold water to notice what lay ahead. Nulato started spearing caribou, and those in front saw him, then, but could not stop or turn—the caribou behind pushed them ahead. Nulato shouted and stabbed at the caribou, but the caribou kept coming, knocked over his kayak, dragged him underwater.

Anvik and I could only watch as the herd swam across the river, as the last stragglers stumbled up the bank, shook water from their hides, ran off into the willows. The caribou had pushed Nulato's kayak onto the riverbank and trampled it to pieces. Eight dead caribou dotted the river.

And Nulato surfaced facedown in the water and did not move.

Anvik shoved his kayak out on the river, rowed quickly to Nulato, and pulled him to shore. Nulato would not move or breathe. I held Nulato's wrist and felt his slow heartbeat till it stopped. Anvik tied Nulato across his kayak and rowed to camp. I ran along the shore, trying to keep them in sight.

The ground was still too frozen to dig a grave for Nulato, so the women washed and clothed the body; the men took kayaks out on the river, found the eight caribou carcasses, pulled them to camp, and dressed the meat. It was dark when they finished. In firelight the shaman beat his drum and danced around Nulato's body, singing songs that would let Nulato sleep. When he stopped, it was quiet. Wood on the fire popped and spat sparks into the air, and the shaman took off his mask and touched it to Nulato's face.

Anvik, Father, and three other men took torches and carried Nulato into the tundra behind camp. Wolves began howling before the men came back.

• • •

For three days Joseph and Kwiguk showed us new things: great farms where Inuit grew foods that gave us diarrhea; plankton induction tanks where men bred plankton in warm water to release in our shallow seas for the whales and fish; crowds of Inuit living in white, stone igloos among trees and streams where it snowed only on holidays.

Joseph showed us lights like stars that were satellites, worlds men had made. "Hundreds of such worlds circle the Earth," he said. "Some are very small, compared to this one. Men bring chunks of rock and ice called asteroids close to the Earth, dig into the rock for the things they trade for money, and melt the ice for water. When the miners finish, other people go and live in the rocks or break them apart to make worlds like ours."

Joseph took us to see the great umiaks men rode between worlds, but he would not take us to the Earth, not even for a day. "It would take three days to get there," he said, though it looked so close. He also took us to the mirrors that powered our satellite and sent light into my level. Even with dark goggles, we could not look at the mirrors themselves. "The light shines through holes timed to open and close in copy of days on Earth," Joseph told us. "Without warmth from this light, everything here would freeze. The air itself would snow down on top of the ice."

"You make winter come?" I asked.

"People like me make your days shorter and shorter so there is less and less light to make heat," Joseph said. "Winter comes for you on the same day every year."

So men like Joseph timed our winters, let us have summer. Knowing that took away my hope for one more warm day before the snow.

•   •   •

"After men not Inuit learned to talk to whales, all whaling on Earth stopped," Joseph said. "You will not be allowed to keep hunting whales, if the whales stay here instead of letting us take them to Earth."

But when I finished school that year, Father planned to take me on my first whale hunt. I had to know, as a man, how to hunt—not just rabbits, ptarmigan, and salmon—but whales.

"Joseph has talked with whales on this satellite," Kwiguk said.

Joseph made the wall in front of us slide back, and we could look through windows into the sea. Dark, huge shapes were swimming there—whales. Joseph had us put on earphones, and we could hear the whales sing. Joseph turned on great lights on the seabed. The whales began to swim away, but Joseph put on earphones and talked to them through a mouthpiece. One bull whale turned and swam slowly toward us. When he bumped the window we all stood up, even Kwiguk, but the glass held. The whale filled the window. He pressed the right side of his face against it and stared at us with one eye.

Joseph smiled. "Come ask the whale your questions," he said, holding out his earphones and mouthpiece. No one moved. Finally Kwiguk walked up to the window, pulled Joseph's earphones and mouthpiece over her head, and spoke to the whale. "Are you happy here?" she asked. The whale sang. A man's voice in our earphones translated: "Yes," the whale had said.

"Do you want to leave here?" Kwiguk asked.

"Only if men keep hunting us."

Kwiguk gave the earphones back to Joseph. The whale went on to talk about the beauty he saw in the sea and of his anger: "Avoid men in boats," he said. "Men kill whales. Men not spare young or old who break water first for air."

Joseph put on the earphones. "What will you do if men keep hunting you?" he asked.

"Kill," the whale said.

I took off my earphones and thought of my father's whale hunt and how the whales would be taken off our world unless we stopped hunting them. But what would we eat? What oil would we burn in our lamps? What would I do at my first whale hunt now that I had heard a whale talk?

• • •

That night, Joseph gave us our parkas and led us to the elevator. No one threw up on the trip back. When Joseph opened the doors we could smell the cold air of home. Kendi and I did not run between the buildings to the school like the rest; we hung back and looked up at the lights in our sky. There were lights there, scattered across the other side of the world. But they were not stars. They were the lights of campfires, and of boats on the sea.

•   •   •

"Come to me when you are sixteen, legal age," Joseph said. "I will take you out, educate you, help you do whatever you want. This world must change, or men on Earth will stop trading with us again."

But I did not care about Joseph's trade. I had only wanted, all my life, to hunt for my family, and now I could not. The very animal we depended on talked, and loved, and plotted revenge.

Kwiguk was angry. "Remember the good things you have with your families. Your ancestors knew what Earth offered, and they rejected it: it was not the Inuit way, not a happy way. Do not let the old ways die."

"But how do old ways die?" Joseph asked. "A culture does not die if it chooses to adapt and change—it becomes something better."

Joseph and Kwiguk told us these things on our last day of school. We were happy for that, at least. All I could think of was going home. But Joseph sat on the desk in front of our class and would not let us go. He looked at us for a long time. "You never know what education will do to you," he said, finally. "You never know what it will make you see. Yours has made you see worlds. Don't give them up."

•   •   •

My parka and trousers stank. I was ashamed to wear them. But when I saw Thule running toward me, her black hair flying back over her open parka hood, I picked her up, swung her around, and hugged her. Her clothes smelled as bad as mine. She did not seem to mind. "What is that, sparkling in the light?" Thule asked, pointing back at the buildings.

"Glass," I said. "Windows."

She looked disappointed. "You already know," she said. I thought of my first year when I'd begun learning new words, and I let Thule tell me the names for the antennae on top of the buildings, the pencils, the toilets.

Thule and I held hands and ran down the valley with the other students. When we got to the seashore, we split into two groups and ran up the beach in opposite directions to where our families camped waiting for us. The sand was wet from a recent rain, and since we were so far north the sand was springy and easy to run in. We hurried around a hill that jutted out into the sea and narrowed the beach. A man stood on the beach, smiling. The others ran past him and called his name: Anvik. Anvik had come to meet Thule and me. He took Thule in his arms and hugged her, dropped her on her feet and hugged me, not caring that Kendi and Nenana were watching. But they ran off. Anvik held me away from him. "You've grown," he said, looking down at my trousers' legs. "And you're through with school. No more of that nonsense."

But I wanted to tell him what I had seen and heard. "We listened to a whale talk, Anvik," I said. He laughed, grabbed my left hand and Thule's right hand and ran, fast, to our camp, pulling us along.

Mother was helping other women cook a feast because, I thought, we had all come home. Kendi's family was there, and Nenana's and Talkeetna's. Fifteen skin tents stretched up our little valley away from the sea. But then I saw Father with the other men sharpening harpoons, knives, and lances.

The feast was not for our return.

"We will leave on a whale hunt tomorrow," Anvik said, his hand on my shoulder.

Mother gave Thule and me a handful of fried minnows. "Anvik is the leader of the hunt," she said, quietly. I could tell from the way she said it that she was so proud of Anvik, so happy. She was the wife of one man and the mother of another. "Anvik brought all these people," she said to me. "It was his doing. His hunt will be your first."

But I did not want a hunt.

"I'll command my own umiak," Anvik said. "Five of my friends will go with me."

I made myself look up and smile. How could Anvik know, after all? Three months before I would have been as happy for him as Mother was—I would have helped him.

And I still would. From what Joseph said, the hunts would end soon enough. With Anvik in his own umiak, my father would need me in his: hunts in the north and south were harder because everything weighed less. Whales moved in ways they could not normally move.

The whales could get away.

If Anvik did not get a whale, he could lead us to Atka to hunt caribou.

Thule hugged Anvik and ran off to find Father. I looked at Anvik.

"I know what you're thinking," he said. "I don't have a wife to give my men." Every leader of a hunt exchanges his wife with his men to cement their friendship.

Mother turned the spit of fish she tended and winked at me. "But if his hunt is successful, the elders will recognize a marriage for him," she said. She nodded at a beautiful girl basting seal roasts over another fire: Taimyr, Kendi's older sister. Taimyr would not look at us.

"Come see our tent," Anvik said.

And I understood. Taimyr and Anvik were friends, and they had agreed to live together. I had known couples to live together till a baby came before the elders recognized them. Mother and Father had done that, and Anvik had gotten them recognized. But if what Mother said were true, the elders would recognize Anvik and Taimyr soon. It would be unusual and wonderful.

Anvik took me into his tent, and it was a fine tent. His whale ribs supported the center, and his scrimshaw hung in rows up the ribs. The seal, rabbit, and caribou pelts on the floor were soft and new. I sat on the pelts and looked at Anvik. All I could think was that he had left home.

• • •

The feasting went late into the night: we ate seal, salmon, caribou, ripe berries. Thule scratched the letters of the alphabet in the sand next to a fire and made everyone laugh, she was so serious. But everyone laughed harder when Kendi, Nenana, Talkeetna, and I tried to tell about all we had seen, heard, and learned.

"You went down through the rock?" Anvik asked.

"The Raven must have spit you back inside," someone laughed.

They thought we'd planned to say the things we said as a joke.

"I'm tired," was all I would say when Mother asked what was wrong.

Suddenly Anvik ran up behind me, grabbed my shoulders, threw me on a blanket. The men picked up the blanket and tossed me in the air. The other children shrieked with delight and begged to be tossed next. I kept trying to stand on my feet:

the men would toss me in the air, and I would try to come down on my feet. Anvik threw Thule on the blanket and pulled me off after they had tossed me seven times. Thule laughed and clapped her hands: having one's brother lead the whale hunt meant less time waiting for a blanket toss.

The umiaks were all drawn far up on the beach. While the men tossed the children, the women danced around the boats singing their magic songs. I left the toss and went to listen to the women sing. Mother held the prow of Father's umiak and sang of life and a safe return. She held the prow of Anvik's and sang the same song twice:

> *Over seas and through all storms,*
> *Alive, and well, and free.*

> *Over seas and through all storms,*
> *And safely back to me.*

The men had piled their harpoons, lances, and knives next to the central fire, and Unalakleet began dancing around the weapons, beating his drum and chanting. One by one, we all went and sat around the fire, ate more meat, and sang with Unalakleet. We sang strong spells, spells that would put the whales in our control or at least make them feel pity for weak men so they would give themselves to us.

But the caribou had had no pity for Nulato; Nulato had had no magic.

Unalakleet stopped, took off his mask, and touched it to Anvik's forehead to bless him. The singing stopped. Unalakleet held the mask to Anvik's forehead for a long time, then swirled his black seal pelt robe around his chest and went to his tent.

Anvik would not look at Taimyr, but she stared at him. After a time she went to the shaman's tent: her last duty before Anvik's hunt. My father began telling hunting stories. The rest took up their weapons and whispered their own charms over them. Mother came for Thule and me. Our tent seemed empty without Anvik, but I was so tired I was soon asleep.

• • •

Father woke me when it was still dark. I dressed quickly. Thule and Mother sat up and watched us leave.

The men had pushed all seven umiaks down onto the water, and Father helped me up into his. Kendi and Kendi's father and three other men were in with us. Anvik pushed his umiak away from the shore and jumped in over the side. Father and five other men pushed out the rest of the umiaks and jumped in. Father sat down next to me, and his boots and the cuffs of his pants were dripping and wet.

I rowed with the other men and watched the fires in our camp merge into one orange light that rose up above our heads. Light came, but the sea was misty and foggy, cold. I did not think we could find whales in such weather. Men in the different umiaks kept calling to each other so we would not get separated.

But after our midday meal the fog cleared, and we could see far out over the ocean. Our seven umiaks were scattered in a long line. We had come to a part of the sea filled with life: seals; plovers, seagulls, and terns overhead, far out from land, hunting fish; even a great bull walrus swimming alone in the water, angry enough to charge our umiak, but lances drove him away. I put my hand in the water, and the water was warm. "We are above one of Sedna's homes," Kendi's father said. Sedna controlled seals, lured men out of their umiaks to drown at her side, and had homes on the seafloor. She kept great fires burning around each house to scare back sharks, and the fires boiled the water, which cooled as it rose to the surface so we could touch it and row across it. Unalakleet often told the story of the day he had hooked a great fish in the warm water above one of Sedna's homes. The fish swam straight down, pulling out all of Unalakleet's line. Unalakleet had been afraid the line would break, but suddenly the fish quit struggling and Unalakleet pulled it in: fried, cooked just right. In its panic, the fish had swum into Sedna's fires.

Kendi smiled at me. I thought of the plankton induction tanks: Kendi and I knew why the water was warm, why this part of the sea never froze and was full of life. The whales would be feeding here.

My father tapped my shoulder and had me pull in my oar. Two men kept rowing, gently. I stood and looked ahead: twenty or thirty sperm whales were spouting, not far away. Our umiak was the closest—we would reach the whales first. Father stood in the prow, harpoon in hand. We came up on the whales slowly, quietly. I imagined them talking to each other. Even so, I put on my gloves, ready to help pull in the rope after the harpoon was thrown, and set my father's lance at his feet.

But the whales saw us or heard us and dropped down into the ocean. Good, I thought. The waves of their sounding rocked our umiak. We all watched the sea. Then I realized the whales had not had time to spout and take in the air they needed. They would surface again, soon. We would be waiting.

• • •

They surfaced behind us. There was no use trying to hide or be quiet. The whales knew we were hunting them. So we rowed hard and fast, and my father watched in the prow. I was soon tired. I hoped the other men were getting tired so we'd stop and let the whales go, but we gained on them—because of our spells or their pity—and suddenly Father stood up and threw his harpoon. Our umiak hit a whale hard, was knocked up into the air and slammed down onto the water but did not capsize. The whale had sounded. Kendi's father laughed as the rope played out over the prow. We held on to the rope to slow down the whale, and the rope burned through my gloves. Our umiak seemed to fly over the ocean, skimming the top of the water. The other men rowed toward us to help kill our whale, shouting happily, each man hoping to be the one to stab its heart with a lance.

Our whale surfaced, finally, far ahead of our umiak but swimming slower. We worked to pull in the rope and got close enough to see barnacles on the whale's mouth and a great scar down its back, relic of some fight. We pulled the rope tight, but suddenly the whale lunged ahead against it, jerked our umiak, knocked Kendi and me to the floor.

"Let the rope hang slack," Father said. He looked unhappy. After a time we pulled in the rope; when it was tight the whale lunged ahead again and again and the harpoon broke free. The whale plunged down into the water.

"He's a smart one," Kendi's father said.

"He's been hunted before," my father said.

• • •

All afternoon and evening we sighted the whales spouting and swimming ahead of us. In the night we let our umiaks drift apart, and one man watched while the rest slept. We kept the whales running, and they were tired.

I tried not to think of the whale we had heard talk, and

Kendi said nothing to me about him. He and I lay together and watched the lights of the Inuit on the other side of the world.

Father woke me in the night when it was my turn to watch. I sat in the prow and looked out over the sea. A strange blue light shone at night on the ocean. I could see far up the sides of the world. Once I thought I saw the jets of whales spouting in the distance, heading back toward land. None of the men watching in the other umiaks called out. Neither did I.

· · ·

In the morning, Anvik harpooned the whale my father had harpooned. We watched the whale sound, swim ahead, pull Anvik's boat over the water. The men in all the umiaks were shouting, rowing hard to catch up. Anvik and his friends dragged in the rope, frantically, and finally the whale could not stand the pain of the harpoon pulling against it, and it surfaced.

It was exhausted. It lay wallowing in the water, spouting. I kept hoping it would get enough air and dive underwater, but Anvik dropped the rope and grabbed his lance. His friends pulled the umiak up to the whale. Anvik stabbed it deep and hard. He pulled out the lance and stabbed it again. Blood spurted across the prow of Anvik's umiak staining it red, staining the water around the umiak red. The whale jerked back and forth. We came up on its other side, and Father stabbed it with his lance.

And the whale sounded. The rope burned out over the prow of Anvik's umiak and knocked one of Anvik's friends into the water. They pulled him back in, red from the whale blood. Anvik smiled and waved at us. His friends were holding the rope, but the umiak was not being pulled ahead. The rope spun out and went straight down. Suddenly Kendi's father and my father grabbed their oars and started rowing away. "Cut the rope and row!" Father shouted to Anvik. Anvik did not understand. The rope quit playing out of Anvik's umiak, and his friends started pulling it in, all slack. When Anvik saw that, he cut the rope and shouted for his men to row, anywhere, in any direction—

The whale burst from the water ahead of Anvik's umiak. It leapt completely from the sea, blood streaming down its sides—something it could not have done, hurt as it was, except in the far north where it weighed less. It twisted in the air and seemed to fall back slowly, seemed to try to keep jumping as if it hoped to reach the oceans it could see on the other side of the world, its flukes jerking up against its sides, twisting, finally, so it would fall back on Anvik's umiak.

Anvik and his friends jumped. The whale hit the umiak, shattered it, went under the water, and surfaced belly up. It turned and spouted blood.

We found Anvik and pulled him in with us. Something had broken inside of him, and his mouth was bloody. I wiped it clean, but the blood came from inside his throat and he coughed and choked. I lifted his head and laid it in my lap. He held my hand, tight. Men in the other umiaks were stabbing the whale again and again.

"Anvik's friends are in umiaks and sitting up," Kendi's father said. Anvik tried to smile. Father, Kendi, and the other men began rowing, fast, for land and our camp. I just sat in the bottom of the umiak and held Anvik's head in my lap.

• • •

Anvik said nothing, to me or to anyone, but he kept coughing blood. All the women, children, and old men ran down to the beach when they saw us rowing in alone. Taimyr screamed and screamed when we lifted Anvik over the side. Mother said nothing, but helped carry Anvik into our tent.

Unalakleet came and held Anvik's head and chanted. Mother and Taimyr held Anvik's hands, and Thule and Kendi stood close to me. I wanted to do something, to try to help. "I'll run for a doctor at the school," I shouted, and I turned to run, but Father grabbed my shoulders and held me back. "It would do no good," he said.

But how did he know? How did he know what doctors could do to save Anvik? "It's not our way," he said, and I wanted to shout at him: "What do you mean, 'this is not our way'—this is Anvik lying here coughing up his blood," but Father looked at me. "Stay here," he said.

Kendi ran from the tent.

• • •

In the evening the other men came with the whale. I heard them grunting and shouting as they pulled it into the shallows by the beach. Anvik opened his eyes and smiled. Suddenly Unalakleet stopped chanting and beating his drum. He left the tent in a hurry, and I did not know why till Mother reached up and closed Anvik's eyes.

Father pulled me to my feet. "Get out and help butcher the whale," he said. He threw back the tent flaps and left. I ran after him.

But he did not go to the whale. He walked out onto the tundra to dig a grave.

The women had fires ready to smoke the whale meat, and the men had stripped off their furs and cut the whale open. They were quiet as I walked up. Two men covered with whale blood waded through the water and heaved a slab of meat down in front of me on top of an untanned skin. I tore off my furs, knelt on the skin, took my knife and started hacking the meat into strips to be smoked.

I hacked at the meat savagely, trying, for all I knew, to hurt the whale. Thule came and stood across from me, and she cried. I would not look up at her. When I had cut a handful of strips, she carried them to the women. I heard her crying as she walked away from me.

And then the men grew quiet, and all the women, and I looked up at Kendi, Joseph, and a doctor: too late. "We might have saved him," Joseph said.

I hated Joseph, then. I suddenly understood what he had done to me. I could never stay here. I would have to go to him when I was sixteen. The women carried Anvik's body into the firelight, and Unalakleet started chanting. I wanted to hack Unalakleet's back with my knife, knock him down, cut open his throat, hold his head back while his blood gushed out onto the ground. But I kept hacking the meat. When I'd cut up my slab, the men threw another in front of me and I cut it apart. Thule carried the meat to the women. I said nothing to Joseph. I do not know when he left.

Late in the night, Thule and I helped our parents and Taimyr carry Anvik out into the tundra. I would not go back with the others. I sat on Anvik's grave and imagined that the lights above me, on the other side of the world, were stars.

NICOJI

I got out of the shower and dressed while I was still wet so that maybe I'd cool off while I walked down to the company store. It was evening and quiet. The store was quiet.

But the ship from Earth had come in.

Vattani was opening a wooden crate with the back of a hammer, and Marcos and Fabio, Vattani's two little boys, were kicking through piles of white plastic packing around his counter. Vattani smiled at me and motioned proudly at his shelves: filled, some of them; restocked, as much as they would be till the next ship.

"Peanut butter!" I said. I grabbed a can of it from the display on the end of the counter. The can was bulged. The peanut butter had frozen in the unheated hold on the way out. But the can felt full. "I'll take it," I said, not asking or caring about the price. Vattani looked at me doubtfully but put down his hammer and keyed in my purchase. I thought of—Morgan, was it?—who said if you had to ask the price you couldn't afford it. Well, I couldn't afford the peanut butter and I knew it so I didn't bother with the price. Besides, they had me. The company had me. What was another twenty or thirty dollars on my bill?

I put the can on the counter and went after the staples Sam and I needed. That's when I saw the company "boy" sitting in the shadows by an open window next to the racks of boots and underneath the hanging rows of inflatable rafts nobody bought because they'd get punctured and the three butterfly nets nobody wanted after the company quit bringing up naturalists. He tapped his gun against his leg and watched me pick up a five-pound sack of rice and a two-and-a-half-pound sack of beans. He moved his chair so he could look at me when I went down another aisle to get a loaf of bread and a jar of vinegar that had an expiration date Vattani hadn't changed. He chuckled when I grabbed a bag of raisins Vattani's wife had dried from the native gagga fruit.

I held out the bag. "Want some?"

He laughed. "We've got apples and bananas in the company house, Jake."

I shoved some raisins in my mouth. "You don't know what you're missing."

"I tried 'em, once."

I thought of different replies to that, communicative things like shoving fistfuls of gagga raisins down his throat.

"How's the college application?" he asked.

My best friend and I had come up, one year out of high school, to earn money for college. I turned and walked back to the counter. "Trouble with shoplifting, Vattani?"

"Less of it. You got your nicoji frozen?" Vattani keyed in the prices of the food I'd picked up.

"Just got in. Sam and I'll eat first."

"Ship leaves in the morning—early. You'll work all night?"

"Sure, work all night."

Vattani stuffed my food in a plastic bag. "You'd better, you and Sam. You missed the last ship, and the price has gone down since then—five cents less per package, now."

"It's the only ship we missed this year. It came early."

"But you missed it, so I had to extend your credit, again. How are you going to pay me back?"

I just looked at him.

"You eat fast and get to work."

I put my right hand on the counter and stared at him. Marcos and Fabio quit kicking the shredded plastic and looked up at us. Vattani waved back the company boy and finally lit the tile under my hand to add forty-six dollars and twenty-three cents to my bill of credit. Then he handed me the groceries. I walked out and let the door slam, listened to the bells over it jangle while I walked down the dirt street.

But I had a can of peanut butter from home, from Earth.

And the sky ahead of me was red on the horizon where the sun was.

• • •

Manoel stopped me just down the street from the store. "Dente," he said in Portuguese, pointing to his teeth. He'd never learned much English. "Raimundo."

"Anda já," I said. He took off down the alley that led to Raimundo's house. I followed.

The company had let Raimundo's teeth rot. Raimundo had asked Sam and me to come help him with his teeth just after we'd gotten in—he thought two Americans would know more about dentistry than the Brazi guys he'd come up with. We didn't. But he was in so much pain I took a pair of electrician's pliers and pulled out the incisor he pointed to. Since then, he'd asked only me to pull his teeth.

Raimundo was sitting on the one step up to his door, holding the right side of his swollen face. He had a pair of pliers tucked between his knees, and he'd stacked alcohol, aspirin, a scrap of clean cotton, and a knife at his side. I put my sack of groceries on the step and looked at him. He handed me the pliers and pointed at the third bicuspid behind his upper canine: black, rotted out in the middle. It must have hurt for weeks. "How can you stand waiting so long?" I asked. But I knew. The company kept promising to bring out a dentist, and a dentist could save Raimundo's teeth if they were still in his mouth.

"Pull it, Jake," he said, his speech thick. He tried to talk out of only the left side of his mouth.

"Let me wash my hands and these pliers."

He grabbed my arm. "Just pull it. Now."

I knelt in front of him. "You take any aspirin?" I asked.

"Six," he said.

Which meant he was hurting bad. He'd generally throw up if he took more than four aspirin—his stomach couldn't handle it. But the company didn't stock any other kind of over-the-counter painkiller. I opened the thinnest blade on the pocketknife, stuck it in the alcohol, and laid it on the cotton. "That's all the cotton you've got?" I asked.

"Manoel packed up the rest," Raimundo mumbled.

That surprised me. Evidently they had their raft packed and ready to go again, though they'd gotten in only a day before Sam and me. No sticking around town for them. "Lean back," I said. Raimundo leaned back against the door frame so he'd have something to push against when I started pulling. "Hold open his mouth," I told Manoel, mimicking what I wanted him to do. He stood left of Raimundo, stuck his fingers between Raimundo's teeth, and held the jaws wide apart. Raimundo grabbed the step with both hands and closed his eyes. I grabbed the tooth with the pliers and pulled hard and fast, to get it over with for Raimundo.

The tooth shattered. Raimundo tried to stand up, but I shoved him back down. Manoel growled Portuguese words I didn't understand—he'd gotten his fingers bitten—but he held on and opened up Raimundo's mouth again. I pulled out the parts of tooth. Only one root came. "I've got to get the other root," I said, and I used the knife to work the root loose enough to grab with the pliers. I pulled it out and laid it on the step with the other pieces of tooth. Blood spattered my arms. Manoel let go of Raimundo's mouth, and Raimundo started spitting blood. I tore off a chunk of cotton, shoved it up where the tooth had been, and had Raimundo bite down.

His hands were white, he'd held on to the step so hard. "You hurt me," he mumbled.

"I'm sorry," I said. "I did the best I could."

He looked at me. Manoel wiped his knife clean on the hem of his shirt.

• • •

I set the can of peanut butter on the table Sam had hammered together from crates Vattani threw away behind his store and listened to Sam whistle while he showered. I was shaking. I'll never pull another tooth, I told myself.

I opened the bathroom door and walked in. Sam stopped whistling. "That you, Jake?" he asked from behind the shower curtain.

"Yes," I said. He started whistling again.

I wiped steam off part of the broken mirror Sam and I had salvaged from the trash heap north of town and looked at all my teeth. They were fine, no cavities.

It was my turn to cook. I went back to the kitchen, dumped three handfuls of beans in a jar, washed them in tepid water from our distiller, and set them to soak on the counter for supper the next night. Then I dumped water and a handful of gagga raisins in a pan and let the raisins plump up while I took a clay bowl and walked out to the freeze-shack for some of the nicoji.

The freeze-shack smelled musty, sweet, like the nicoji. "Light on," I said. I heard a rustling in the shadows and flipped on the light. The help had all scurried under boxes or stacks of burlap sacks. Three help peeked out at me.

"Sorry, guys," I said. The help hate light, even the dim light Sam and I had strung in our freeze-shack.

"It's Jake," some of them whispered. "Jake."

I walked to the far wall where we hung our sacks of nicoji and lifted one down from its hook. It was wet and heavy. I set it carefully on the dirt floor and untied it. Nicoji were still crawling around inside. I put my hand in the sack, and a nicoji wrapped its eight spindly legs around my little finger. I lifted it up. It hung there, its beady eyes looking at me. I flicked it in the pan and picked out eight more nicoji that were still moving, since they'd be the freshest, set the pan on the floor and started to tie up the sack, thinking we shouldn't eat too many ourselves, not now, but then I thought why not? We'd had a good catch. Even Vattani would be proud of Sam and me.

Not that it mattered how well Sam and I did.

So I put four more nicoji in the pan, threw one or two nicoji in each corner of the freeze-shack, and hung the sack back on its hook. The help waited till I switched off the light to scramble out after the nicoji.

· · ·

Sam was still in the shower. I banged on the door. "Supper, Sam!" I yelled. Whenever we first got back in town, he'd stay in the shower just letting the water run over him, trying to feel clean; then, after he'd taken all the water in the rooftop storage tank, if it didn't rain, we had to go to the well half a mile away for cooking water and to the company bathhouse if we wanted a bath—five dollars each.

I dumped the water off the raisins, poured in a cup of vinegar, sprinkled sugar and a dash of salt over that, and turned on the heat underneath the pan. When the raisins started bubbling, I washed the thirteen nicoji, chopped off their heads and stiff little legs and tails, gutted them, rinsed the blood off the bodies, dumped them in with the raisins and vinegar, and set them to simmer. The photograph of Loryn, my girlfriend back home, had fallen out of the windowsill onto the stove. I dusted it off and stuck it back in the window.

Sam padded out from the shower, still wet, toweling his hair dry. When he saw the can of peanut butter he just sat down and held it.

"It's been two years," I said.

· · ·

We ate our nicoji over rice and, though the nicoji had made me a slave, I still loved the taste. "They never get 'em like this back home," I said, "fresh."

Sam nodded. We finished the nicoji and carried the peanut butter and bread to the veranda and sat on the steps. The gravitational wind was blowing, and it felt cool, off the sea. We sat facing into it. The moon was so big, it didn't pull in just tides: it pulled the atmosphere along with it, and we could count on relief from the heat at least twice a day. I tore the bread into thin pieces. Sam pushed up the tab on top of the can, broke the seal, and carefully peeled back the lid. I wiped the peanut butter stuck to it onto a piece of bread, tore the piece in two, gave Sam half, and we ate without a word.

One of the help wandered out, dragging the garbage sack from the kitchen. The help were famous for scrounging through garbage sacks and trash heaps. This help had on someone's greasy old shirt that hung in tatters, open. Whoever had thrown it away had cut off and saved all the buttons.

The help dumped out the garbage and rummaged through it looking for the heads, legs, and tails I'd cut from the nicoji we'd had for supper. Little eight-legged "ants" had swarmed all over the nicoji hard parts. The help let a few ants crawl on his fingers, and he watched the ants run up and down his hand. He ate the ones that started up his arm. Eventually he settled back to eat the nicoji, ants and all, watching Sam and me. Suddenly he stuck his fingers in the peanut butter. "Hey!" I yelled. I swatted his hand away, but he lifted it up with a look of horror on his face. He sniffed the peanut butter on his fingers, wrinkled his nose, and looked at Sam and me eating peanut butter on our bread. He tried to shake the peanut butter off and finally ran to the street and rubbed his fingers in the dirt till they were clean. He came back for the nicoji and walked away, disgusted, leaving the garbage scattered. Sam and I shoved the garbage in the sack and sat back down.

The night had cooled off. There were clouds around us, and lightning, and when it rained it wouldn't matter that Sam had taken all the water. The moon was rising. It filled a third of the sky, shining red through the clouds.

"You boys still eating?"

It was Vattani walking home with his two sons, holding their hands. "Go help your mother home from the bayou," he told them. The boys ran off. Senhora Vattani washed other teams' clothes in the bayou. Sam and I washed our own clothes, to save money, and Senhora Vattani used to hate us for cheating her out of work, at least till we started bringing her new plants from the pântano for her garden.

Vattani marched up to our veranda.

"You let my friend vagabundo buy a can of your peanut butter," Sam said. "Muito obrigado."

"Vagabundos—both of you," Vattani said. "The ship will leave in three hours. Other teams have already taken their nicoji to the company house."

"You told me the ship would leave in the morning," I said.

Vattani shrugged. "I was wrong. Ships keep their own time."

Ships keep the company's time, I thought.

"Thanks for the warning," Sam said.

• • •

I wrapped the peanut butter in a towel to keep off the ants and grabbed our butcher knife to cut the nicoji with. Sam used his pocketknife. I got our two buckets, one to fill with disinfected water to rinse the nicoji in after we'd gutted them, the other to throw the guts in. We went out to the freeze-shack, pulled down our sacks of nicoji, and set them by the freezer. The freezer was a rectangular machine that misted the nicoji with water and packed them in square, five-pound blocks that were wrapped in plastic and lowered into liquid nitrogen which, at minus 195 degrees Fahrenheit, flash-froze the nicoji, forming ice crystals too small to rupture the cells, preserving the color, nutritive value, and taste. The company shipped the nicoji to a station above Earth where they were graded, UNDA-inspected, given a final packaging, and shipped down to market as one of the most sought after luxuries.

We'd hung dim red lights over the table where Sam and I sat to do our cutting. After we turned on the freezer and adjusted the nitrogen pump, we turned off the other lights in the freeze-shack and the help came out. Sam and I had twelve help following us around just then. We'd had as many as thirty. They'd take turns feeding nicoji bodies down the hole on top of the freezer till the weights registered five pounds and a red light started flashing; then they'd jump from the stool and reach their leathery little hands around Sam and me very carefully, very quietly—holding their breath, almost—and snatch the piles of heads, tails, and legs. They didn't like the guts as much as the hard parts. We could hear them munching and chittering in the corners all night every night we worked the freeze-shack. By morning they'd be sick from eating so much.

"Slow down," Sam said. "Leg." He pointed with his pocketknife to a bit of leg I'd left on the nicoji I'd just cut. The company inspectors had opened a package from our last shipment and found a tiny bit of chitinous leg. They docked half our money for that. You couldn't train the help to reject a nicoji that still had part of a leg or tail—they liked the stuff—so you had to make sure yourself. Some teams had so much trouble with the inspectors that they worked together, one team to cut, the other to inspect what had been cut. Sam and I weren't that good yet, hadn't started making enough money to be in danger of paying off Vattani and buying a ticket home.

One of the help started parading around the freeze-shack rattling the two peach pits we kept in a can. I got up and took the can away from him and hung it back on its nail. Sam and I'd each gotten a peach our first Thanksgiving out but didn't plant the pits. It was too hot here, though when we were going to get someplace on this planet cool enough to plant peaches I didn't know.

"I got a letter," Sam said when I sat back down.

I looked up. I hadn't, again. Even Loryn hadn't written for seven months.

"My family got the nicoji I sent for Christmas," Sam said.

It was soon Christmas, and the company would ship nicoji at reduced rates to our families so they would think we were making lots of money and were all right—sent the packages with company versions of our letters.

"Think Vattani got his camera fixed?" I asked.

Sam shrugged. Vattani had had a camera our first year out, and Sam and I cleaned up, rented clothes in Vattani's store to dress up in, and had our pictures taken to send home—we'd sat in the back of Vattani's store in rented clothes holding up handfuls of nicoji we'd caught ourselves. The company'd loved it. We'd been out two months.

Sam started sucking his finger. "Something bit me," he said.

"No nicoji," I said.

He nodded. He stirred the pile of nicoji in front of him with his knife. One started crawling away, and Sam stabbed it and held it up on the end of his blade—a nicoji shark: a carnivore that had evolved into looking like a nicoji. It had been in heaven, trapped in that sack with thousands of nicoji, and it was fat. Sam flicked it to the ground. One of the help stomped it with his heel to make sure it couldn't bite, then started tossing it in the air. He'd throw it so hard it would hit the ceiling and slam back down on the dirt.

Another help started squealing and jumping up and down—the freezer was out of plastic to wrap nicoji in. I ran for some plastic while Sam turned off the freezer and made the help stop pushing nicoji down the chute. I brought back three boxes, loaded one in the freezer, and we started up again. You couldn't train the help to go after plastic.

"Got enough plastic?" Sam asked.

"Most of last month's," I said.

Sam laughed. It was another way the company kept us. We had to pay rent on the freezers and go to Vattani's store for plastic and liquid nitrogen and company-approved disinfected water to mist the nicoji with.

Sam started humming the tune the company played on its ads back home—"Make a million; Eat nicoji. Spend a million; Beat the times"—and the rain started: a few drops hit the tin roof of our freeze-shack like bullets, then a downpour came in an explosion of sound that made me remember Javanese rock concerts. The help covered their ears and ran under crates, sacks, and our chairs, chittering loudly, trying to be heard over the rain. But the rain could fall for hours and Sam and I had a deadline to beat, so I kept cutting nicoji and Sam stood up to feed nicoji to the freezer.

The help quit chittering, suddenly.

I looked up. Sam looked up, and then we heard a pounding on the door. I ran to open it, and Sam switched off the freezer.

It was Raimundo, wet to the skin. He stepped just inside the door, brushing water from his arms, his pants dripping on the dirt floor. I pushed the door shut.

"I owe you," Raimundo said to me. "I've come to pay you back for helping me with my teeth."

I didn't know if he meant he was going to beat me up for the pain I'd caused him, or what. He walked to where Sam sat, and I followed. "Turn on the freezer," he said. He wanted noise. I thought the rain made enough noise, but Raimundo wanted more. Sam turned on the freezer.

"A new company's set up base on the mesão," he said.

We just stared. The mesão was a huge mesa rising out of the pântano two weeks south of us—solid land to build on, but days away from nicoji marshes, we were told, and out of our concession anyway. The company had its concession only till scientists decided whether the help were sentient or merely imitative, and it could keep its part of this world only if the help weren't sentient. I wondered if the coming of this second company meant ours had finally bought off the scientists and had their "decision."

"The new company's Brazilian registry and will buy your contracts and give you citizenship. It pays well. Its town has cinemas, more stores than one, good doctors, and women."

"How do you know?" I asked.

"I met one of their teams in the pântano. They had new equipment—prods that shocked nicoji out of the mud before the tide."

"And they told you this—about the cinemas and the women?"

"Do I look like a fantasist? Do I look like my brain is full of lagarto poison?"

I looked at Sam.

"Manoel and I are poling south to this new company. I spit on American Nicoji for keeping me here three years and letting my teeth rot."

He spat on the floor. I hoped, for his sake, that there was a new company with a dentist. "Come, too," Raimundo said. "You won't need your insurance, then."

Sam laughed.

"Do you still have your insurance?"

I nodded. The option to buy life insurance from firms not owned by the company was the one real benefit the company-controlled union allowed us. Sam and I had named each other the beneficiary of our policies.

"So if Sam dies, you get to go home?" Raimundo laughed, asking me.

"And vice versa," I said.

"Aren't you afraid he will kill you in the night?" Raimundo asked Sam, pointing his thumb at me.

Sam smiled.

"If they let you go home," Raimundo said.

Everybody wondered if they'd really let us go home, where we could talk and dry up their supply of workers. I knew only one guy who'd left: Ben Silva. He'd scrimped and saved and one day made enough from a catch to pay off Vattani and buy a one-way ticket halfway home. That was good enough for him. They'd made him wait three days before letting him up to the ship, and he sat the whole time on the steps of the company house, afraid they'd leave him if he wasn't ready the minute they called. He hadn't bought another thing, not even food, worried he wouldn't have enough money for something he touched that they'd charge him for and that they'd cancel his ticket before he could borrow money to pay off Vattani again. Sam and I took him some food on the second day. He said he'd write us a letter and say, "The nicoji here tastes like duck liver," which would really mean he'd made it home in one piece, alive. We never got a letter.

"Will you come?"

I looked at Sam. We were both thinking the same things. We'd been Americans all our lives, and it might be fun to be Brazis for a while—the average person had three different citizenships in his lifetime because of company transfers. We even spoke a little Portuguese. But getting American Nicoji to sell our contracts was the problem. If it wouldn't, we'd be in big trouble when we got back here. And if we broke contract and stayed with the new company anyway, we'd have to stay with them forever no matter what they were like. Breaking contract would ruin our work records. Only renegade corporations would hire us after that. It was also nearly hurricane season, and we usually stayed close to the company town then. Besides, Raimundo had been quick and free with his story, and we'd learned not to trust anyone who was easy with information. Our first month out, an older team had given Sam and me directions to a nicoji hole they knew about, and we'd followed their directions to one of the worst holes in the pântano. I wondered if Raimundo was setting up an elaborate joke on me to get even.

"Does this company have a station?" I asked.

"Claro que sim, Jake—of course."

"Why haven't we seen it in the night sky?"

"They positioned it a few degrees below the horizon. American Nicoji already had the spot above us."

Sam and I just looked at him.

"The new company pays experienced guys more—they located so close to us, on the very edge of our concession, to draw us all off to work for them."

I looked down and scuffed my right shoe on the ground.

"Oh, I get it," Raimundo said. "Don't trust me. Don't come

with someone who's had the way pointed out to him. But when I do not come back from the pântano, think of what I said and head for the south edge of the mesão. We'll party in the new town."

He kicked a nicoji tail to the help crouched under my chair. "Ten cents less per package, this ship," he said. He turned and walked to the door. I let him out and watched him run under the eaves of our house and up the street, splashing through the rain and mud.

"Vattani said five cents less," I told Sam.

• • •

If Raimundo's story were true it meant a way out—a new company that would buy our contracts gave us a place to start over. If it paid a fair price for nicoji, Sam and I could earn passage home someday.

We got back to work. Most of the help crawled out from under the sacks and boxes and chairs after the rain stopped. I wasn't paying much attention to anything but my thoughts— just automatically cutting off nicoji heads, legs, and tails; gutting the bodies and rinsing them; stacking the bodies to one side and sliding the hard parts to another; thinking of movie theaters and dentists—when one of the help started screaming. Sam switched off the freezer, and I jumped up. The help stuffing nicoji down the chute had his hand caught, had probably dropped a nicoji down the chute after the red light started flashing and tried to grab it back. I ran to his side, and he quit screaming once he could see that Sam and I knew what had happened to him. He was shaking so bad the stool he stood on shook, and when I leaned against him to look down the chute, he rubbed his head on my shoulder.

"Hand's caught in the wrapper, Sam, and bleeding."

Sam ran for the alcohol. I flipped the wrapper setting to retract and pulled back the wrapper's arms. The help flipped out his hand and jumped down from the stool. Before he could run away, I grabbed him and pulled the melted plastic from his hand. Sam came and dumped alcohol over the cuts. The help howled. I smeared on an antibacterial cream that must have felt good because he calmed down while I bandaged his hand. Sam started cleaning the freezer. Two of the help's fingers were broken, and he'd have bad bruises. I made little splints for his fingers and sent him off with four uncut nicoji in his good hand.

• • •

We worked till half past midnight, then put on our insulated gloves, boxed up our packages of nicoji, and carried them to the inspectors. Sam and I were the last team in line. Eloise Hansdatter was just ahead of us, gun strapped to her leg, careful to watch us walk up, make sure who we were. The few women up here had to be careful. She was telling a team of Brazis about a scam of lagarto that had crawled onto the lower branches of the tree she was sleeping in. "Poison was rank on their breath," she said. "I started to hallucinate just breathing the fumes—saw talkative naked men all around me in the trees. I had to kill the lagarto just to make the men shut up." The Brazis laughed. I smiled at Sam. Eloise worked alone and would not stop talking when she was in town because for weeks at a time she had no one to talk to but herself. Even so, you had to like her.

"Freeze all your nicoji?" she asked Sam and me.

Sam laughed.

"Thought not," she said. "Me either—which made my help happy: they know I'll give them what's left when I'm out of here."

She didn't mean just out of the company house—she meant out of the town. Eloise never slept here. She'd take out her raft, drift down different bayous, and spend the night guarded by her help.

The company had strung one light bulb over the door, and the guys standing in the light were swatting bugs. Something dropped into my hair and crawled inside my shirt and down my back. I started squirming, and it started biting. "Something's biting my back, Sam!" I said.

He got behind me, shoved his boxes against my back, and smashed whatever was biting me. "Why did they put up this light?" I asked. No one had ever kept a light outside before.

"My help couldn't stand it," Eloise said. "They're off in the shadows. When it's my turn to go in, I'll have to go get my boxes from them." She'd worked with the same group of help ever since she'd come up, and they always carried her boxes to the company house for her. They were jealous little devils that would hiss at you if you sat too close to Eloise and throw trash at you if you stayed too long in the freeze-shack she ran with two of the other female teams. But they only treated you that nice if Eloise actually let them know she didn't mind that you were there. If she did mind, or if the help thought she was in any danger, watch out. Just before Sam and I came up, two guys tried to jump Eloise, and her help practically bit them to death before she could pull the help off and keep them off—one of the guys had an eye chewed right out of its socket and he'd had to start wearing a patch. For her sake, I was glad Eloise had her help. Guys talked about poisoning them so they could have a little fun with Eloise, but no one ever tried it.

Agulhas, tiny bugs with eight needle-sharp suckers spaced evenly on their bellies, started swarming over our feet and crawling up our legs. Eloise tried to keep them brushed off her legs and ours, but she couldn't do it—there were too many bugs. That was it for me. "Turn out the light!" I yelled. Other guys and Eloise started shouting the same thing.

A company boy shoved out through the door. "Shut up!" he yelled.

"The light's attracting bugs," I yelled back.

"Then complain to your union rep when he comes next month. He insisted you guys needed this light."

The union rep hadn't asked us about putting a light outside in the dark.

"Think of this as your bonus for being last in line," company boy said. "More bugs to swat." He laughed and turned to walk inside.

"Just turn it out!" I yelled.

"And what will we tell your union?" He swatted his neck, looked at his hand, and rubbed it on his pants.

"Tell the guys in there to hurry," Eloise said.

"Oh, you want me to tell the inspectors they're too slow? You want them to hurry and maybe not figure the right price for your nicoji but at least get you inside and out of the bugs?"

Nobody said a word to that.

Sam and I finally got inside and onto a bench where we swatted the agulhas on our legs and sat with our cold boxes steaming beside us on the bench and under our feet. I pulled off my shirt and had Sam try to see what bit me at first, but he'd smashed it so bad he couldn't tell what it was. He brushed off my back, and I shook out my shirt and put it back on.

A company boy walked up and down the aisle in front of us, leering, swinging his billy club onto the palm of his hand. The company boys needed clubs. The company house saw trouble.

"Next."

We set our boxes on the counter. The inspectors took them to a table and tore into one, tossing random packages of nicoji onto scales and then into a microwave. They cut open the thawed packages, and nicoji juice spurted out over the inspectors' plastic aprons. One fat inspector kept shoving our raw nicoji in his mouth four at a time, chewing and swallowing. He started into another box.

"Hey!" I yelled. "That's one already."

He jerked his thumb in my direction. "You guys get the special treatment after last time."

Sam grabbed my arm. I could hear the company boy walking up behind us, slapping his club onto his palm. I wanted to shove the club down his throat, but I knew better than to try it. The inspectors had our nicoji.

They tore open packages from each box. When they finished, the fat inspector stuffed his mouth full of our nicoji again, counted the packages left whole, thought for a minute, then sputtered a price. A different inspector keyed the money into our account and printed out a receipt. Sam put it in his shirt pocket. We turned to leave.

"This way, farm boys."

Company boy stood in front of us, pointing down a hallway with his club. Farm boys? At least I'd had a job before coming up here—at least I hadn't been a thieving street thug.

"Yeah," I said, and I started to brush by. I always walked out the front door.

He grabbed my shirt collar. "You hard of hearing? I said this way." He tried to shove me in the direction he wanted me to go. Six more company boys ran up. Before I could do anything, Sam grabbed my arm and pulled me down the hall. The company boys followed. I shoved Sam away from me, mad that he'd stopped me, even though I knew fights only got us trips to the correction field and made us poorer after we'd paid for damages and the company boys' medical bills.

Eloise staggered out from a room at the end of the hall, holding the back of her right wrist. Two company boys shoved her through a door and out of the building. The company doctor met us in the room Eloise had been in. He'd flown down from the station. He hardly ever flew down. "This won't take long," he said. "It's for your safety, sons."

He called everybody "son" though he looked so small and scrawny he probably couldn't father anything.

"What's for our safety?" Sam asked.

"These implants—locators," he said, holding one up. "Help us find you if you get lost in the pântano."

He was going to implant a locator on the back of our wrists.

"They're really quite simple," he went on. "The bottom of each locator is coated with a mild acid that quickly destroys the underlying skin, allowing the locator to replace it. The surrounding skin eventually bonds to the edges of the locator, making it a permanent, if shiny, part of your wrists—quite a comfort, I'm sure, when you'll be . . . away from here."

Sam and I stared at him.

"These locators run on minute amounts of power drawn from the natural electrical impulses in your bodies, so they quit functioning if you're killed or if they're removed."

A warning: don't cut them off. They'd have a fix on your last location and come looking. The doctor stepped up to a chair. "If one of you'd please sit here and let me disinfect your wrist, we'll get started."

Neither of us moved. Two company boys grabbed my arms and dragged me toward the chair. "Scared of a little pain, Jake?"

one sneered. "Don't worry. We'll hold you like your mommy used to when the doctor'd give you shots in the ass."

"Freeze you," I said. I broke away, slammed my fist on the guy's nose, and heard it snap. He fell into the doctor, and they both fell in the chair. Sam kicked the table and knocked down the implanter, scattering locators all across the floor. The other company boys ran in. I knocked one down, but two grabbed my arms and shoved me up against the wall. The guy I'd hit on the nose, his face bloody, kicked me twice in the stomach. Someone hit the back of my head with his club, and I fell to the floor. I couldn't get up. I started smashing locators with my fist, but I felt a sting in my leg and the room went black.

• • •

I came to, covered with agulhas, lying in mud in the circle of light in front of the company house. On the back of my right wrist, bloody, was a locator. It felt tight in the muscle when I moved my hand. I tried to sit up but then dropped back, dizzy from the drug they'd put me out with.

"Hey, one of them's awake," somebody yelled from back by the company house. I heard steps splashing through the water toward me. I turned to see who was coming, but all I could see were his legs. He kicked Sam in the ribs. Sam rolled over next to me, sprawled an arm across my chest. A company boy crouched down, unbuttoned Sam's shirt pocket, and pulled out our receipt. "This will cover half the cost of what you two pulled in there," he said.

He stood up. "Get out here! These two are waking up."

I heard guys running through the water. I tried to sit up, but I couldn't. I kept blinking, trying to see. Two guys pulled me to my feet, and two others pulled up Sam. They dragged us down the street and into the correction field south of the garbage dump.

"Put 'em in here."

They tore off our shirts and shoes and made us crouch down into narrow metal boxes and clamped our wrists above our heads and our ankles to the floor. Some guy stood to one side and recited legal stuff at us—about how the company was empowered and obligated to keep law and order, about how we'd known this when we'd signed contracts with the company, and how we'd agreed to abide by its rules and regulations and accept its punishments.

"Let me out!" Sam yelled.

They were making examples of us: look what happened to Sam and Jake when they tried to get out without a locator. Better get the locators on your wrists. What's acid eating a little of your skin compared to this?

I heard the doctor talking: "Hearts are OK—I checked them when they were out. No danger with these two."

"Son of a bitch!" I yelled. "You castrated, excised, son of a—"

They slammed down the box lids and turned on water.

"Let me out!" Sam yelled.

We had no light in the boxes. They filled the boxes with so much water I had to tip my head back to keep my nose out. The doctor lifted up the lids and looked at us, then dropped them back down. He and the company boys stood around the boxes, talking.

"There's something alive in here!" Sam yelled.

A company boy laughed.

"Get it out!"

I heard Sam thrashing around. Something settled onto my shorts and started crawling up my stomach. Its eight, feathery legs tickled across my skin. I tried to hold myself very still.

Whatever was on me had stopped moving and clung to the hair on my chest. After a while, it crawled onto my neck and up under my chin, just at the edge of the water. I couldn't stand it. I shook it off, and it settled back down onto my stomach and bit me. I could feel it sucking blood through the skin. I thrashed around in the water and tried to shake it off, but I couldn't. "It bit me!" I yelled. "Get it off."

"2:25," the doctor said. "Write that down."

He lifted up the lid. "Just got to get a blood sample," he said. He drew blood out of my neck. He took blood from Sam after he got bit. "Nothing to worry about, boys," he said. "You're just helping me with a little research. Back in an hour to check your blood." All legal, according to our contracts: criminals could be used in nonlethal scientific experiments. The doctor dropped down the lids, and we heard him and the company boys walk away.

• • •

The doctor checked our blood at three hourly intervals, then drained out the water. He left the lids open, and in the waning red moonlight I could see the bloodsucker. Its head was buried in my skin. The eight spindly arms around its head clung to my belly, and its bloated body had flopped down against my stomach. The doctor looked in at me, then soaked a piece of cotton in alcohol and touched that to the back end of the bloodsucker. The bloodsucker pulled out its head, fast, and the doctor tore it off me, threw it in the mud, and treated the bite. Then he got the bloodsucker off Sam and took care of him. He closed the lids and left us shivering in the wet boxes.

The help found us sometime before dawn. I heard them chittering. "Lift up the lids," I said.

"Jake!" one of them said. "Jake!"

The lids were locked down. "Wait for us by the house," I told them. But I didn't know if they'd wait for us, and we needed them. "Eat the nicoji we left in the freeze-shack," I told them. "It's yours."

We wouldn't have frozen it. The company paid only a third of the normal price for packages that came in after the ship had gone—barely enough to cover the cost of plastic wrapping and liquid nitrogen. They claimed it wasn't fresh. The help ran off.

It rained most of the day, so it never got too hot in the boxes. The company boys pulled us out that night, after twenty-four hours. Sam and I couldn't walk. They dropped us in the mud. A company boy threw our gloves, shirts, and shoes in the water beside us and stomped off, splashing water in our faces. I grabbed our gloves and held them on my chest so they wouldn't get wet inside. After a while I pulled Sam up. "Let's go," I said. But we didn't go home. We staggered down the streets through red moonlight to Raimundo's house. He'd told us the truth about there being a new company. American Nicoji didn't put locators on us for our safety, to help us if we got lost. They wanted to keep track of us, keep us from defecting south to the new company.

Raimundo was gone.

• • •

We decided to sleep in our own house that night and head out in the morning. The help were waiting for us. They hadn't been able to get the sacks of nicoji down from the hooks, so we still had nicoji to eat. I took down a sack and gave it to the help.

"And we've got this to finish," Sam said, picking up the can of peanut butter I'd wrapped in a towel.

But the towel was covered with ants.

Sam dropped the towel on the floor. The can was thick with ants. Sam took out his pocketknife, scraped off the top layer of peanut butter where the ants were, and flicked the ants off the sides and bottom of the can. I brushed off the table. We sat and ate the peanut butter with our fingers.

In the night, the help who had gotten his hand hurt crawled on top of my chest and patted my face till I woke up. "Yeah?" I whispered, trying not to wake Sam. The help held up his hand. "Being better," it chittered.

I knew it would be. The help had such fast metabolisms— they healed faster than anything I'd seen.

"What you want me do nice you?" the help asked.

"Let me sleep."

He patted my face. "What you want most? What you want most, Jake?"

I closed my eyes. "To go home," I said.

He scampered down off my chest and hardly made a noise as he ran out across the straw sleeping mats Sam and I had woven.

• • •

I lay there and thought of home. I remembered one day in particular, the day that started Sam and me toward this place. Sam and I had climbed into a truck with Loryn, my girlfriend, to eat lunch. We'd been running potato harvesters while Loryn drove one of the trucks we dumped the potatoes into. It was a cold day, and the sky was overcast and gray. It looked as if it might snow.

We pulled off our gloves and hats and opened our sacks. We had the same things for lunch: roast beef sandwiches, potato chips, apples, hot chocolate. Loryn sat in the middle. "Hitachi Farms got their last spuds in at 11:00," she said. She heard things like that in the pits when she dumped her potatoes.

"Beat us again," Sam said.

"They beat everybody, again," Loryn said. "CitiCorp and UIF don't expect to get done till next week. They're hoping for snow."

The potatoes wouldn't freeze under a blanket of snow. They could still be dug.

"We'll finish today," I said.

We worked for Westinghouse Farms. In the spring, we'd tried to get on with Hitachi, but the Supreme Court had struck down Idaho's intrastate labor laws and Hitachi had brought in cheap contract labor from California and didn't hire local help. All the corporate farms were watching Hitachi's profit margin. If it was good enough, every farm would switch to contract labor, and Sam and Loryn and I'd either be out of work or we'd have to sign five-year contracts with one of the agricultural labor pools and forget doing anything else. You couldn't get ahead on contract labor. You'd have to sign up for another five-year stint, then another and another till you died. So every Idaho farmhand worked hard, trying to make our farms beat Hitachi.

From where Loryn had parked the pickup, we could look down over the dry farms to Alma, the county seat, built on bluffs above the Snake River. The clouds above the city had broken, and Alma looked blessed in the light, the white houses and churches shining, surrounded by dark fields. But the clouds closed up again, and it started to snow. The snowflakes melted on the windshield, the hood of the truck, and the ground. I downed the rest of my hot chocolate, shoved my half-eaten sandwich back in my sack, and looked at Sam. He had two more bites of his sandwich to go. Loryn just held hers. "Trouble," she said.

I looked up from pulling on my gloves. A Westinghouse pickup pulled to a stop in front of the truck. Sam and I climbed out. Loryn slid over behind the wheel. Floyd Johnson, one of the foremen, climbed out of the pickup. So did Doug Phillips, from Hitachi. Loryn climbed down from the cab when she saw Doug Phillips. The other drivers got out of their trucks and hurried over.

"Hitachi bought us out," Floyd said. No explanation. We'd had no hint Westinghouse was selling out.

"I hope I can welcome you into Hitachi," Phillips said. "We got Hitachi equipment and teams headed here to finish digging these spuds, but we could use all of you running the old Westinghouse equipment. Just go down to the pits first and sign the contracts we got waiting there."

"Five years?" I asked.

"Standard."

I looked at Sam and Loryn.

"We'll take everybody but you, Sam," Phillips said.

Because Sam had sent away for a copy of *Corporate Feudalism* after the county library wouldn't order it in. It was all I could figure. The book said we were no better off than feudal serfs who gradually—and probably without realizing it at first, if ever—gave up their freedoms in return for physical protection. Relatively recently, our ancestors had once again given up the freedom to control their lives—had let corporations in effect buy them—this time in return for economic well-being. Corporations now had the land and the wealth and hence the power, and most men and women had become merely productive or unproductive units tallied in offices continents away. We were serfs, again, serving a corporate aristocracy. The first serfs cast off their chains after a thousand years of wearing them. When would we find the courage and vision to cast off ours, the book asked. Sam had passed that book around to too many people, and when Westinghouse found out about it they'd nearly fired him. Now Hitachi wouldn't take him.

"You'll all get paid for the work you've done here," Floyd said.

Loryn, Sam, and I drove back into Alma. Loryn and I wouldn't sign Hitachi's contracts, and none of us knew what we were going to do. We passed the Hitachi equipment and workers headed for our fields. One of their harvesters got caught in a rut in the muddy road and veered into our truck. We skidded off the road into a ditch. The cab filled with freezing water, and we couldn't open the doors because the ditch banks were snug against the truck. I held my breath and tried to kick out the windshield, but it wouldn't break though I kicked it, and kicked it, and kicked it—

•   •   •

I sat up. It was still night. I'd gone to sleep and started dreaming. We hadn't been forced into a ditch to drown. Sam and I ended up here. Loryn got work with a feed supply franchise, but it didn't pay much and in her last letter she said she might be getting a new job. She hadn't said what. I wondered what she was doing. My stomach felt tight like it always did when I thought about signing contracts with labor pools.

Sam was gone. I heard someone in the freeze-shack, so I stumbled out there, rubbing my eyes, blinking in the light when I opened the door and walked in. Sam looked up and smiled. He was sitting on the floor, getting ready to drain the liquid nitrogen from the freezer. "Just in time," he said. "I need help with this nozzle."

"What are you doing?"

"Packing up everything we've paid for."

I laughed. We hadn't talked about going to the new company

to check it out, but we hadn't needed to. We were going, and we both knew it, hurricane season or not. We'd head south as far as we could without upsetting American Nicoji, then we'd cut out the locators and head for the new town. If we didn't like what we saw, we could always come back, face the correction fields and fines.

Sam had me hold a wrench clamped on the bolt below the nozzle so the hose on the nitrogen can wouldn't turn while he screwed the nozzle in place. Once done, he pulled the drain lever, and we sat on the ground with the can between us, listening to the nitrogen hiss into it.

"I dreamt it was snowing," I said.

"Here?"

"Back home."

We looked at each other.

"You scared?" I asked.

"Just about hurricanes. I can take the rest."

Hurricanes scared us. One had slammed into the coast three hundred miles north of the company town two years ago, and we'd had waves forty feet high. The company had evacuated us up to the station. I did not like to think how high the waves would get under the storm itself.

"We might have the help for company," Sam said. The help always left us at the start of hurricane season. They'd go south with us as long as we went south, but if we turned north, east, or west it was good-bye for three months. We thought they probably went to the mesão to wait out the storms. Now we'd find out if that was true.

"I want to chance it," Sam said.

So did I. "Where are the help?" I asked. We needed them to carry stuff down to the raft.

"I shooed them out before I turned on the light," Sam said.

I hurried outside and looked around. I couldn't see any help, so I took down a sack of nicoji and scattered nicoji over the ground. The help immediately came out of the shadows. I let them eat, then Sam and I handed them our nets, fish trap, cooking gear, and clothes. They chittered off through the trees, happy to be going, happy we were going in the dark. And they'd be happy we were going south. They couldn't carry the heavy stuff—the plastic and the cans of liquid nitrogen and the waterproof chest—so Sam and I ended up carrying those and the medkit and guns. I wrapped my picture of Loryn in a scrap of plastic and put it in my pocket. Sam got the mirror and shower curtain from the bathroom. We had to take everything with us when we left or expect it to be gone when we got back, so it didn't look odd for us to pack up everything we owned. Anybody who watched us would think we were just heading out again to catch nicoji, but with luck Sam and I were saying good-bye to this place and that did not make me feel sad.

I took a plastic bag we'd gotten in Vattani's and walked behind the freeze-shack to pick a bagful of alma leaves. Alma was a pungent little plant Sam and I grew on the wood slats of the freeze-shack's back wall. The leaves were an almost-black dark green, as long and wide as my fingers. We always took a bagful with us into the pântano and dried them on the raft. The Brazis had convinced us to do this: they thought the leaves were rich in iron and vitamins. We'd crumple the dry leaves over our beans and rice and give them a kind of nutty taste. I filled the bag with alma leaves and turned to see what was left of the orchard we'd tried to grow.

The mango tree was still alive, waist-high now. The company had given us a mango once at Christmastime, and we'd planted the seed. The apples were all dead. They'd been our biggest failure. The help loved to chew on the saplings. We couldn't stay up all night to make them stop, so we'd given up on apples. The two avocados were nearly as high as my head, so I started to think maybe Sam was right and we'd planted them too close together. But we were Idaho farm boys—what did we know about avocados? The Brazis couldn't tell us how to plant them. They were city boys used to buying avocados in a feria, so Sam and I just stuck the seeds in the ground as far apart as looked right to us and hoped for the best. Now we might never know how they'd turn out.

The help had been "planting" again. I kicked eight tin cans and a frayed length of wire out of the dirt past the avocados. We couldn't keep such trash cleaned out of the garden. The help would put it right back. When we'd water or weed in the evenings, the help would pour water over their cans and sit and stare at them as if they expected something to happen. They just didn't believe, yet, that you first had to grow food from plants and then put it in cans.

Something was glittering in the little mango tree. I walked over to see what it was. The help had put pottery shards on all the branches. I wondered what kind of fruit they expected to grow from that, or whether this was part of some religious ritual with human trash.

• • •

The help had dumped our gear on the raft and were chittering in the trees. The raft's logs felt cool under my feet. Sam's and the helps' and my feet had worn the logs smooth, and we hardly ever got slivers anymore. The raft was longer than it was wide and held together with three-sided crosspieces driven through notches we'd cut top and bottom in the ends of each log. It was sturdy and not really tippy once you learned how to handle it. We set the two cans of liquid nitrogen toward the front of the raft for balance, since the back end was a little heavier, and packed everything else in our waterproof chest. I put my picture of Loryn in there.

Sam untied the raft and jumped on. I poled us out on the bayou. Sam grabbed his pole, careful of his sore wrist, and we were off. The help followed in the trees. After two minutes we could not see the lights of the company town, could hear only the regular thumping of the generator, and that, too, faded quickly. Red moonlight skittered on the water. Otherwise, the bayou was dark. The leaves of all the trees around us started rustling—the gravitational wind was blowing off the land, cool on the back of my head, in my hair. The tide was starting out. Sam and I were alone, again, in the pântano—Portuguese for swamp; that's all the Brazis had called it: swamp. So many Brazis had come up at first—before American Nicoji bought out Nicoji de Tocantins, the Brazilian corporation granted the original monopoly up here—that their names for places stuck. The maps in the company house showed tens of thousands of miles of pântano. It was so flat that even where we were, one hundred miles from the sea, when the moon pulled the tide in through the mass of vegetation, the water covered all the muddy land. We'd sleep on our raft tied to the top of a tree or in the trees themselves. The help would crowd with us on the platforms we made in the branches, not sleeping, since they slept in the day, but watching Sam and me while we slept.

The trees started shaking and a roar swept over us: a ship had taken off. We watched it climb into the sky, red-orange glares under its wings. Two help fell from the trees into the water. One grabbed my pole, and Sam pulled the other onto the raft. We lifted them back up to the branches. I could see the help with the hurt hand still up there—he'd hung on. His white bandage flashed through the trees ahead of us till dawn began to light the bayou and the help crept into the shadows to sleep. They'd catch up with us. They knew the route. We had no open water to cross for two days, so they didn't have to keep up. But when we came to open water, in the daylight, we'd have to bundle them up out of the light, put them on the raft with us, and pole them across to the next grove of trees.

• • •

Late in the afternoon, it started to rain. The help had come down to sleep on the raft, but now they sat up and peeked out from under the sacks they held over their heads and stuck their tongues out to catch the cool rain. It rained harder and harder, so Sam and I decided to find shelter and wait it out.

We poled our raft up against the roots of an old tree. The roots towered over our heads. We turned on our guns, listened to them hum for the three seconds it took them to warm up, then fired into the shadows under the roots. Nothing bellowed or splashed into the water, so we used the guns to burn through enough roots to let us pole the raft under the rest to the calm water against the trunk.

It was dark under the roots. Before Sam could pull the lights out of the chest, the help swarmed into the roots to look around. The help with the hurt hand came back and tugged on my shorts. "Got nothing here, Jake," he said. "Nothing."

"Fine," I said. Sam and I shined the lights around anyway. Some guys told stories about waking a sleeping scam of lagarto when they went under roots like this. Sam and I'd never had anything like that happen. A few times we'd heard something around the tree swim away from us. That was all.

So we sat there in the dark, shining our lights, making the help screech when we'd shine the lights in their eyes. The forest canopy above us and the roots let very little rain drip down. It thundered, and the sound of it boomed out across the pântano.

I started thinking about Alberto Goldstein, the Brazi Jew who got under a tree like this once and found a perfect Star of David growing in the bark. He took it for a sign that he was going home. He told us he didn't plan to stay in Brazil—he'd go to Israel, and after that, if he could manage it, to one of the Israeli stations in the asteroids. Nice as all of us goyim were, he said, he'd spend the next Passover with his people in Jerusalem.

He disappeared one month after that. He was working with two other Brazis. Cliff Morgan and Doug Jones found the Brazis' raft tied to the side of a tree below a platform they'd built. Up on the platform was all the Brazis' gear, packed in tidy piles, their guns laid out in the sun to recharge. No sign of the Brazis. No sign of a struggle. Cliff and Doug looked for them for two days and finally gave up, took their gear back to the company town, and gave it to the Brazis' friends.

I shined my light up the tree trunk. No Stars of David grew there. Just muddy, black bark. Sam took a nap, but I kept shining my light around, looking. Soon the rain lifted, and we floated the raft back out on the bayou. The help climbed up to the forest canopy and followed us along there, it was that dark under the rain clouds.

• • •

When the sun started down and the water began to rise, we were in the right place. We laid our poles across the raft and let the raft rise up among the empty boles of a great grove of mature trees. Only young trees had branches below the night waterline. Sam and I had a platform in an old tree thick with branches growing straight out across the water. Some teams got used to traveling at night, but Sam and I stuck to the day so we could see. We weren't sure enough of the things that hunted in the dark.

I tied our raft to the tree, and Sam and I climbed up to the platform, twenty feet above the water. Somebody had slept there since we'd last used it. They'd left the platform covered with leaves. The leaves had rotted in the rain, and ants were thick in the rot. I stepped out on the platform, but Sam pulled me back. "Booby-trapped," he said. He pointed to a branch on the outer edge of the platform. It was cut partway through.

"Who'd do this?" Sam asked.

I hung on to a branch and stomped on the log. It snapped and dropped into the water. Sam and I stomped on each log, and half of them broke in two.

"I didn't like this place anyway," I said.

"Who wants to sleep with ants?" Sam asked.

We dumped the rest of the logs in the water to get rid of the ants and built a new platform on the other side of the tree. Sam climbed after the wide leaves we slept on. I let down our fish trap and pulled up one nicoji and a long slimy thing with eight stubby legs that flapped around in the trap till I threw it out. The nicoji surprised me, but only one came up so I decided no big colonies had moved in nearby. The third time I dropped the trap I brought up six sadfish. Sam and I laughed at their melancholy faces and ate them. By the time we finished washing our dishes and tying everything down on our raft, it had been dark for an hour.

Our help came chittering up through the trees. They leaned

down from the branches to smell us, then scampered around the platform and the raft. I opened the waterproof chest, pulled out the bottle of gagga raisins, and gave some to the help. They loved the raisins.

Sam took out his glasses and flashlight and read a few pages from his one book, *Pilgrim's Progress*. He'd read that book five or six times—twice to me out loud. The wife of our first company inspector had given it to him. It had bored her. When we settled down to sleep—a flashlight in one hand to scare off the littler things that might crawl up after us, our guns strapped to our sides for the rest—the help settled down around us to watch.

• • •

In the night, something bellowed, far-off, a hollow sound like a foghorn's, deep and huge. The help patted our faces to make sure we were awake, listening. They were terrified, but they made no sound. We heard nothing else unusual for half an hour, and I was drifting off to sleep when it bellowed again, closer. Sam and I sat up. The help climbed quickly and silently into the branches. I occasionally saw pairs of their round eyes looking down at us. The help with the hurt hand inched down the tree to the water and rubbed mud and slime over his white bandage, to hide it. I thought we ought to take it off if he was going to do that, but he climbed up the other side of the tree and disappeared. We heard nothing else. Sam and I finally lay back down. I kept thinking of all the things we'd seen that the scientists had never seen, and of all the things we'd heard but never seen.

• • •

We got up in the dark when the wind started and the tide turned. The water hissed away through the trees. We were quiet then—night things were still out—and we had to be careful not to let our raft get tangled in branches below the nighttime waterline. Our raft had got caught, once, thirty feet above the mud, in a snag of dead and dying branches that hadn't yet fallen off the trunk of a young tree just starting to grow above the waterline. We foolishly tried to shove the raft free with our poles—and let the water drop farther and farther away below us till we could see mud. We couldn't cut the raft free, then. We were afraid the fall would break it apart. So we tied the raft to the tree trunk to keep it from floating away when the tide came back or from falling to the mud if the dead branches it was caught in broke away, grabbed our stuff, and spent the day in the part of the tree above the waterline. In the evening, when the water came up under the raft, we cut it free, floated it up on the tide, then over to a mature tree that wouldn't still have branches below the nighttime waterline.

But we didn't get caught this time. By dawn we'd almost dropped down, and in the light we felt safer. We set our guns in the light to recharge.

My hand with the locator felt stiff and sore. Sam kept rubbing his. I wondered what would happen after we'd gone as far south as we dared go with the locators on and we cut them out. I wondered how long it would take to get to the new company town. "Women, Sam," I said.

He smiled. "More than one, I hope," he said.

I laughed and remembered the "shore leave" the company'd sent us on when we were out one year. They'd flown us up to their station and given us a tiny room together. The fridge was stocked with fruit from home—apples, oranges, even a peach. We sat on the beds to eat the fruit, and someone knocked on the door. I opened it. A pretty girl stood there in a tatty white dress with a red sash around her middle, barefoot. "Oh, there are two of you," she said, and her face went red. The company was so cheap it had sent one girl for the two of us. We had her come in. She ate an apple, and we laughed for a while. "Well," she said when our conversation lagged. She smoothed out her dress and looked at us. I couldn't do anything. The girl was willing to take on both Sam and me—it was her job—but I was just a year away from Loryn, and Loryn had promised to be true to me, and I'd promised to be true to her. I'd even carried Loryn's picture up with me in my pocket. So I left the girl with Sam and went to the observation deck to watch clouds blow over the seas below us and to look at my picture of Loryn. "Yeah, women," I said to Sam.

I wondered what Loryn was doing now, and whether she was thinking of me.

•   •   •

We traveled south for a week to the nicoji colony Sam and I'd discovered on our last trip—the best we'd ever found. It was on a huge hummock rising seventeen feet out of the pântano—a mile square, Sam and I figured—and when the tide was out hundreds of thousands of tiny, black holes covered the mud below the trees, holes that marked where the nicoji burrowed down for the day. When the tide came in and covered most of the hummock, the nicoji swarmed out. Since only Sam and I knew about the colony, it hadn't been overharvested, and in three nights we'd catch more nicoji than our raft could carry south to the new company town, a decent catch that would pay our way.

We got to the hummock about midday, so Sam and I tied up the raft and lay down on our stomachs to sleep since we'd have to work hard all night. The help scampered out from under the sacks we'd covered them with and clambered up the trees to the shadows. On their way, some poked their hands down nicoji holes and tried to pull up a nicoji. The first few caught one or two—muddy and gasping in the air and light—and carried them up the trees to suck them clean, spit out the mud, and eat them. The rest had a harder time. The nicoji sensed the vibrations of the help walking on the mud and burrowed deeper and at angles from their original tunnels. The last help off the raft didn't catch any nicoji.

• • •

Toward evening, I woke up and then woke Sam. The water was rising and the wind was blowing. We floated up with the tide and poled our raft toward the center of the hummock to a place the water didn't cover—a dry place twenty feet square— and tied our raft to a tree on the shore. We'd dug three pits there that filled with water, where we kept our nicoji alive in burlap sacks till we were ready to go.

Sam and I stripped down to our shorts and started stringing out our nets. The help came up through the trees, slowly, climbed down and chittered around behind us on the grass. It was work time now, and that never made them happy.

"Fix net? Sam and Jake fix net?"

It was the help with the hurt hand. He was picking up sections of the net and inspecting it.

"Yes, we fix," I said, and then I laughed. I was talking like the help.

"You got hole here."

He held out a section of the net to me and, sure enough, he'd found a hole. I got our hemp from the raft and mended the tear.

When the sun was nearly down, the water around us started

to boil: the nicoji were swarming to the surface after bugs that sailed on the surface tension. The nicoji never jumped out. They just stirred the water and sucked the bugs under. We watched the water carefully, and the help were watching it, trying to see if anything had swum in around the island hunting for something more substantial to eat than nicoji. The water looked fine. Sam and I took opposite ends of the net, our twelve help picked up the middle, and we waded into the water, mud squishing up through our toes.

The nicoji hardly swam away from us. Sam and I waded up to our chests in the water and the help swam bravely, holding their sections of net in their teeth and keeping it from getting tangled. When we started back for shore, dragging in the net, it got so heavy Sam and I couldn't pull it and we had to let some of the nicoji go. After we got the net on shore, the nicoji swarmed out and tried to crawl to the water, their tails arched high over their backs. Sam and I scrambled after them, filled two burlap sacks, and dropped the sacks in the pits. We broke the necks of all the nicoji sharks we saw to cut down on the competition. The help sat and shoved whole handfuls of nicoji in their mouths, gorging themselves contentedly.

The water looked fine. We watched the help, and they seemed willing to go again, so we went, this time on the other side of the island. By the time we'd dragged that net to the beach, dumped the nicoji in sacks, carried the sacks to the pits, and straightened out our nets, it had been dark for half an hour. Sam and I shone our lights across the water. The water bubbled away with the nicoji but nothing more, nothing bigger. We'd usually drag in two or three nets, then pole out the raft, watching and taking turns using a smaller net to catch nicoji. Wading through water in the dark was too dangerous. "Time for the raft," I said.

"But look at the nicoji," Sam said.

There were so many nicoji so easily taken.

"Let's get one more net," he said.

I nodded. If something came after us, it usually got tangled in the net while we climbed on the raft, or on shore, or up a tree. So we went. But this time we only waded out till the water came up to our bellies. The help swam past Sam. Sam and I started pulling in the net.

And the water stopped boiling. All the noise in the treetops quit, suddenly, as if the silence had been commanded.

Sam and I kept hold of the net—letting the nicoji swim out underneath and above it but keeping the net between us and whatever had come hunting—and started walking backward toward shore, slowly, disturbing the water as little as possible. I looked back but could see nothing on the shore or in the water behind us.

The help suddenly dropped the net, swam to me, and bunched up around my legs. They'd never done that before. We'd always held the net together till every one of us got on the raft or on shore. It was something new, then, out there.

"Sam—" I said.

Something dark rose out of the water in front of him.

"Run!"

Sam turned to run but the thing lashed out at him, and he screamed and fell in the water.

I stumbled to the raft for my gun and waded out after Sam. Sam was floundering in the water. I splashed up to him, and he hung on around my waist. "Its tongue's around my leg!" he yelled. I held my gun ready to shoot whatever had his leg, but I couldn't see anything. It was under the water. I started dragging Sam to shore, and it rose up, dark and huge. Lagarto. It was a lagarto with its hallucinatory poison on the needles in its tongue. It had been waiting for the poison to work before pulling Sam to its mouth and teeth. It roared and lunged for Sam's foot.

I shot the lagarto in the head. The light shaved off its forehead and snout, cauterizing the wound so there was no blood. It slumped down in the water, dead, but still holding Sam with its tongue. I pulled the light through the water to cut the tongue, sending up clouds of steam. The tongue snapped loose. Sam and I fell back.

I pulled Sam to the muddy shore, part of the tongue still wrapped around his leg. Sam sat up and tried to pull off the tongue, but I grabbed his hands. "Don't touch it!" I yelled. I wound a scrap of burlap around my right hand, tore off the tongue, and threw it in the water. Lagarto needles had punctured Sam sixteen times. Four had broken off in his skin. Red streaks ran up his leg already. I knelt in the mud, wrapped burlap around my fingers, and pulled out the four needles, then took Sam's pocketknife, cut his leg, and started sucking and spitting out blood and venom, fast, trying not to swallow anything. "Help us!" I called to the help, but not one would come near Sam and me.

Sam started hallucinating, pointing, mumbling something about a woman in white with a red sash around her waist and a leaking can of oil. I looked where he pointed and saw such a woman standing back in the huddle of help, but she wasn't holding an oilcan——she was holding a dog, and she wore red slippers, not a red sash. "You're wrong, Sam," I said. "She's got red slippers and a little dog, too." As soon as I said that, I realized what was happening, and I slapped my face and stumbled to the raft. I was hallucinating now; I'd swallowed some of the poison. But lagarto poison in my stomach would only make me sick and crazy, not kill me. I had to give Sam a shot of antibiotic and antivenin before I went out of it. By the time I found our medkit, Sam had crawled partway to the raft, knowing what he needed. I ripped open the kit and spilled the syringes and vials in the mud. My eyes weren't focusing. Our vials of medicine were held in a padded metal case, and I had to open it and look closely at each vial before I found one that read Instituto de Butantã, the antivenin center back in São Paulo that developed our medicines. I tore the plastic cap from a syringe, shoved the needle in the antivenin, and filled the syringe. I grabbed Sam's arm and stuck the needle in it—but my own arm stung and I realized I'd shot my own arm, so I pulled out the needle and pinched Sam's arm; mine didn't hurt so I knew I had Sam's. I gave him the shot. I wanted to give him another since I didn't know how much I'd shot in my arm, but I couldn't find the right vial again, and then the woman put down her dog and started walking toward me, smiling, holding out her hand—

• • •

I came to my senses just after dawn when I threw up. I could see it wasn't the first time Sam and I had vomited. I was holding Sam's head in my lap, patting his cheek as if I were one of the help.

The help were gone, off to the shadows. Why had they run from the lagarto? I wondered. They'd seen Sam and me kill twenty lagarto. And why had they given no warning?

Sam's leg was swollen and red. He was sleeping deeply, sweating. I put down his head and staggered back to the raft after the medkit, thinking I had to make some kind of bandage for Sam's leg. I remembered where the girl had stood, and I couldn't help looking for tracks. There were none. There were no dog tracks. But I looked at the mud flat where the water had been the night before and saw the carcass of the lagarto, partially eaten. Who knows what had crawled around Sam and me, feeding on that thing in the night.

When I found the medkit and started back for Sam, I heard a rustling in the tree above me and looked up. The help were all there, in the shadows. Help-with-the-hurt-hand climbed down the branches toward me, shading his eyes from the light.

"Sam die?" he asked.

"No. Sam's alive, barely."

I started off for Sam, but the help started cooing sadly, as if they were disappointed. I looked up again.

"You not get insur-nance then, Jake? You not go home?"

It took a minute for that to sink in. The help had all been in the freeze-shack when Raimundo talked to Sam and me about our insurance, and they must have understood that I'd get to go home if Sam died. Then I remembered Help-with-the-hurt-hand waking me up in the night to ask what I wanted most—and what I'd answered. "You bastards!" I yelled. I picked up a stick and threw it at them. They clambered higher in the branches, chittering confusedly. I kept throwing sticks, and they finally climbed into other trees and hid in the shadows.

I dumped alcohol over Sam's leg, and that woke him up. He swung his arm over his eyes to keep off the light. "Where is she?" he asked.

"In Kansas," I said. I smeared an antibacterial cream over Sam's leg and bandaged it. I'd have to keep changing the bandage and the cream, and I hoped I'd have enough of each to keep Sam going till I got him to a doctor. I picked our syringes and vials out of the mud, washed them off, gave Sam a shot of antibiotic, and put the medkit back on the raft. I dragged the raft down to the water and tied it to a tree, went back for our bags of nicoji and dumped them on the raft. When I went back for Sam, the help had crawled into the tree above him, chittering.

"Where you go?" one called.

"You go to hell!" I shouted. But I thought about that and changed my mind. "No," I said. "Go back to the old company. You deserve it."

I knew they couldn't understand the irony of what I said, that they'd never understand my actions, but I didn't care. They'd slop across the mudflats to get off the hummock, then wander back to wherever it was they lived. When they got hungry enough they'd find some Brazi team to work for. The Brazis could have them. I dragged Sam onto the raft, untied it, and poled us out on the bayou, heading south. Tomorrow we'd cut out the locators, and if we didn't bleed to death we'd find Raimundo. Otherwise, we'd join Dorothy and Toto in Oz.

HOW WE PLAY THE GAME
IN SALT LAKE

The people in my section of the baseball stadium were all missing teeth. I noticed that right away. Everybody, except for the eleven people I'd come with, could have starred in one of those dental hygiene movies they show in health classes.

A little Mexican girl turned around and smiled at me when I sat down. Her front teeth were gone. She was a kid, so I didn't think it strange for *her* to be missing teeth. I smiled back and wondered whether Mexicans teach their kids to believe in the Tooth Fairy. The Tooth Fairy had been busy, if the people around me were any indication. The girl's mother spoke to her in stern Spanish and made her turn around. The mother's side teeth were gone.

Some chubby, stubbly faced guy sat down next to me on my right and spilled popcorn into his lap and on the floor. He stuffed the pieces on his pants into his mouth and started gumming and sucking on them, making watery noises. "Going to be a great game," he said, sucking in after the last word. I just stared at him. He held out his hand. "Dave," he said.

I shook his hand. "Mike," I told him. Dave had no teeth that I could see.

"You come here often, Mike?" he asked.

"No," I said.

"Didn't think so," he said. "Never seen you before."

This was going to be my first baseball game since high school. After graduation I'd sworn never to sit through another ball game, but here I was. I hadn't even had to pay for my ticket, which seemed right considering how much I'd hated team sports as a kid—always the last one picked, a handicap to my team no matter what we'd played, sidelined with thick glasses.

"I wouldn't miss a game," Dave said.

I nodded and stared straight ahead. I hoped he wasn't going to try to talk to me through the whole game. I pretended to be interested in our team, the Salt Lake Buzz, warming up in front of their dugout, and I started to get interested, really, which continued to surprise me. I'd been manning the Utah AIDS Foundation hot line the afternoon some guy from the Buzz had called, and not to ask about safe sex. "Hey, would you guys like a few tickets to our next game?" he'd said. "It's division playoffs, Vancouver in town. The Twins general manager will be here to watch, maybe tap Cordova for major league play next season."

The Minnesota Twins sponsored our minor league team in the Pacific Coast Northern Division. They took our best players east and paid them big salaries. Cordova was evidently our best player.

I'd told him we'd love tickets, but what I hadn't told him was that the minute he'd asked I'd wanted tickets for my partner Ryan and me. It had surprised me, but I'd wanted them. It would be something out of the ordinary that we could do, something I could give Ryan. The guy from the Buzz had asked how many, and I'd asked how many could he send, thinking people might get into this, a lot of dying people on social security and tight budgets might like to watch a baseball game if the tickets were free. There were a lot of us with AIDS in town, a lot of people like me failing therapy with partners sick of taking care of us. He'd said he could send twelve. I'd passed the information to Carla, the activities director, and put Ryan's and my names on the sign-up sheet before I'd left from my shift.

But Ryan wouldn't come with me. I was sitting in cheap seats at the far end of right field with Carla and ten guys I didn't even know.

I felt the top of my head burning in the late afternoon sun. I pulled my cap out of my back pocket and put it on—not much hair left.

"You're cute," the guy to my left said, one of us with Foundation tickets.

I just looked at him. We'd never met. I wasn't sure where he was headed with that comment.

"I'm down from minimum security," he said, completely open about his situation. "They let me out for Thursday support group, but group got canceled this week since most guys signed up to come here. I have to meet the prison van as soon as the game ends."

"I'm sorry you have to go back there," I said. I wondered what he'd done. It bothered me at first that he talked about coming from prison like he'd have talked about getting off work early. No big deal. But then I thought maybe nonchalance was the only way he could face telling somebody he was in prison. Maybe nonchalance was a wall against how people must react to him. It started to remind me a little of the times I'd had to tell someone I have AIDS.

"Are you new to the group?" he asked.

"No," I said. "I don't go to a support group anymore." I'd attended a support group for three years. Fourteen of the twenty-one people had died, and after the social worker who led it died, the rest of us disbanded. I hadn't been able to join a group after that and face getting close again to people who were all going to die.

He sucked Pepsi through the straw in his drink, kept looking at me. It was strange and flattering. It felt odd to have somebody think I was worth looking at. When I looked at myself in the mirror, I didn't see that anymore. All I could see was a man with that starved, prisoner-of-war look people with AIDS get toward the end. The guy slouched in his seat and put his leg tight against mine. I didn't move my leg.

The players were doing something down below, the two teams huddling around their coaches, the Salt Lake Buzz in black and white striped uniforms on this side of the field, the Vancouver Canadians across the field in robin's egg blue. Salsa music blared from the loudspeakers. People were hurrying to their seats, spreading blankets to sit on because the metal seats were hot in the sun. About two-thirds of the people in this section were Hispanic, and I wondered if they were related to guys on our team, guys with last names like Brito, De la Rosa, Jimenez. I watched everybody around me laughing, smiling, calling to each other in Spanish and a little English, waving. All of these people—Hispanic, Anglo, young, old, middle-aged, teenagers—were missing teeth. I turned around to look at the people behind me. Same thing.

"Get a load of this," the guy to my left said.

Three rows below us, one of the fattest guys I'd ever seen was trying to fit into a seat. He had to tuck himself down. His wife tried to help, pulling on his shirt and pants. When he'd finally squeezed all the way in he turned around, happy to be here and not embarrassed. I was glad he managed that. He smiled to no one in particular. Some of his teeth were missing.

Was it poverty? Were these people not able to afford dental care? I felt sorry for them, but glad they could at least find a few dollars for something like this ball game to take their minds off toothaches.

The music changed to something orchestral and grandiose, the introduction to the National Anthem. At that moment, the guy from prison touched my hand, down at my side. People probably couldn't see. I didn't want to lead him on, but I didn't move my hand. It wasn't right to touch like this since I was in a committed relationship, never mind what that relationship had become, so I had to let him know. But it had been a long time since anybody had wanted to touch my hand. "What's your name?" I asked him.

"Ned," he said.

I told him my name, then leaned over to him. "I have a partner," I whispered.

He moved his hand, looked away, sucked more of his Pepsi.

"I wonder why sometimes," I said.

He smiled, a little pride saved. I wished he hadn't moved his hand. Ned was a handsome guy. It didn't hurt to admit that. If things had been different, if I weren't committed and if he weren't in prison, I'd probably have gone with him for a beer after the game, maybe on a date Saturday night.

The National Anthem began. Everybody stood. A tenor with

the Utah Opera Company belted out the song. I was impressed. Most people put their hands over their hearts. Everybody pulled off their hats.

And the game began, Vancouver first up to bat. They soon had a guy on every base, then one Canadian struck out. Another walked to the plate, tapped it with his bat, stood ready for the pitch. The people around me sat absolutely still, absolutely intent on the game. Even Dave quit sucking on his popcorn. "Tucker's one of their best batters," he whispered to me.

Tucker swung. The ball cracked against his bat, arched up high, landed in left field. Brito scooped it up, a Canadian touched home plate, one point for their team, Brito slammed the ball to third base, but the Canadian there was safe, Tucker already on first. The bases were loaded again. Another Canadian stepped up to bat.

"Men's room call," Ned said. Dave and I moved our knees so he could get by. Ned's shoes crunched the popcorn Dave had spilled on the floor.

The little girl turned around in her seat. She looked down at the crushed popcorn. Dave didn't say a word. He just held out his popcorn bag. She ate a handful, all smiles. "I'm Maria," she said to me. She evidently knew Dave. He let her take another handful. "This is my momma, and my sister Lucia is sitting next to me." Lucia looked back at us. She was maybe sixteen, quite an age difference between these two sisters.

"How old are you, Maria?" I asked.

"Five," she said. "And that's my brother playing ball. If he does good enough in this game, we're moving to Minneaxolis."

"Cordova's the brother," Dave said to me. "Right outfield."

It was just like I'd thought: relatives in the stadium. The

Canadians scored one more point and were out. It was 2-0, and Salt Lake's turn at the bat.

Ned came back. He didn't say a word. We just watched the game. By the end of the fourth inning it was Vancouver still in the lead, 5-1. "I have a bad feeling about this," I told Ned, and I wasn't the only one. Lucia and her mother were fingering rosaries. There was a kind of intent murmur in our section. People in other sections were streaming up and down the aisles, carrying armfuls of hot dogs, nachos, drinks, throwing things around, standing and talking. I wondered why they'd come if they weren't going to watch the game.

Cordova hadn't scored a point yet. He'd struck out twice. An old lady walked up the stairs and spoke with Mrs. Cordova in hushed Spanish. She handed Mrs. Cordova a white envelope and walked down the stairs to her row. Lucia stared at her mother. Her fingers stopped moving across her rosary. The wife of the fat man in the row in front of the Cordovas turned around and handed Mrs. Cordova an envelope. Somebody tapped me on my shoulder and handed me an envelope, pointed to Mrs. Cordova. I passed it to her. Dave took a folded white envelope out of his shirt pocket and gave it to Mrs. Cordova. He looked at me and shrugged. "Cordova's game's about to improve," he said. I had no idea what he was talking about.

Lucia suddenly stood, took Maria's hand, led her past their mother to the stairs. "Candy!" Maria said, waving to us.

"Did you give them money for candy?" I asked Dave, thinking I could contribute a couple of dimes, maybe a quarter. I'd brought a pocketful of change to buy a Pepsi and a hot dog.

Dave burst out laughing, slammed his hand over his mouth to keep gummed popcorn from flying into Mrs. Cordova's hair. "Don't think so," he said.

I tapped Ned. "Let's get a hot dog," I said.

"No money," he said.

I knew exactly how much I had in nickels, dimes, and quarters, all I'd been able to scrounge together to bring to the game. "I can spot you," I said. I couldn't buy a Pepsi that way, but there were drinking fountains.

He followed me out. "This is weird," I said.

"What, that we're losing?"

We passed a little boy hurrying down the stairs with a white envelope in his hands, his momma calling directions to him in Spanish from four rows up.

"Have you noticed how all these people are missing teeth?"

Ned looked around. "Now that you mention it."

The concourse was crammed with people, the lines for food too long—but how could you go to a baseball game and not eat a hot dog? We waited it out. I bought two hot dogs slathered in green pickle relish, onions, cheese, ketchup, mustard. As we walked back, I could smell the sweet mustard.

We passed Maria, jumping up to look over a banister at people in the costlier seats, and Lucia, not far away, crying behind a pillar in shadows. "Are you all right?" I asked her.

Lucia looked at Ned and me, then recognized us. "I must be brave, señor," she said, that was all.

When we got to our seats, it was Vancouver still in the lead, 6-1. Mrs. Cordova had spread an old white sheet on the narrow metal walkway in front of her daughters' seats. Mrs. Cordova and the lady who'd been sitting next to Lucia were opening what was now a big stack of white envelopes and emptying the contents—cornmeal, sugar, pepper, dried herbs, dried flowers—into their left hands, spreading everything in geometric patterns on the sheet.

"We won't lose," Dave said.

I took a bite of my hot dog. Lucia came back, leading Maria by the hand. When their mother and the other lady had emptied all the envelopes, Mrs. Cordova stepped into the aisle and Lucia and Maria crawled across her seat into theirs, Maria first. They knelt in their seats so their legs wouldn't hang down and disturb the patterns on the sheet. Lucia now sat next to her mother.

One Salt Lake player had struck out, a second had walked to first base. Cordova stepped up to the plate. "Lucia," Mrs. Cordova said, then she took a pair of needle-nose pliers out of her dress pocket. Maria covered her eyes. Lucia leaned forward. Mrs. Cordova reached into Lucia's mouth with the pliers. I heard a crack, and the bloody pliers came out with a tooth. Mrs. Cordova dropped the tooth onto the sheet. The ball cracked against Cordova's bat, and he ran. Our man on first base ran. Lucia let her tears and blood spatter the sheet.

I felt sick to my stomach. I couldn't believe what I'd just seen. Lucia was spitting blood onto different parts of the sheet. But something was happening in the other sections of the stadium. People were standing and throwing their arms in the air, then people next to them would stand and throw up their arms. I looked at them, then at Lucia, who was coughing now, then at them, then at Cordova running around the bases. The people in the section next to ours stood and threw up their arms, then waited for us. We just stared at them. Our man who'd been on first base touched home plate. The other people in the stadium realized no one in our section was going to throw his or her arms in the air, so they skipped us. People across the field started doing it again.

"The wave," Ned said.

Cordova touched home plate. He'd hit a home run. *Then* people in our section stood and applauded and cheered. We were the only ones in the stadium who'd seen what had happened. The wave stopped. Everybody in the other sections was trying to figure out why people in our section were standing and applauding, out of turn with their wave. Lucia and Mrs. Cordova didn't stand. Few of us around them did. Mrs. Cordova pressed a strip of thin cloth into Lucia's mouth and Lucia bit down hard.

I sat there with a half-eaten hot dog in my hands. Dave had quit gumming his popcorn. "Why?" I asked him.

"Cordova hit the ball, didn't he? Got a home run, didn't he?"

What were the Cordovas involved in—Santeria? Espiritualismo? Macúmba?

"You watch," Dave said. "Cordova's good. He hits plenty of balls on his own. But when the chips are down, when a lot rides on a critical play with no room for error—" He paused. He didn't need to finish his sentence. But I wasn't sure I could accept his explanation.

"Just Cordova?" I asked.

"Haven't you looked around? Of course not. I've been coming here for years. I've helped these people once in a while, but I don't have much left to give them."

He'd never had money, so he'd given them his teeth.

"There's more than just good ball riding on this," Dave said. "There's Lucia's college, the mother's gallbladder surgery, glasses for Maria. Cordova out there is responsible for this family. He can't lose his job, and if he gets good enough, if he makes it to Minnesota, he'll have money to buy them artificial teeth and anything else they might need. The whole family will have made it and moved away."

Part of me wanted to leave. Part of me wanted to get up right then and carry my hot dog to the trash can at the top of the stairs and drive home to an empty apartment. Ryan wouldn't be there. When he came home he wouldn't care about what I'd seen, probably wouldn't even ask. Another part of me thought that what the Cordovas were doing should be true, that sacrifice and pain should result in something good. I wanted to live in a world where you could change outcomes if you sacrificed. I looked down the row at everybody else from the AIDS Foundation. They all looked sick.

Lucia leaned back. She'd wiped her face clean.

"Sounds weird," Ned said. "But I sort of understand this. I've seen old guys in prison save their cornbread from supper, grind it up after it's dried, and sprinkle it on their windowsills, thinking it will help them get out. But they're all still in prison. Maybe they need to add blood."

I kept thinking about what I'd seen, and about glasses, the Minnesota Twins, old men in prison. "Does it always work?" I asked Dave. He shook his head no. The game went on. Vancouver stayed ahead, and at the bottom of the eighth it was 7-4. At one point, Dave stuffed what was left of Ned's and my hot dogs into his popcorn bag and carried them to the trash can. No one had moved the sheet. Vancouver didn't score during their ninth turn at bat. It was the bottom of the ninth inning, and we had to make four points to win.

We got men on first and second bases, and Brito hit them in though he was tagged out on second.

Two points to go. I looked around to see whether anyone else were spreading a sheet, but Mrs. Cordova's was the only one.

De la Rosa made it to second base. Cordova stepped up to

the plate, tapped it with his bat. A lot of people were looking at Lucia, Maria, Mrs. Cordova. A hush fell over our section. Cordova swung and missed. The catcher threw the ball back to the Canadian pitcher.

Lucia leaned forward. Her mother took out her pliers, then put them back. "No, hija," she said. "No, Lucia."

Cordova swung and missed a second time. Lucia reached for the pliers.

"Take one of mine," I said.

The Cordovas, Dave, and a lot of other people looked at me. What they didn't know was that I wouldn't need my teeth much longer. Like Dave, I couldn't give them money, but I could give them this.

Cordova swung and tipped the ball, but the umpire called it a foul ball.

"Move," Dave told the Cordovas. He got them out of their seats. Mrs. Cordova handed me the pliers. I hurried into her seat. "I don't think I can do it myself," I said.

"I'll help," Ned said. He climbed into Lucia's seat and crouched there. "Take a back one," I told him. He was quick. He cracked out a tooth, dropped it on the sheet, and Cordova hit the ball. I leaned over the sheet to let my blood spatter it. I was surprised at how much blood there was. I was surprised at how bad it hurt. I was trying not to cry.

"Hijo bendito," Mrs. Cordova said softly. "Hijo bendito." She handed me a strip of white cloth, and I shoved it where my tooth had been. Carla was there, and she helped me wipe my face. Somebody else from the Foundation wadded up the sheet and hurried it to the trash can, since nobody else should touch the blood on it.

People started standing, clapping, cheering. Others were

rushing out to their cars. Dave slapped me on my back. "We won!" he shouted over the noise. We'd won. Cordova was at the fence, and Lucia was there. He reached through the wire to touch her fingers.

Dave handed me a can of Pepsi. "Here," he said. "Get the taste out of your mouth."

"Where did this come from?" I asked.

"Somebody behind us."

I took a drink, but still tasted blood.

"I have to go," Ned said. "I can't be late to the van. I hope I didn't hurt you too much."

We followed him out. I was shaking, but I could walk. It felt better to walk than to sit. I dropped the Pepsi in the trash can at the top of the stairs. I had blood on my pants. People were touching me, saying things to me in Spanish as they passed by.

"Why did you do that?" Carla asked.

"We won, didn't we?" Dave said. He was still with us.

Mrs. Cordova hurried up to me, carrying Maria. "Gracias, hijo," she said to me. "Gracias."

Lucia was biting down hard. There were tears in her eyes. I knew what she was feeling. She tried to smile at me.

It was slow going. The rich got out first. But in the sunset were hints of green, low on the mountains in the east. There is a magic in the world, I thought. I was still part of it for a time.

Ned waved and ran to his van. I wondered if I'd see him again. Maybe I could get his address and write, I thought. Maybe that, at least.

Carla told me good-bye. "Come to the support group next Thursday," she said. "I'm sure people want to talk to you after what you did today."

"No," I said. I wasn't ready for that. But as I watched her

walk away, I thought of my dead friends. They'd have joined another group if they'd have lived. They'd have kept trying. Maybe I should too, I thought.

"Good luck to you, Mike," Dave said. He held out his hand. "We play the game pretty well, when all is said and done."

I shook his hand. "It's not what I expected," I said.

"It never is," he said.

HOMELESS, WITH ALIENS

No. 1: If you become homeless, find ways to stay warm.

The morning the aliens flew into Salt Lake City, I became homeless. It was my choice. Most middle-aged women probably wouldn't have made that choice, but I did. I hadn't known what I would do till then, but in the news from other cities I'd seen what the aliens would likely do. When the sirens and bells went off it suddenly occurred to me that if I left practically everything—my books, furniture, clothes, food, condo, pickup—and went to live on the streets the aliens might leave me alone, might pass me by, might not think I was trying to stop them from taking whatever of mine they could possibly want because it would look like I didn't have anything to want and I might not get one of their sharp little hands shoved between my ribs and my heart torn out and my breasts and tongue slashed off and eaten.

I was wrong, of course, at least about being left alone.

I kept my gear organized on shelves, and it didn't take me long to shove what I'd need into a backpack and two shopping bags and head out the door—which I locked behind me, not wanting to make it too easy for them if they wanted in. The street was wild with traffic, people heading any way they could out of town. Other people stood at open windows in their apartments and condos in the fall cool looking out over the valley or staring up, not knowing what else to do, and I thought: I've at least got a plan.

But it wasn't much of one. I didn't know what to do next. I'd never asked myself what a homeless person did after locking the front door for the last time, except find food and stay warm.

I started downtown, which is where most homeless people ended up, but as I walked along I watched twenty silver, oval ships settle into position above the skyscrapers. By the time I'd reached the bottom of Second Avenue, I'd decided I wasn't taking another step in that direction. The mouth of City Creek Canyon is right there, ending in a new little park with stone bridges and manicured trees. I started up City Creek toward the Watershed Protection Area in the hills north of town. I'd feel better with rock at my back at night anyway, not cement or brick. People had called me crazy, but I truly lived for my days and nights hunting fossilized insects on the Mongolian steppes or in the Utah backcountry. I wished I was out there now, either place, away from this city and the aliens—

And right then three aliens rushed out of the white and peach gingerbread Victorian on Canyon Road, hands dripping blood and mouths chewing and arms full of dolls and cooking pans and an unopened twelve-roll family pack of toilet paper. There was screaming coming from that house. I stepped off onto the grass while the aliens ran down the sidewalk. One stopped to stare up at me, the one with an undressed brunette baby doll crying in his arms and Nurse Barbie and Malibu Barbie. I dropped my bags at his feet and started to take off my backpack. I was shaking so badly I could hardly pull the straps over my shoulders, but he turned to run after the others. People made a wide path for them all.

Someone actually fired a gun—some fool on the seventh floor of Canyon Road Towers started shooting at those three aliens and maybe hit one: the gray-green little bastard with the toilet paper dropped to his knees, then got up and kept hold of the toilet paper and started running again as if nothing had happened. I grabbed my bags and ran in the opposite direction.

I was no doctor. I could not help in the gingerbread Victorian. They needed medical help there, not a paleontologist. Other people were running into that house who maybe could help if there was anything to be done, and I heard sirens—the phones were still working to call 911. People would probably let an ambulance through, panicked though they were.

But what was heading this way once shooting started was anybody's guess. We all knew from the news, at least we all should have known after what happened to every army in the world, that the last thing you wanted to do was shoot at them.

I headed straight up City Creek through Memory Grove, but once past the city I cut up to the ridge-line trail and took the high ground. I did not want to be down in the canyon for anybody, including aliens, to see coming. I wanted to see things coming my way first.

By nightfall, I was twelve miles out of town. I'd tied my shopping bags to the back of the backpack, and I walked along across a little plateau fragrant with fall wildflowers—and one of their ships settled onto the flowers and grass ahead of me, scorching them and sending up a smell of burning.

I thought I was too tired to run, but run I did. A bright light followed me, and aliens followed, running fast, closing the distance. What did I have that they wanted, I wondered, and I hoped it wasn't my sweaty breasts. I dropped my pack and ran on about twenty feet, the light trained on my every step. It was no use. I sank down in exhaustion and shaded my eyes. Seven aliens swarmed across the grass and tore open my pack and threw my gear around and strapped my clean bras on their heads and chittered and ripped and tore and scattered and one of them came up to me and said "Got rocks?" I picked up pebbles from the ground and tossed them at his feet. He kicked them back, stepped closer to stare me in the face, and took hold of my breasts. "Got bug rocks, Missy?"

"Not here!" I said, shoving his hands away.

He kicked my legs, hard. I tried to stand but the others swarmed up and held my shoulders down, bras waving back and forth on top of their pointy little heads. One of them noticed the ants. I'd sat down maybe three steps from an anthill, and we'd stirred them up in the night. The first alien cooed and put his hands down near the ants and let them crawl over his skin. He held up his arms in the moonlight, and all the aliens cooed and went to touch his arms and pass ants onto their hands and fingers. They stared at them, transfixed.

I crawled away, then stood and walked back toward the city. They didn't follow. When they were out of sight, I ran—down into the canyon, into the brush, into the trees along City Creek. What had they meant about bug rocks, I wondered— and had they meant fossils? Did they somehow know I studied fossils—and how would they have known that? How would

they have known I was a paleontologist? I had no way of knowing the answers, and I ran and ran, and walked, and ran.

And sometime around dawn I thought I hadn't done too
badly my first night as a homeless woman. I'd run and walked all
night, and because I'd never stopped moving I'd stayed warm.

No. 2: If you become homeless, look a little crazy.

The shelter was not deserted, and when I went there for
food the next night they had food to give me: an apple, half a
Swiss cheese and mayonnaise sandwich. I couldn't go home—
if there was any chance the aliens knew about my work and
wanted something from me, I could not go back to my condo.
They'd look for me there. They might be waiting there. I could
not go to my friends. If the aliens could find me in the hills,
they could find me in the city. Staying with friends might put
them in more danger than they already were. I had no money
or credit cards since I'd left my wallet in the backpack, so I was
truly homeless—me and half the city now after all the burning.
I looked like I'd been homeless for years: I was dirty; my
clothes were dirty; and I had nothing, not even a shopping bag.

"They're sleeping three to a bed upstairs and all over the
floors," the lady at the shelter told me, "but I'm sure we can
find you a space."

"I don't want a space," I told her. I took my food outside and
ate it standing on the sidewalk, hands unwashed, smoke rising
from the City County Building, the State Capitol, Primary
Children's Hospital, ZCMI Mall, the old Mormon Assembly
Hall, Canyon Road Towers, countless homes. The streets were
deserted of cars: the aliens had started blasting cars from their
ships—the highways were choked with wreckage—so I was
stuck in the city with everybody else still alive.

I went back into the shelter for a blanket. "Why are you here?" I asked the lady at the desk. "Why did you come to work?"

"What else was I supposed to do?" she said.

I had no answer to that.

"Be careful out there," the lady told me.

"You be careful in here," I said. I walked away through the smoke, the screams, the sudden silences, sticking to shadow to avoid the little gray-green forms darting in and out of buildings. I eventually camped underneath the bed of an overturned pickup without bodies in it, but the night was so cold I couldn't sleep. I lay shivering in my blanket, hungry and miserable, thinking of nights like this I'd spent in the San Rafael when despite the snow I'd stayed there digging fossils so delicately preserved you could study the antennae of the termites, the multifaceted eyes of the beetles, the patterns in the wings of the giant dragonflies.

And a light settled onto the street beside me.

Oh God, I prayed, trying to crawl out from under the pickup—help me, God—but aliens swarmed on both sides and I was trapped there, aliens reaching hands in toward my chest and chittering and saying things in English.

"Got rocks, Dr. Massey?"

"Bug rocks."

"Rocks."

I blinked tears out of my eyes, determined at least not to cry out of fear in front of them. They chittered on about bug rocks. "You want fossils?" I asked them. "Rocks with insects in them?"

"Bug rocks, Dr. Massey."

"Bug rocks."

"Will you leave Salt Lake if I give you bug rocks?" I asked.

I don't know why I said that, but I was scared; I was desperate; and I wanted them away from me. It wasn't the first time I'd bargained with thieves, either. I'd once been fool enough to barter through an interpreter with brigands on the Mongolian steppes, us broken down and stuck in the mud, them driving an ancient jeep and riding horses. Now I found myself bargaining with these thieves. They chittered amongst themselves, and one spat at me, eyes big and bright in the light, glaring and angry.

"I know where to find bug rocks," I said. "I've found lots of them and I'll give them to you, but if I do, you have to leave this place and never come back. Otherwise, find them on your own and good luck."

Suddenly they all left, but the light didn't. I watched their spindly legs scurry away out of sight. After a time, I peeked out from under the pickup. One of their ships was hovering maybe eight feet above the street. The aliens were heaped on top of each other under it, not moving, chittering softly and squirming around. One looked up at me. "Warm," he said, patting the pavement next to him.

And so it was. I could feel the warmth from the ship. I didn't think they'd sleep in that warmth if it were radioactive.

They all sat up. "Rocks, rocks, bug rocks, rocks, rocks," they chittered at me.

"You'll leave this city? All of you?"

"Yesssss," they said in unison.

"Do you want them now, or in the morning?"

"Morning," one said.

"Morning, morning," they chittered.

Then they settled back down, but a lot of them kept looking at me. "Warm," one said.

"Warm here," another said.

"Warm, Dr. Massey."

"Is the warmth radioactive?" I asked.

"No!"

"No, no, no," they said.

I cursed all the papers I'd published. I cursed the species of fossilized insects I'd classified. I cursed myself for a fool and thought how crazy I must look to anybody who might be watching, but even so I took my blanket and walked over to them and lay down on the pavement in the light of their ship and the warmth from it and the warmth from all their little alien bodies and I slept and they slept.

No. 3: If you become homeless, watch your back.

We walked to my lab. They didn't offer me a ride in their ship, and I didn't ask for one. People stared at us as we walked along, me in the lead and seventeen gray-green little aliens fanned out behind me, streetlights blinking off as we went ahead in the brightening dawn. We made quite a parade.

Along the way, we passed a discount electronics store. It had one TV still running in the busted-out window display. The *CBS Morning News* was on, broadcasting from Boise, and I didn't care what the aliens thought, I stopped to listen. The news showed the horrors the aliens were committing in Chicago, Delhi, Arusha, São Paulo, North Platte; then the announcer read a list of seventy cities where the same things were happening. A red dot blinked on a world map with every name, Salt Lake one of those dots. The broadcast moved to a panel speculating about why the aliens had left our satellites alone, then they started showing pictures of the Serengeti Plain littered with the corpses of thousands, maybe tens of thousands, of wildebeests—all dead. No one knew why.

"You did this, too, didn't you?" I said to the aliens.

"Did what, Dr. Massey?"

"What?"

"Did what?"

They hadn't been paying attention to the news broadcast—they'd been tossing around shards of broken glass—so I pointed to the TV and made them look at the dead animals. "As if you haven't done enough to us, you've killed the animals in Africa. Why? Why did you have to do that?"

"Not us, Dr. Massey."

"Not us, not us, not us," they chittered.

"What then?" I asked. "Those animals were doing just fine till you came." I didn't mention poachers or madcap dictators willing to turn national parks into private hunting reserves.

I turned and started walking again. "Not us. Not us," they kept saying, and I ignored them.

We reached the University of Utah campus, and most of it was still standing—but what a mess it was: papers and books and chairs scattered everywhere on the lawns and all the windows busted out. My office was what you'd expect—if a cyclone had hit it, it would have dealt a kinder blow. The lab was in worse shape. "What *did* you need me for?" I asked. "You mean to tell me you couldn't find your precious bug rocks after you made all this mess so you had to come find me to sort it out for you?"

They actually looked abashed. I didn't know how far I could push them, but I was angry at what they'd done and at what they were doing—to me and to everyone, to the animals in Africa.

We were standing in what had once been a decent, even decently funded, paleontology lab, a huge, cavernous warehouse of a building where my preparators and I and all the other professors and their preparators and the curators had stored and studied and labeled and taken notes for articles on all the specimens we'd found in Mongolia and Patagonia and Utah. My colleagues and I had stored our specimens in trays and boxes on metal shelving fifteen feet high, and the aliens had knocked those over like dominoes. All the specimens lay heaped on the floor amidst the twisted shelving, looking like nothing more than dusty rocks. The electricity was on, but the lights flickered and I didn't trust them. I did not want to walk back into the black cave the building would become if the lights went out, alone as I was with aliens. They'd scattered amongst the piles of rubble, picking up rocks and looking at them and tossing away anything that didn't interest them longer than two seconds.

"Be careful with those specimens!" I said, but none of them would look at me or stop throwing fossils.

One of them touched my hand. I jerked it away, surprised. "Bug rocks," he hissed.

"You'll get them," I said. "But in this mess you've made, it might take me a while."

Someone screamed. Six aliens started jumping up and down on rocks not far away, hissing. I rushed over. "Don't hurt them!" I shouted. "If you hurt these people, I will not help you get bug rocks."

The aliens quit jumping, but they kept hissing and pointing and curling their sharp, long fingers. It was Ann Sanders, one of my preparators, and a young man, both of them wrapped in blankets. I walked through the ring of aliens after them. "Stand up," I told them, and when they did I put my arms around them. "Now walk out with me."

We stumbled over the fossils and shelving to the front of the room, the aliens following, hissing. "These people work for me," I told the aliens, which was partly true, at least in Ann's case. "You must not hurt them."

If anything, the aliens hissed even more.

I turned around to face them. "Are we agreed?" I asked. "Or do I leave you now?"

"Agreed," one of the aliens finally hissed.

"Agreeeed," they all said.

"Then stop hissing," I said. "We humans have work to do. Stay out of our way."

I don't know who looked more surprised at my orders, the aliens or Ann and her boyfriend. I needed things from my office. "Come with me," I told the two humans. I couldn't just send them after a flashlight and the recording gear—I wanted to keep them in sight to make sure they were safe. "We'll be right back," I told the aliens.

Of course they followed us.

"You must be Tom," I said to the boy as we walked along.

He nodded. "But Dr. Massey, how——"

I told them what had happened and about the bargain I'd struck. Eventually we found my flashlight under books thrown on the floor, and the mike I clip to my collar, and the little recorder I use to record my comments and ideas while I work. Then I walked Ann and Tom to the front door where I could watch them walk away across the lawn and watch the aliens to make sure they didn't run after them. It was the best I could do for their safety. When I couldn't see Ann and Tom anymore, I went back to the lab and started stepping over the piles of stones—all of them fossils, some of them priceless—heading for my section. The aliens began sorting through the fossils again on their own. "Dinosaur rock," they'd say in disgust, then throw the fossil against the wall.

"Reptile rock," they'd chitter before throwing a specimen onto the floor.

"Dinosaurs, dinosaurs, dinosaurs," they'd chant, and then spit.

That they knew about dinosaurs at all made me wonder. "How do you know so much about past life on this world?" I asked them.

They just looked at me. They wouldn't answer. Answering my questions, after all, was not part of our bargain. I started looking again for my fossils, and they went back to throwing around dinosaur bones. When I needed help, they helped me pull aside the twisted and bent shelving, and I found my specimens. I'd know them anywhere, of course, even in a mess. "God damn you—you broke this one," I said, and I held up the two pieces of what had once been a perfect *Meganeura monyi,* a giant dragonfly, with its three-foot wingspan. I handed the pieces to one of the aliens. "You broke off the right wing," I said.

All the aliens sucked in their breath and held it. The hands of the one I'd handed the giant dragonfly to were shaking. "Don't drop it," I said. "Put it down if you can't hold on to it."

He did set it down, and he stood watch over it while the others cleared a space on the floor where they set out all the specimens I handed to them. It was a small, precious collection—precious to me, anyway. Insects are such poor candidates for fossilization that there never have been many to study, not in the ambers, not in the rocks. It was how I'd made a name for myself. I'd discovered the earliest fossilized termites—in Permian rock, something people had had theories about but hadn't proved. The oldest rock they'd found termites in before my work was Early Cretaceous. My termites had been a new species, too, and huge. I was giving up these specimens and others to buy Salt Lake and me a little time, but I hated to do it. I didn't hand them everything.

They stared at the bits of ancient life I did give them in awe, and they chittered softly, almost reverently, around them. Their fascination with insect fossils made their disdain for every dinosaur fossil seem odd. Why the difference? Why hate one kind of ancient life and love another? Wondering that made me wonder how much they knew about dinosaurs, anyway. I figured they knew a lot.

"You know what killed the dinosaurs, don't you?" I said.

They deflected my question. "Bugs not dead," one said.

"Got ants, got dragonflies, got beetles—"

"Yes, but we don't have the great reptiles, do we? Or the great amphibians—what about them? You know what happened, don't you?"

They stopped chittering.

"Tell me," I said.

They said nothing.

"Did an asteroid or a comet kill them?" I asked.

They were quiet for a time. "All die off," one said.

"I know that," I said.

"Mammals now."

"Mammals!"

"Mammals die, die, die," they chanted.

"Why?" I asked.

They just looked at me. Then they started picking up the fossils and heading for the doors. Eventually I followed them, turning out the lights as I went. When I walked out onto the sidewalk, they were gone. Not a thank-you. Not a good-bye. Not a good luck to you, mammal, because you'll need it.

I looked up at the sky and wondered what they knew that

we didn't. What was maybe sneaking up on us that drove them here to take what they could while they could? Or what had they loosed upon the Earth that was killing all mammals? Thinking those thoughts—wondering those things—my mammal body shivered and grew cold.

No. 4: If you become homeless, guard personal space.

They didn't leave. Their ships hovered over downtown through evening and into night. I grew more and more angry at the sight of them, and I started thinking: what do I have to lose? I headed downtown.

Downtown was deserted, busted-out windows and wrecked cars and bloated bodies everywhere. I wondered if the aliens hated cars so much because bugs splatter across their windshields—because cars are bug killers. I walked under seven of their ships and shouted up at them, but nothing happened. I started hearing what I thought was chittering in the dark, but it wasn't them, it was the TV in the discount electronics store playing news bulletins: aliens in Paris, aliens in San Antonio, aliens in half the world, all the adult sheepdogs in Tierra del Fuego and Australia dead overnight, and the adult sheepdogs in New Zealand and Idaho and Wyoming sick and listless and dying, too—but no infection, no canine pandemic, no poisoning that anybody could detect. Something had just turned off in the sheepdogs of a certain age and they died. Everybody blamed the aliens, but I wondered. For as long as I remembered, whales had beached themselves around the world for no clear reason. Last Christmas, my father had told me the American Cattlemen's Association had reported the fourteenth year of drops in live births in cattle. Human sperm counts had been dropping for decades. What was going on with class Mammalia?

And how did insects fit in?

I found the aliens in Liberty Park, or rather, I found my fossils set out in a neat row on the sidewalk and I knew the aliens could not be far. They were attracting moths with a light and catching the moths in jars. "Punch holes in the lids, or they'll die," I told them. "They have to breathe."

They hissed greetings at me: "Dr. Massey, Dr. Massssssey, Dr. Massey."

"We had a deal," I told them. "Why haven't you left?"

"Got catch bugs!"

"Take live bugs!"

"Bugs, bugs, bugs, bugs, bugs," they said.

I started helping them, the sooner to get rid of them. We caught ants underneath picnic tables. I took them to garbage cans where they caught flies. Their hands were so fast they could follow the sound of a cricket and snatch it out of the shadows.

And the puzzle started to come together in my mind. I turned on my recorder. "You want live bugs and stone bugs," I said.

"Yes, yes, yes," they chittered.

"You want specimens of the one thing that's never had a truly big die-off on this world—insects."

They stopped whatever they were doing to stare at me. I was lying, of course: Earth evolved *two* types of life that haven't, as far as we know, suffered a mass extinction—we have class Schizomycetes, the bacteria, besides class Insecta. But I did not want to give them ideas. Mammals also haven't gone through a natural extinction on the scale of the dinosaurs, but the aliens seemed to think such a thing was upon us.

"Smart mammal," one hissed.

"Smart, sssmart, smart," they hissed, then they were quiet, staring at me.

"On any world," one said, finally.

That stunned me. Evidently, at least as far as these aliens knew, insects were the only species *anywhere* to be so lucky. Nowhere else had anything like them to study. It was clear now why the aliens had come to Earth. "So it won't be just amphibians, reptiles, now mammals," I said. "Your day is coming, too?"

They held up their jars with insects in them. "Maybe not," one said softly.

"Maybe not, not, not," they whispered.

Theories flashed through my head. Perhaps DNA combines and evolves and works for, oh, one hundred, two hundred million years in a given class, then it gets too garbled—its combinations produce more errors than viable organisms—and the class dies off. "It's the DNA, isn't it?" I said. "It never was an asteroid or a comet."

"DNA, Dr. Massey."

"Sssmart mammal. Smart."

"DNA."

So they'd come here to study a species that hadn't suffered a mass extinction—probably to try to find a way to extend the life of their own species, or maybe class. We should have known what they knew, I thought, and maybe we would have realized it on our own, given time. We'd known for decades, after all, that dinosaurs in Australia had survived millions of years after the comet or asteroid or whatever hit the Earth had done its damage. Something else had reduced class Reptilia to the comparatively few examples we presently have. I turned the recorder back on. "How long does a die-off take?" I asked.

But I had almost all the answers from them I was going to

get. They ignored that question. I tried one more. "What mammals will likely survive?"

They wouldn't answer that, either, or so I thought. I gave up and turned off the recorder, something I've always regretted. One of them hissed, at that moment, unrecorded: "Ratsssss."

No. 5: If you become homeless, keep secrets.

By morning they had lots of bugs, and by noon they kept their part of the bargain. They never came back to Salt Lake City, but they spent most of the year terrorizing the rest of the planet; then they spent two years collecting on Mindanao, in the Amazon Basin, in the ruins of Shanghai and Isfahan; then they all left. I spent a year in Isfahan with all the teams trying to figure out what was unique about insects there—living or fossilized—and we came up empty-handed. But there was something, we figured. We just hadn't found it yet. Shanghai ended up having eight aquatic insects, two flies, one cockroach, one beetle, and two moths all endemic to the city—and who would have imagined such a thing? I'm leaving for Shanghai next fall to study the fossilized insects they're finding in the quarries the aliens left behind.

And they'll be back, we figure—they, and others like them. When they come, we hope to show them a few surprises. One will be a planetary defense system. Another will be that we'll still be here. A third will be plenty of other mammals besides rats with us. The aliens have their insect specimens to work with. We have everything on the whole Earth—with at least two types of persistent life to compare. We'll find the antidote to DNA meltdown, too. We know now what to look for. We know how little time we have. We know how hard and fast we have to work.

When I walked into my busted-up condo the day the aliens left Salt Lake, I had an idea what I'd find missing. The TV, the VCR, the microwave, the computer were all still there, if shattered and ripped apart counts as still being there. It was my personal collection of fossils that was gone: my own *Meganeura monyi* I'd displayed so proudly on a stand on the piano, the *Acrididae* from their display cases, all the *Mastotermitidae*. The only thieves I knew who'd take fossilized bugs and leave television sets weren't from this world.

Early the next morning, I walked up into the hills to see if any of my gear was worth retrieving. It was. My backpack was thrown off in the scrub oak and still there. My bras were tromped down in the mud, but washable. The tin cooking gear was scattered here and there. I picked it all up.

Something had been eating the food. From the little tracks, I knew it had been rodents—not rats, I was too high up, but deer mice. What a feast they'd had: lentils, bread, dried hummus, salt. I didn't begrudge them any of it. I sat there and looked at their tracks and hoped we'd find the antidote in time for them to survive with us.

The aliens hadn't found what I'd hidden in the backpack. There's a pocket inside it, camouflaged at the bottom, a good place for passports and cash. I unzipped it, and what I'd packed into it in my haste that morning was still there: my lovely little section of fossilized termite mound, a hundred million years old, the termite pupae still in their home after all this time. I held them, and sat in the westering sun, and listened to the pleasant buzzing of mosquitoes and flies.

BRIGHT, NEW SKIES

I took my broken goggles to the UV-protective goggles store built into the dike across from the World Trade Center. The wheelhouses of two Siberian cargo ships, docked behind the store to unload wheat, towered above the dike, and I could not stop looking at them because I remembered the days when America exported wheat to my country of Siberia, not the other way around. When Mother could get American wheat, she would bake it into bread early in the morning, and she would laugh at my five brothers and me after the aroma made us tumble out of bed and hurry into the kitchen, rubbing our eyes. "What will this country come to," she'd say, "if capitalist bread can pull even young communists out of bed?"

But that was a long time ago.

"Lady, either go in the store or get off the sidewalk."

Complete stranger. High voice but a man, I guessed—I

could not see under his burnoose for physical confirmation. His New Jersey accent told me nothing more than place of origin. I forced myself not to appear startled—not to show any sign of weakness in front of him. The science of biology can teach you that, teach you not to startle, but to observe and record. Biology had startled me many times, but I had flinched only once, not very long ago. I did not flinch in front of this man. I pulled my chador tighter around me and walked toward the store, wary of the man behind me on the sidewalk, listening for any sound that he was moving toward me. I was in a good part of New York City, I kept telling myself. Nothing bad should happen to me here.

But part of me kept saying that this was New York, not Irkutsk, that I was in a temperate land now, not a polar, and that things were different here. You never knew. The very conference on ozone depletion I had come to speak at had collapsed, and in a world where things like that could happen despite the desperate evidence outside the conference doors, anything at all could happen. Anything.

Bells jangled when I opened the door. The store was cool. The man did not follow me inside. I closed the door and looked back out at the man as I did so. He was standing there, watching me. Sunlight glinted on goggles under his burnoose. He could have easily walked around me, so I did not know what made him angry enough to order me off the sidewalk. Maybe he belonged to one of the sects that kept women indoors where their skins would never burn and he thought I should not be out like this.

"Can I help you?" asked a clerk, dim in her chador in shadows behind a counter, Greenwich Village accent.

I considered asking her to call the police, but I decided to calm myself. The man outside could be merely a religious fanatic, not a pervert, in which case a three-cabbie cab would do as well for me as the police if I needed help leaving this place: one of the expensive cabs, with a driver, a bodyguard riding shotgun in the front passenger seat, and the bodyguard's rifle that Americans counted as the third cabbie. I realized the man could also be following me, keeping tabs on where I went; the worst that would happen then would be that more company executives would track me down and try to talk to me, try to pay me money for what I had discovered, as if that were what I would want—me, from Siberia, a woman with memories of an old-fashioned, communist mother who would have been ashamed of me for taking it. My discoveries were worth more than money: they were worth the sight in animals' eyes. I could stop the rush of blindness in all species. But even so, I could not decide whether to announce my discoveries. I would have to change a species forever to save its sight—genetically enhance it; ensure, through adaptation, the final destruction of the world we knew and the creation of a new one. I could not sell such techniques for money. If I decided to use them, I had to give them to a company that would use them well, and quickly, and sell its procedures cheaply. Doing that, at least, would have made my communist mother proud.

"Can I help you?" the clerk asked again, genuine concern in her voice this time. I let the kindness of her concern wash over me.

"Yes," I said, but then I stopped. It was a day for worries, and maybe even shock. On the counter next to the clerk stood a stuffed penguin wearing Xavier-Briggs UV-protective goggles, smiling as if it were as happy on top of a glass case as it would have been on a beach, and all I could do was stare at it. I hadn't seen a penguin, alive or stuffed, since I'd left Antarctica one year before. "Who did that to a penguin?" I asked. I did not have to add: one of the last penguins.

"It's not real. Feel it. It's fake. Marketing ploy—you've seen the TV ads? But the stuffed animals they make these days look so real, don't they?"

I nodded and forced myself to look away from the penguin, pulled my broken goggles out of an inside pocket of my chador. That made me remember to throw back the hood, take off my borrowed goggles, and run my fingers through my hair. I was always forgetting to throw back the hood of my chador when I walked in a store, and I wasn't always in a hurry.

"Prescription or merely protective?" the clerk asked.

"Protective. My eyes are still good."

"Lucky you. We have to send out for prescription, and that can take an hour. Go ahead and look around at what we have in stock. Try on anything."

I walked off down an aisle of goggles, wondering if she'd said "lucky you" because I wouldn't have to wait or if she meant to comment on the fact that my eyes were still good. I glanced back out the door. The man was still standing on the sidewalk, looking into the store. If he worked for Xavier-Briggs or some other company that had hired him to follow me—and if I could prove it—I'd sue them for harassment. I passed cases of diamond-studded goggles, then rows of fluorescent orange and green goggles. I needed a pair of good work goggles.

The clerk walked over to me. "Should I call the police about that man outside? Is he a threat to you?"

"I don't know," I said. "He ordered me off the street, and that was the first time I heard his voice. I remember voices, so I don't know him. But he's just standing there, looking at us."

"I'm calling the police."

She called them on a phone on the wall behind her cash register, then she walked to the front door and locked it. "They're coming," she said.

The man just kept standing on the street, looking into the store.

"I'm sorry," I said. "I did not come here to disrupt your business."

"It happens," she said with a shrug. "But I have your accent now. You're from Siberia, aren't you?"

So she played the game, too. Picking out accents was a game I'd played with expatriate friends I made at Columbia when I was a visiting professor there. We tried to learn what we could about a person from the voice, now that people everywhere hid in clothes for protection against the sun. Voices told more about people than I ever imagined. I could now hear if a man were fat or if a woman were anorexic or if someone were developing skin cancer, all from the voice. My mother claimed to be able to tell what kind of skin cancer people were developing, just from the words they spoke about other things.

"Yes. I'm Siberian," I said. "From Irkutsk."

"You came for the conference?"

I nodded.

"What do you study?"

"Ecosystems, and how to adapt them to the new world."

"Ah, that explains why the penguin upset you. They aren't adapting, are they?"

"I will not buy anything made by Xavier-Briggs," I said, looking back at the begoggled penguin on the counter. All my life I had talked about adapting, with all kinds of people about all kinds of adaptations. I walked down an aisle, looking at the goggles. I saw goggles with little gold crosses on the sides, and I thought of the finely wrought Russian Orthodox church near my mother's house and how I had talked with her about adaptation there. The communists had made it into a museum, and my mother was proud of that. She used to take me there to see the art on display, art confiscated from private owners after the revolution and now set out for all the people to see. One day we arrived early in the morning. The curator was just opening for the day, and we met him outside on the steps. He was scraping wax off the steps and sweeping up the remains of candles that had burned down in the night. "They make such a mess here," he said.

"Who?" I asked, in my little girl's voice.

My mother looked sharply at me. "The superstitious in this town who won't give up trying to worship here," she said.

"Why?" I asked. "It's a museum now. Why do they want to burn candles on the steps?"

"Because they think this place is holy, whether we call it a museum or not," the curator said, and he swept the candles into a garbage pail and we all walked inside. I thought and thought about those people, whoever they were, trying to do on the steps what the church had been built for, and thinking about them and their disappointments made me cry. Mother took me outside, and we sat on the steps while I stopped crying. There were still flecks of wax on the steps by my shoes. I reached down to brush them away, into the grass. My mother was not cross with me. "A lot of people cried when we made this place a museum," she said. "But a new world had come to us back then, and we all had to adapt to it. In the case of the people who valued this place as a church, we had to force the adaptation, for their own good. It's turned out all right. Forced adaptations might be painful at first, but only at first. In a generation, no one will think of this place as anything but a museum."

In spite of those words, I'd gone on to spend my life trying to keep things the way they were, trying to find ways for the natural world to survive as it was without changing it to fit new realities. How I had failed. If I had listened to my mother all those years ago, I would have known that I would fail.

"Have you seen these?"

The clerk held up a pair of goggles with tiny aquaria in the temples. Little blue fish swam in them behind tinted glass.

"We import them from Taiwan," she said.

I took them out of her hands. "How do you feed the fish?" I asked.

"The tops open, here." She opened one for me, then closed it again. "We sell little boxes of food for the fish, along with the goggles."

I tried them on and looked in a mirror. The goggles looked terrible on me, but they were fun. "How much are these?" I asked.

"Four hundred ninety-seven dollars. Plus tax."

I took off the goggles and handed them back. "What I really need is something that can get knocked around in the open," I said. "Work goggles."

"I carry a Swiss line that might be just the thing for you."

She led me to a back corner of the store, and I could hear water there, and distant booms from the unloading of one of the Siberian ships. We were evidently standing at the edge of the dike, fifteen feet below the new sea level. I touched the wall. It was cool but not damp.

The Swiss goggles were fine: black, sturdy frame, scratch-resistant lenses. "I'll take them," I said, and someone knocked on the door. We both looked at the door. Three men in suits stood there. Customers, I thought.

"Meet me at the cash register," the clerk said, and she hurried to unlock the door.

I carried my goggles to the cash register and looked at the penguin. I couldn't help it. It looked so real, and so silly in its goggles. I almost touched it to see if it were fake, after all.

"You can save that species, can't you?" the clerk asked me, back now, at the cash register.

"What do you mean?" I asked. The men in their goggles and burnooses had walked up with her and the man with the Jersey accent was with them, and suddenly I knew. These were all company people. Probably Xavier-Briggs. I did not know what was going to happen. The police were not coming. The clerk had obviously never called them. Her call had brought these men.

"Why don't you do something to save the penguins?" the clerk asked me.

"I would have to destroy them—turn them into something different—to save them," I said. "I'm not sure it's worth that."

"Gifts of nocturnal eyes and nocturnal biorhythms would save the species from extinction," one of the men said.

"No," I said. "The penguins would still be extinct. I would just have created a new creature on their basic frame."

"So you can do it."

So I'd been tricked. I was admitting too much of what I could do and what I hesitated to put into practice. I put the goggles on the counter.

"No, they're yours." The clerk pushed them toward me. "We'll buy you anything you want from here." She'd kept the Taiwanese goggles with aquaria, and she tried to hand them to me, too. "You at least would take good care of the fish," she said.

I would not touch the goggles. I would not be bought with gifts or money.

"Only the species that can adapt will survive, and not all the ones we need are going to make it," the clerk said. "We have to help them."

And make billions in the process. I'd heard it so many times before, from so many companies. Whoever could finally save the cows alone would make billions. My communist mother, the year after the Soviet Union ceased to exist, when she finally gave up hope of it ever coming back, looked at me and said the only people who would survive now would be the ones who adapted to money-grubbing. "Adapt," I spat the word out. "You want me to use what I developed to change the natural world so it can adapt to the ugliness and desperation uncontrolled capitalist corporations brought on the earth. And that hasn't changed, has it? You are all still uncontrolled. All I might do if I work with you is prolong a species' suffering."

"You don't believe that," the clerk said. "You were stunned by a stuffed penguin. You came in here to buy goggles to protect your own eyes. If you didn't want to live in a world that might still include penguins, in whatever form, you wouldn't be here to take care of yourself."

I looked down and said nothing. This clerk could read more than accents. And this was an odd conversation, for me. Yes, they had tried to buy me with gifts of goggles. Yes, that gift implied much more. But they hadn't yet talked about what more it implied. They had talked mostly about saving species. These people were a little different, after all. "How do I know any of you will let me give eyes to the penguins?" I asked.

"We have a list of species to save first," the clerk said. "We could let you add some of those you love most to that list. If we start research and testing on your processes now, perhaps by spring we could have cows in fields again."

At night, grazing on the tough grasses inheriting the earth. All the delicate and beautiful soft grasses were gone.

"Your penguins could be next," one of the men said.

"Will you at least talk with us?" another asked. "Xavier-Briggs' bioengineering division is second to none. We can do this work faster than anyone else. You must want things to move quickly now."

"I'll think about this," I said.

"Others will eventually discover what you have," the clerk said. "You should act now while you have a chance to shape the world in ways you want it shaped."

"I'll need time to think about all this," I said. "Let me pay for the goggles and go." I took my credit card from my purse and held it out to the clerk. I knew now that she was no mere clerk, but she had been minding the store, so she had probably been trained to make sales. I was suddenly chilled to think how closely these people had watched me and how accurately they had anticipated my actions and how quickly they had set up this elaborate ruse to talk to me.

The "clerk" took my card and deducted fifty-nine Siberian dollars for the Swiss goggles from my account. I left the Taiwanese goggles on the counter, put on my new goggles, and walked out of the store. No one offered me a ride; I would not have accepted if they had. None of them asked where they could find me. I was sure they knew how to find me. I walked along, trying to imagine adding the names of six or seven species to a list of a handful to be saved, and wondering how I would choose and whether I should attempt to set up an entire little ecosystem of saved species that could prey on each other in the new world.

A wind had started blowing, from inland up the Hudson, and it was dusty. I had half an hour to get to the Central Park entrance on Seventy-ninth Street, meet the three people I'd flown over with, and go to the Metropolitan Museum of Art to see its controversial exhibit "The Green Hills of Earth: Landscape Painting before Ozone Depletion."

•　•　•

My mother had never joined any of the new political parties in Siberia. After the breakup of the Soviet Union, she never voted again. As I walked along the streets of New York after leaving the goggles shop, I remembered standing once in front of our house in Irkutsk, watching people walk to the church/museum to vote in a confusing election with candidates from fifteen political parties, and my mother would not go. I could not understand that. She had talked to me so often about how communists could force successful adaptations in society, but now she would not adapt herself to a new society. Remembering that made me suddenly realize that she had been just like me— or that I was just like her, after all: we both wanted the world to stay the way it had been. My mother's world had been communist, and she hadn't wanted it to change. All those years ago, I felt her watching me when I finally set off down the street to vote, and I seemed to feel her eyes on my back again as I walked down these streets in New York City. I felt it so strongly I turned around once, and an old woman was behind me, but she was black and dressed in an ankle-length black skirt and a long-sleeved, green silk blouse and burnoose, the kind of fine clothes my mother could never have worn because she hardly saw such things in the stores of Irkutsk through most of her life and when they did come she didn't have the money. The black woman smiled at me, and I hurried on to the park.

Savka Avilova, my old friend, stood waiting in front of the park entrance. I could tell it was Savka, even in his abayeh and burnoose. He always stood in a crowd with confidence and interest. I walked straight over to him. "Nadya, how could you tell it was me?" he asked.

I just smiled. "Where are the others?"

"Inside. Come with me to get them."

I looked up at the protective dome that covered the park. "No," I said.

Savka grabbed my arm and pulled me closer to the entrance. "Smell the air," he said.

The air flowing out of the park smelled of growing plants. Humus. Faintly of lilacs, though it was not their season.

"Come in," he said.

"No," I said again. "Take away this dome and the plants in there would die. I don't find that beautiful. I remember those trees growing without domes over them."

Savka left me and went in after the others. I walked away from the park entrance, back to where the air smelled of dust and exhaust and people who could afford to bathe only once a week, even in summer heat. I bought the week's *Time* at a newsstand. The cover story was on the new coastal settlements in Antarctica after the ice cap had melted. I didn't turn there first. I started reading about the underwater Swedish cities, and the underwater mines they were developing, and their under-water farms. The Swedes all planned to move into the Baltic. A hundred feet of seawater was the best defense against UV radi-ation for any fair-skinned man or woman.

I had started reading about the state of Missouri's plans to build a dome over all of Saint Louis when a blind woman walked by, tapping the sidewalk with a metal rod torn from some rusted machine. "I'm hungry and thirsty," she kept saying. "Will someone please buy me food?" No one bought her any food. None of the street vendors handed her anything, especially not a glass of water. She kept tapping her way down the sidewalk. "I'm hungry and thirsty," she said again and again. Midwestern accent. She'd come here from some desertified part of Iowa.

I bought a hot dog and a Coke and carried them to the blind woman. "Here's some food and drink," I said. I told her what I'd brought. She reached out above the food, so I put it in her hands. She did not wear goggles. There was no need. Her eyes were UV-blinded, white, the color fading from her irises, like my mother's eyes before she died of skin cancer. My mother had looked at me with those fading eyes and asked me to drive her to Lake Baikal one last time, before she couldn't see it anymore. We spent the day on a rock high above the lake, watching the sunlight on the water, and the clouds reflected there, and when my mother spoke to me that day it was the first time I could hear the skin cancer in her voice: low, and dark behind her words.

"Nadya," Savka called, behind me.

I turned. Savka waved to me. The other two were with him. I left the blind woman and walked back to them: Yegor Grigorovich, Gomel State University, specialist in the treatment of advanced skin cancers; Aruthin Zohrab, Novosibirsk State University, noted for his work in developing UV-resistant strains of wheat; and Savka, Moscow M. V. Lomonosov State University, dreamer, theorist, believer in man's ability to restore the ozone layer.

"You were talking to that blind woman?" Aruthin asked.

I nodded.

"Have you read a newspaper today?" Yegor asked. "The U.N. Commission on Blindness estimates fifty million people have gone blind in China. Another hundred million may go blind in the next ten years."

"How can that country go on with so many blind people?" Aruthin asked. "What will they do with them?"

Nothing, I thought. Nothing. I remembered the first time my mother and I had seen a blind Chinese. He had walked across the border and all the way to Irkutsk, somehow, in the fall ten years before. Mother took him into our home. Neither of us spoke a word of Mandarin, and he knew no Russian. I made him some tea and put the warm cup in his hands, and he held it and tried to stop shaking from the cold. We let him sleep by the stove after supper. He kept holding the teacup—he wouldn't let go of it. In the morning, he was gone. He hadn't taken anything. He'd set the teacup in the middle of the table. We looked for him, but we couldn't find him on the streets around our house or downtown.

"The museum is just up the street," Savka said. "We should get in line."

We started walking toward the Metropolitan. A line of people stretched from its doors, down the steps, and up a hundred feet of the sidewalk. Everyone in line was waiting to see "The Green Hills of Earth."

"There are still lines," I said. "After five months of exhibition."

"A silly exhibition, fifty years too soon," Aruthin said. "Most of us in this line can remember the Earth as it was. I am going because I love the Constable landscapes on loan here, nothing more."

"At least now we can appreciate your Constables," Yegor

said. "Landscape art was undervalued before ozone depletion."

They went on like that, the two of them. Savka and I stood behind them, in line, listening to them talk about art, moving forward step by step.

"What made you give up?" Savka asked me, quietly, suddenly.

"I haven't 'given up'!" I said. I was angry with him for asking such a question, for suggesting such a thing. "My life has been the study of biological diversity and how to preserve it. I will not give up on that."

"But you wouldn't come into the park to see the diversity preserved there."

He couldn't see the world the way I saw it. He thought that domed park a good thing. "We had so much," I said to Savka. "And we have lost so much."

We listened to Yegor and Aruthin talk about art, and to the noise of the traffic on Fifth Avenue. We didn't talk for a time. But I knew Savka well enough to know he wouldn't let this conversation just end. He noticed the *Time* I was carrying.

"You were in Antarctica, weren't you?" he asked. "What is it like?"

"Cold," I said.

"Just cold?"

Where could I start? He was reading me like I knew he could. I'd seen things in Antarctica I hadn't told anyone about. "There's still a lot of ice—at least it seems that way to me," I said. "The sea is completely free of ice."

"Where were you?"

"At Mirnyy. I was there in the summer, so there was always light, glinting off the ice. The glare is softer in the mornings, and the ice looks deep blue then—almost purple."

We walked ahead slowly, maybe five feet, then I looked at Savka and decided to keep talking, to tell him about what had made me flinch in Antarctica: make him see that I hadn't given up though I'd been hurt. "I walked out my first morning there," I said. "I wanted to look at the sea. The morning was quiet. There was no wind. Then I realized it was too quiet—no seabirds were hunting fish. There were no birds at all, I thought, at first.

"But there were still some birds. There were still penguins. I came around a bend in the beach and saw hundreds of them lying there, blind, starving. Many had already died, and the stench was terrible. I knew the penguins were starving when I went to Antarctica: the phytoplankton extinctions led to the extinction of krill the penguins fed on and there was nothing left for them to eat. But it never occurred to me that the penguins would go blind. I hadn't realized how the suffering of their looming extinction would be compounded. Two chicks had just hatched, and I watched them stare up at the sun and try to walk, and I realized they were being blinded, even then, just out of their eggs. I knelt so that my shadow was over their heads for a time and tried to think of a way to save them, but there was no transport for them to a zoo and no way to nurse hatchlings at the base. I had to leave them. I stood up and looked around and I was standing in the middle of all those hundreds of dead and dying penguins, and I could do nothing for them. Nothing, Savka. Nothing."

I'd twisted my *Time* into a tight roll. I unrolled it, then rolled it back the other way to try to get the bend out of it. It was something to do with my hands.

"You two are a somber pair," Aruthin said.

"Here is the museum entrance," Yegor said. "Get out your money."

We paid and went inside, staying in line for "The Green Hills of Earth." After a time I asked Savka and the others to save my place, and I walked off toward the ladies' room. But once around a corner, I just sat on a bench and looked at the crowds of people coming in to see paintings of an old Earth.

Someone tapped my shoulder, and I looked up at somebody in a burnoose, wearing goggles inside the museum. "Are you just going to sit here, lady, or will you come with me now to talk to the Xavier-Briggs people?"

It was the man with the Jersey accent. I was sure he was a man, now, after his touch. I did not scream. I did not cause a scene. I did not even get very angry. I just knew, then, that it was time to talk with them, time to start my work. In his abayeh and burnoose, the man looked like a medieval monk waiting to receive my confession. But I had nothing to confess, except that I was tired: very, very tired of working for something that would never be. The world would all change now, and I would help mold that change. That was my choice. I did not know what my mother would have thought of my decision. But I was younger than she, and maybe different from her after all, because I was voting again—I realized that now—I was voting in the new world I would help to be born.

I sat up straight, threw back the hood of my chador, pulled off my goggles (I'd forgotten to do all that again, once inside), and spoke to the man. "Wait for me outside," I said. "I want to look at these paintings. Then I will go with you to talk to your people."

I tried not to imagine him smiling in the shadows of his burnoose.

I looked away and imagined, instead, the *Sphe[isciformes noc-turnalis* that would come, the nocturnal penguins, with their large owl eyes and their thick lids, waking at dusk to tumble into a dark sea. There they would feed on UV-resistant krill I would develop, if I could, and if not krill, something. I would find something to change for them so they could eat in the blackness of their new world.

I took my place in line and went with Savka and Aruthin and Yegor to look at Constable's *The Hay-Wain* and *The Grove at Hampstead* and the soft sunlight in those paintings. We walked along past the works of so many other landscape artists, and somewhere between Frederick Church's *Heart of the Andes*, with its sumptuous trees, and Van Gogh's *A Cornfield, with Cypresses*, I opened my *Time* to the article on Antarctica and looked at each photograph. In years to come, the photographs from Antarctica would look very different. These had no penguins.

THE THING ABOUT BENNY

Benny said, apropos of nothing, "The bridge is the most important part of a song, don't you think?"

"Oh, yeah," I said, me trying to drive in all that traffic and us late, as usual. "That's all I think about when I'm hearing music—those important bridges."

"No, really." Benny looked at me, earphones firmly covering his ears, eyes dark and kind of surprised. It was a weird look. Benny never has much to say, but when he does the company higher-ups told me I was supposed to take notice, try to figure out how he does what he does.

The light turned green. I drove us onto North Temple, downtown Salt Lake not so far off now. "Bridges in songs have something to do with extinct plants?" I asked.

"It's all in the music," he said, looking back at the street and sitting very, very still.

"Messages about plants are in the music?" I asked.

But he was gone, back in that trance he'd been in since L.A. Besides, we were minutes from our first stop. He always gets so nervous just before we start work. "What if we find something?" he'd asked me once, and I'd said, "Isn't that the point?"

He started rubbing his sweaty hands up and down his pant legs. I could hear the tinny melody out of his earphones. It was "Dancing Queen" week. Benny'd set his player on endless repeat, and he listened to "Dancing Queen" over and over again on the plane, in the car, in the offices we went to, during meals, in bed with the earphones on his head. That's all he'd listen to for one week. Then he'd change to a different Abba song on Sunday. When he'd gone through every Abba song ever recorded, he'd start over.

"Check in," Benny said.

"What?"

"The Marriott."

I slammed brakes, did a U-turn, did like he'd asked. That was my job, even if we were late. Benny had to use the toilet, and he would not use toilets in the offices we visited.

I carried the bags up to our rooms—no bellhop needed, thank you. What's a personal assistant for if not to lug your luggage around? I called Utah Power and Light to tell them we were still coming. Then I waited for Benny in the lobby. My mind kept playing "Dancing Queen" over and over. "It's all in the music," Benny'd said, but I failed to understand how anybody, Benny included, could find directions in fifty-year-old Abba songs to the whereabouts of plants extinct in the wild.

Benny tapped me on the shoulder. "It's close enough that we can walk," he said. "Take these."

He handed me his briefcase and a stack of World Botanics

pamphlets and motioned to the door. I always had to lead the way. Benny wouldn't walk with me. He walked behind me, four or five steps back, Abba blasting in his ears. It was no use trying to get him to do different. I gave the car keys to the hotel car people so they could park the rental, and off we went.

Utah Power and Light was a First Visit. We'd do a get-acquainted sweep of the cubicles and offices, then come back the next day for a detailed study. Oh sure, after Benny'd found the *Rhapis excelsa* in a technical writer's cubicle in the Transamerica Pyramid, everybody with a plant in a pot had hoped to be the one with the Cancer Cure. But most African violets are just African violets. They aren't going to cure anything. Still, the hopeful had driven college botany professors around the world nuts with their pots of begonias and canary ivy and sword ferns.

But they were out there. Plants extinct in the wild had been kept alive in the oddest places, including cubicles in office buildings. Benny'd found more than his share. Even I take "Extract of *Rhapis excelsa*" treatment one week each year like everybody else. Who wants a heart attack? Who doesn't feel better with his arteries unclogged? People used to go jogging just to feel that good.

The people at UP&L were thrilled to see us—hey, Benny was their chance at millions. A lady from HR led us around office after cubicle after break room. Benny walked along behind the lady and me. It was *Dieffenbachia maculata* after *Ficus benjamina* after *Cycus revoluta*. Even I could tell nobody was getting rich here. But up on the sixth floor, I turned around and Benny wasn't behind us. He was back staring at a *Nemanthus gregarius* on a bookshelf in a cubicle just inside the door.

I walked up to him. "It's just goldfish vine," I said.

The girl in the cubicle looked like she wanted to pick up her keyboard and kill me with it.

"Benny," I said, "we got a bunch more territory to cover. Let's move it."

He put his hands in his pockets and followed along behind me, but after about five minutes he was gone again. We found him back at the *Nemanthus gregarius*. I took a second look at the plant. It looked like nothing more than *Nemanthus gregarius* to me. Polly, the girl in the cubicle, was doing a little dance in her chair in time to the muffled "Dancing Queen" out of Benny's earphones. Mama mia, she felt like money, money, money.

I made arrangements with HR for us to come back the next day and start our detailed study. The company CEO came down to shake our hands when we left. Last we saw of Polly that day was her watering the *Nemanthus gregarius*.

ABBA, FÄLTSKOG LISTING 47: "DANCING QUEEN," DAY 3.
DINNER.

The thing about Benny is, he never moves around in time to the music. I mean, he can sit there listening to "Dancing Queen" over and over again and stare straight ahead, hands folded in his lap. He never moves his shoulders. He never taps his toes. He never sways his hips. Watching him, you'd think "Dancing Queen" was some Bach cantata.

I ordered dinner for us in the hotel coffee shop. Benny always makes me order for him, but god forbid it's not a medium-rare hamburger and fries. We sat there eating in silence, the only sound between us the muffled Dancing Queen having the time of her life. I thought maybe I'd try a little conversation. "Hamburger OK?" I asked.

Benny nodded.

"Want a refill on the Coke?"

He picked up his glass and sucked up the last of the Coke, but shook his head no.

I took a bite of my burger, chewed it, looked at Benny. "You got any goals?" I asked him.

Benny looked at me then. He didn't say a word. He stopped chewing and just stared.

"I mean, what do you want to do with your life? You want a wife? Kids? A trip to the moon? We fly around together, city after city, studying all these plants, and I don't think I even know you."

He swallowed and wiped his mouth with his napkin. "I have goals," he said.

"Well, like what?"

"I haven't told anybody. I'll need some time to think about it before I answer you. I'm not sure I want to tell anybody, no offense."

Jeez, Benny, take a chance on me why don't you, I thought. We went back to eating our burgers. I knew the higher-ups would want me to follow the lead Benny had dropped when we were driving in from the airport, so I tried. "Tell me about bridges," I said. "Why are they important in songs?"

Benny wouldn't say another word. We finished eating, and I carried Benny's things up to his room for him. At the door he turned around and looked at me. "Bridges take you to a new place," he said. "But they also show you the way back to where you once were."

He closed the door.

I didn't turn on any music in my room. It was nice to have it a little quiet for a change. I wrote my reports and e-mailed them off, then went out for a drink. I nursed it along, wondering where we stood on the bridges.

Abba, Fältskog Listing 47: "Dancing Queen," day 4.
UP&L offices.

World Botanics sends Benny only to companies that meet its few criteria. First, they have to have occupied the same building for fifty years or more. You'd be surprised how few companies in America have done that. But if a company has moved around a lot, chances are its plants have not gone with it. Second, it's nice if the company has had international ties, but that isn't necessary. Lots of people somehow fail to tell Customs about the cuttings or the little packets of seeds in their pockets after vacations abroad. If a company's employees have traveled around a lot, or if they have family ties with other countries, they sometimes end up with the kind of plants we're looking for. UP&L has stayed put for a good long time, plus its employees include former Mormon missionaries who've poked around obscure corners of the planet. World Botanics hoped to find something in Utah.

The UP&L CEO and the HR staff and Polly were all waiting for us. You'd think Benny'd want to go straight up to the sixth floor to settle the *Nemanthus gregarius* question, but he didn't. Benny always starts on the first floor and works his way to the top, so we started on floor 1.

The lobby was a new install, and I was glad Benny didn't waste even half an hour there. Not much hope of curing cancer with flame nettle or cantea palms. The cafeteria on the second floor had some interesting *Cleistocactus strausii*. Like all cactus, it's endangered but not extinct in the wild yet. There are still reports of *Cleistocactus strausii* growing here and there in the tops of the Andes. As far as anybody can tell, it can't cure a thing.

We didn't make it to the sixth floor till after four o'clock, and you could tell that Polly was a nervous wreck.

But Benny walked right past her *Nemanthus gregarius*.

"Hey, Benny," I said in a low voice. "What about the goldfish vine?"

Benny turned around and stared at it. Polly moved back into her cubicle so she wouldn't block the view, but after a minute Benny put his hands in his pockets and walked off. Well, poor Polly, I thought.

But just before five, I turned around and Benny wasn't behind me. I found him at the *Nemanthus gregarius*. Jeez, Benny, I thought, we need to know the name of the game here. Declare extract of *Nemanthus gregarius* the fountain of youth or tell Polly she has a nice plant but nothing special. I steered him out of the building and back to the Marriott.

ABBA, FÄLTSKOG LISTING 47: "DANCING QUEEN," DAY 4. DINNER.

I ordered Benny's burger and a steak for me. We sat there eating, the only sound between us a muffled "Dancing Queen." After last night, I was not attempting conversation.

I'd taken time before dinner to look up *Nemanthus gregarius* on the net. It is not endangered. It grows like weeds in cubicles. It can't cure a thing.

I didn't know what Benny was doing.

He sucked up the last of his one glass of Coke and put the glass down a little hard on the table. I looked up at him.

"I want to find a new plant and name it for Agnetha," he said.
"What?"

"My goal in life," he said. "If you tell anyone, I'll see that you're fired."

"You're looking for a new plant species in office buildings?"

"I'd actually like to find one for each of the four members of Abba, but Agnetha's first."

And I'd thought finding *one* completely new species too much to ask.

"When Abba sang, the world was so lush," Benny said. "You can hear it in their music. It resonates with what's left of the natural world. It helps me save it."

It was my turn to be quiet. All I could think was, it works for Benny. He's had plenty of success, after all, and who hasn't heard of crazier things than the music of dead pop stars leading some guy to new plant species?

When I wrote up my daily reports that night, I left out Benny's goals. Some things the higher ups don't need to know.

ABBA, FÄLTSKOG LISTING 47: "DANCING QUEEN," DAY 5.
UP&L OFFICES.

We spent the day looking at more sorry specimens of *Cordyline terminalis*, *Columnea gloriosa*, and *Codiaeum varigatum* than I care to remember. By the end of the day, Benny started handing out the occasional watering tip, so I knew even he was giving up.

"Nemanthus gregarius?" I asked in the elevator on the way down.

Suddenly he punched 6. He walked straight to Polly's cubicle and stuck out his hand. "I owe you an apology," he said.

Polly just sat there. She was facing her own little Waterloo, and she did it bravely.

"I thought your *Nemanthus gregarius* might be a subspecies not before described, but it isn't. It's the common variety. A nice specimen, though."

We left quickly. At least he didn't give her any watering tips.

ABBA, FÄLTSKOG LISTING 47: "DANCING QUEEN," DAY 5.
WANDERING THE STREETS.

The thing about Benny is, if it doesn't work out and we've studied every plant on thirty floors of an office tower without finding even a *Calathea lancifolia,* he can't stand it. He wanders up and down the streets, poking into every little shop. He never buys anything—he isn't shopping. I think he's hoping to spot some rare plant in the odd tobacco or magazine shop and to do it fast. I have a hard time keeping up with him then, and heaven forbid I should decide to buy something on sale for a Mother's Day gift.

We rushed through two used bookstores, an oriental rug store, four art galleries, three fast-food joints. "Benny," I said. "Let's get something to eat."

"It's here," he said.

"What's where?"

"There's something here, and we just haven't found it."

The Dancing Queen was resonating, I supposed. Shops were closing all around us.

"You check the Indian jewelry store while I check Mr. Q's Big and Tall," he told me. "We meet outside in five."

I did like I was told. I smiled at the Navajo woman in traditional dress, but she did not smile back. She wanted to lock up.

I made a quick sweep of the store and noted the various species of endangered cacti and left. Benny was not on the sidewalk. I went into Mr. Q's after him.

He was standing perfectly still in front of a rack of shirts on sale, hands in his pockets.

"These are too big for you," I said.

"Window display, southeast corner."

Well, I walked over there. It was a lovely little display of *Rhipsalis salicornioides*, *Phalaenopsis lueddemanniana*, and *Streptocarpus saxorum*. Nothing unusual.

Then I looked closer at the *Streptocarpus saxorum*. The flowers weren't the typical powder blue or lilac. They were a light yellow.

The proprietor walked up to me. "I'm sorry," he said, "but we're closing. Could you bring your final purchases to the register?"

"I'm just admiring your cape primrose," I said. "Where do they come from?"

"My mother grows them," he said. "She gave me these plants when I opened the store."

"Did she travel in Africa or Madagascar?"

"Her brother was in the foreign service. She used to follow him around to his postings. I don't remember where she went—I'd have to ask her."

"Do you mind if I touch one of the plants?" I asked.

He said sure. The leaves were the typical hairy, gray-green ovals; the flowers floated above the leaves on wire-thin stems. It was definitely *Streptocarpus*, but I'd never seen anything like it described.

"I think you should call your mother," I said, and I explained who Benny and I were.

The store closed, but Mr. Proprietor and his staff waited with us for the mother to arrive. The whole time Benny just stood by the sale rack, eyes closed, hands in his pockets. "You've done it again," I whispered to him.

He didn't answer me. Just as I turned to walk back over to the cape primrose, he opened his eyes. *"Streptocarpus agnethum,"* he whispered.

And he smiled.

ABBA, FÄLTSKOG LISTING 32: "I HAVE A DREAM," DAY 2. AGNETHA'S GRAVE.

The thing about Benny is, he's generous. He took me to Sweden with him, and we planted *Streptocarpus agnethum*, or "dancing queen," around Agnetha's gravestone. Turns out the flower wasn't a cure for anything, but it was a new species and Benny got to name it.

"Agnetha would have loved these flowers," I told Benny.

He just kept planting. We had a nice sound system on the ground beside us, playing her music—well, just one of her songs. It talks about believing in angels. I don't know if I believe in angels, but I can see the good in Benny's work. Nobody's bringing back the world we've lost, but little pieces of it have survived here and there. Benny was saving some of those pieces.

"These flowers are so pretty," I told him.

Of course he didn't say anything.

He didn't need to.

WITH RAIN, AND A DOG BARKING

I don't hear most noises in Salt Lake City. I've gotten used to city noise, and my mind ignores all the sirens, the engine back-fires, the startup of traffic when the lights turn green. I only realize how surrounded by sound I am when I go home to Idaho and walk out in the night and hear how profoundly still it is. But in Salt Lake last April 15th, at 11:30 at night, I realized the Barretos' black Labrador had been barking next door for some time. I remember the date and the time because I had just finished my taxes and had gotten up to get my coat and the car keys, turn off the lights, and drive down to the post office.

I walked outside and looked over the fence to see if anything was going on in the Barretos' yard. I try to watch the Barreto place since Elicardes died of a heart attack in March. Besides, you learn early when you grow up on a farm that you should not ignore a persistently barking dog. Dogs bark for reasons:

sometimes reasons you can ignore, like a homeless person looking for aluminum cans in the trash, and sometimes not. You'd better find out which.

I couldn't see the dog at first, it was that dark outside, but I could hear it barking in the Barretos' back yard. It had been raining, and the grass was wet. I put my tax envelopes in the car, then walked back along the fence between our places looking for what, I asked myself—a stray cat? A prowler? The dog knew what was normal and what wasn't, so something was going on.

But I couldn't see a prowler. There wouldn't have been a place for one to hide, really, in the Barretos' back yard. They had a flowering plum tree in the back corner between our yards, two spruce pines in the opposite corner, a swing set and a sandbox. The dog was barking by the plum tree, so I walked back to it. I couldn't make out anything up in the tree, but I could see the dog. He was standing close to the trunk of the plum and barking. I whispered his name: "Lucky."

He stopped barking and looked at me. I crouched down and stretched my hand between the slats of the fence. "Here, Lucky."

He walked over and smelled my hand. He knew me. I petted his head, and he licked my hand. He was shaking, wet from the rain. I looked up at the tree, but nobody was in it. I could have seen that. I thought maybe a cat could be hiding up there. Lucky usually didn't bark at cats—he actually seemed to like them—but maybe this was one he didn't take to for some reason. "Quiet down, Lucky," I said, and I left to mail my taxes. He was barking again when I got back.

• • •

In the night, Edwardo, the youngest Barreto boy, opened his window and shouted for the dog to shut up. He didn't shut up.

I realized he was making more of a whine now. I got up and looked out my kitchen window into the Barretos' yard. The dog was standing on the back step, whining at the tree. A light was on in the Anderson's, the house on the other side of the Barretos'.

Maria came out again and talked to Lucky in a low voice and petted him. She walked over under the plum tree, looked around, and after a few minutes walked back inside her house. The dog was quiet while Maria was outside, but he started barking as soon as she closed the door.

• • •

In the morning he was still barking and whining. I watched him for a minute from my window. He was sitting on the back step where it was dry, still barking at the plum tree. I drank a glass of orange juice, pulled on my boots and a hat, grabbed a broom, and walked out under the branches of the plum that stretched over the fence and shaded part of my yard, too. The morning smelled rancid, like the city. Petals were falling from the tree in the still air, and they mottled the grass. I thought it was early for the petals to fall. Maria walked out when she saw me poking around in the branches of the tree, knocking rainwater down on top of me. It would run down the broomstick onto my hands and up my sleeves.

"What's up there?" Maria asked.

"I don't know," I said. The dog had followed her over and had stopped barking as if he were confident we were finally going to do something to put a stop to whatever was bothering him.

"I came out earlier and looked," she said. "I couldn't see anything."

I couldn't see anything either, or drive anything out with my broomstick. "There has to be something up there," I said. I jumped over the fence and started thrusting my broomstick up in the branches on the Barreto side, but I could see there was nothing up there. The tree wasn't that tall. I didn't scare anything out. The dog started whining, then barking. He left us and walked back to the steps, sat there alternately whining and barking. Maria and I just looked at him.

"I'll go get the boys off to school," she said. She took the dog in the house with her.

• • •

When I got home from work that afternoon, the dog was outside again, and barking. My friend Ellen was coming over for dinner, and I needed to start cooking, but I thought I'd take a few minutes with the dog to try to calm him down. I didn't want him barking during dinner. I hurried to change clothes. The old shoes I'd worn the night before were covered with a dusty film from the rain. I'd seen that sort of thing plenty of times. See it once, and you'll never stick your tongue out in the rain again, like you can in the country. I brushed off the shoes and went for the dog.

"I walked him twice today—once in the rain," Maria said when she handed me the leash. "But maybe you can do something."

Lucky was glad to get out of the yard. He kept running ahead, pulling on the leash, then he'd suddenly stop and look back at me as if he were relieved to be away from his house, as if he wanted to say thanks. Dogs do things like that. They feel emotions, like relief, and—maybe because we're both mammals—we feel the same things, and we recognize similar emotions. Some say we just anthropomorphize the animals, but I don't think so. Lucky was relieved. I petted him when he'd stop to look at me. "It's all right, boy," I said. "We'll work this out of you."

I started running, and he darted out ahead of me, pulled on the leash for a while, then matched his speed to mine so we could run together. We ran east down Arapaho, north across Apache, then west back up Shoshone. I tried to dodge the puddles, and so would Lucky, usually, but sometimes he'd run right through them and splash us both. Good, I thought, the exercise should make him tired and calm him down.

The air stank, and I was surprised the rain hadn't cleaned the air. Life in the city, I thought. I started thinking maybe the guys who jogged around with breathing masks over their noses might be smart after all. Who knows what I was breathing into my lungs?

Three blocks along Shoshone, Lucky started to slow down. And bark.

"Stop it, Lucky," I said.

He stopped and whined and would not go forward.

"Come on," I said, tugging on the leash. "We've got to get back."

He growled at me. I began to wonder if he were sick. "Lucky?" I said. I walked back to him. He didn't growl as long as I didn't try to make him go forward.

I looked around the neighborhood to see what could be making him act like that. But I couldn't see anything unusual or anything that could be connected with the Barretos' back yard.

Except the four cherry trees on the corner of Shoshone and Blackfoot, three houses down from us. The trees were in bloom, and the petals were falling around the trees, carpeting the grass. Was this dog upset by flowering trees? Allergies? He didn't seem stuffed up at all, or sick. Just on edge. Besides, how would a dog associate allergies with flowering trees? He wouldn't.

Still, I seemed to have no choice but to walk him away from the trees, east back down Shoshone. I turned south on Nez Perce so we could get back to Arapaho. There were cherries in bloom behind a green house on our right, and Lucky whined when we walked past them, quickened his pace so we'd get by faster. He barked out loud at three pear trees planted in a row in front of a house across the street. When we got back to Arapaho, our street, and started toward our houses, he whined and barked and was shaking when I handed him over to Maria. I walked into my front yard and looked at the two plum trees I had planted there then, regular plums, not flowering ornamentals. They had been blooming and had been a mass of color for nearly a week. The grass around them was thick with fallen petals.

• • •

Ellen got to my place around seven. I shook out her umbrella while she hung her coat in the hall closet. It had been raining again for nearly an hour, though now it was letting up. "What a night," she said.

She had rain misted on her chin and lips, and the water caught the light when she smiled.

"Your chin is red," I said, touching her.

"Cold," she said.

I got her a towel and watched her dry off and wondered again why our relationship hadn't gone anywhere. We were just friends, now—we'd tried dating, but it hadn't worked, and she was one of the few people who managed to stay in my life as a friend after something like that. I wanted the dinner to be nice for her.

"Baked Danish ham," I said. It was glazed and beautiful. I let it keep cooking on low heat in the oven while we sat down to eat the salads.

Ellen took hold of my hands. "They're all red," she said. "Have you been working outside?"

"No," I said. But I remembered poking around in the tree with the broom that morning, knocking rainwater on my hands. Ellen's chin was still red. I got up and looked at the broomstick in the laundry closet. It was covered with a dusty film like my shoes had been. I could rub it off with one finger.

"You'll have to put some lotion on your hands," she said.

Maybe more than that, I thought. I sat back down and told her about the rain, that maybe there was something in it. We were quiet for a time. Ellen touched her chin.

"What's that noise?" she asked.

"The dog next door? You remember Lucky—"

"No. The high-pitched whine. Did you have an alarm system put in here?"

Ellen could hear high-pitched sounds I could never hear, like the whine of alarm systems in department stores. The clerks said a few people, especially children with their good ears, sometimes commented on the sound. Ellen wasn't the only one. A year ago, she'd insisted on having her desk at the paper moved farther away from the water fountain because it emitted a high-pitched whine no one else could hear but which bothered her.

"No alarm," I said.

"What's on?" she asked, looking around the kitchen.

"I left the oven on low heat," I said. I got up and turned it off.

"I still hear it," she said. "It's faint. Could it be from out-side?"

She got up and looked out the kitchen window.

"Come outside with me," I said. "I wonder if you'll hear this sound under the plum tree."

I found us both hats to wear, and we kept our hands in our pockets. The sky was just dripping now. Occasional raindrops hit our hats when we walked outside, that's all. We walked back under the plum, getting our shoes wet. Lucky was whining on the Barretos' back steps, and he ran toward us when he saw us walk out, pawed at the fence. I reached over and petted him.

"The sound is louder here," she said. "Much worse. Can't you hear it?"

I shook my head. "But this dog's been going crazy since last night," I said. "Barking and whining at this tree."

"It's no wonder," she said. "The sound would drive me crazy. It fluctuates a little, but it's pretty constant."

"So what's up there?"

She was looking at the tree. "No one spot emits the sound," she said. "It's as if the whole tree is resonating."

I had her walk out in my front yard.

"Your plum trees are doing it, too," she said.

•   •   •

I tried putting on music to drown out the sound, but that didn't work. I could tell the sound still bothered Ellen, so we aban-doned dinner at my place and drove to a little Vietnamese restaurant in a shopping mall a mile from my house—with asphalt parking lots between us and most trees. Ellen couldn't hear a whine inside the restaurant. But she called me later from her apartment to tell me she could hear dogs barking down the street near Liberty Park, which had apricots and cherries and plums in flower.

I walked back outside, not under the plum trees where rainwater might drip on me, but near them, and tried to hear their resonations. I couldn't. But I could hear Lucky trying to bark, though he was mostly hoarse now. There were dogs barking down the street past the Andersons' and some big dog with a deep voice barking two or three streets south.

That night, I lay in bed and listened to dogs barking all over the city.

•   •   •

In the morning, all the petals had fallen from my fruit trees. By night, when I got home from work, the leaves had started to fall. Ellen called to say that she had gone for a walk in the park at noon and that the fruit trees were resonating there, too, and dying. The leaves were falling off them.

I changed clothes, and Edwardo and I wore hats and gloves and took Lucky out for a walk. The dog didn't want to run, just walk. His paws seemed to hurt him, and I tried to steer him away from the puddles of water. He seemed exhausted, though calmer. And maybe with reason, I thought. The sound might have lessened. All the fruit trees down Arapaho and back up Shoshone had lost their petals and were losing their leaves.

•   •   •

Maria kept Lucky in her house, and he lost whole patches of fur. The boys tried to brush him at first, but his skin was tender and it hurt him, so they just let him shed. Maria swept up after him. After a few days, though, he didn't seem to mind being outside again. The sound was over, by then. We were right about the rain, that it had caused the rashes on our skin, and Lucky's shedding, and more. The rashes, at least, soon cleared up. All the news in the papers and on TV was about the new compounds in the rain, a result of many things—loosened regulations on emissions from cars; dust blown in from the National Toxic Dumping Grounds in the west desert; pollution from the Geneva steel mill in the next valley over; and possibly the resumption of poison-gas testing at Dugway Proving Grounds, though the media could never fully confirm the rumors of that connection. The compounds killed seventy-four thousand trees in Salt Lake in a matter of weeks, including most of the fruit trees. They stood without leaves all around us and made it look as though a new winter were coming, not spring.

"And I heard it," Ellen said to me when we went walking in the park past all the dead trees, crunching dry leaves under our feet in late April. "I heard the sound the trees made when they died."

And the dogs had heard it.

You think you understand the world. You think things work in certain ways, that they do only certain things. Then the trees make noise when we kill them with toxic compounds. It was the chemical reaction, the news said. The sound was a result of the chemical reaction going on inside the trees, the reaction that killed them.

I chopped down the plum trees in my yard and in the Barretos', had them hauled away. Maria and I didn't burn the wood, like some people did. We didn't want to risk breathing in whatever might have been in the smoke.

I washed my car every day after I knew what was happening, but the paint still faded in places. The whole neighborhood got out hoses, and we sprayed down our houses, but we were too late there, too. Most of the houses ended up with yellow spots all over them, and we had to repaint later in the summer, after the rain stopped.

And I didn't plant fruit trees back in the front yard. I planted junipers, a hardy desert tree that had stood up under the new rain, at least for now. New antipollution regulations had stopped the problem, we were told. It would be safe to plant fruit trees again. It wouldn't happen again in Utah. But I wondered. So I stopped trying to grow fruit myself, decided to buy it instead from the country, where I hoped it would be cleaner away from the city, where I hoped the world still worked like it had when I was a boy, and the trees didn't cry out before dying.

THE SOUND OF THE RIVER

It was the physical presence of the Sahara surrounding Niamey, the heat and the dust and the sand of it, that never let anyone in the city forget that Niamey had no water of its own. By the end of my third week there, getting water for drinking, cleaning, and bathing had become an obsession with me, an obsession shared by everyone else. It got so that just before dusk I would stand on the balcony of my third-floor hotel room and watch the road south of town for the dust of the water trucks lumbering up from the coast. Watching from the third floor gave me an advantage. At the first glimpse of dust, I would pull on a shirt and hurry out to Sekondi Usala, a water seller whose friendship I tried to cultivate—and I'd get there before most of the other people.

I preferred buying my water from Sekondi Usala. He seemed honest, and once he had even sold me a liter of first-grade drinking water before the sun had set—but only once. "You Americans suffer more in our heat," he'd told me when he'd handed me the water, and he hadn't charged extra for the evaporation when he'd measured it out.

So it happened that on the Friday of my third week in Niamey I caught an early glimpse of the dust of the water trucks south of town and arrived at Sekondi Usala's door before the sun had fully set. I carried two empty three-liter plastic water bottles with me. I wanted to be sure to get water for a weekend bath.

"Go away," the gatekeeper told me in French. "We will not sell water until ten."

"So I will wait here in line," I said. I was going to take a bath that night. I hadn't been able to get enough water midweek to take a bath, and I'd tried washing with beer I'd saved from a lunch at the Canadian embassy.

"You will not wait here," the gatekeeper said. "Sekondi Usala will not have it."

"I am his American friend," I said. "He will let me wait."

"Indeed, he will not have it. Sekondi said to me: 'Tell my American friend to wait in the museum. All people not from Niger go to the museum, but he does not go. Tell him to wait there until we sell the water.' And so I have told you."

The gatekeeper would not look at me or talk to me after that. He brushed flies away from his eyes and watched his feet.

So I walked away slowly, back up the street. It was not a good idea to anger one of the major water sellers of Niamey, one who was evidently a Nigerophile proud of his country's past and the museum that preserved some of it.

I leaned against the wall of a house two houses down from

Sekondi Usala's. The gatekeeper did not look at me. I looked at my watch: 7:30. Two and a half hours till I could buy any water. Other people were standing up and down the street in the lengthening shadows, waiting. None of us in line, of course. Sekondi Usala wouldn't have that.

I looked back at the gatekeeper. He was looking at me, then. "The museum will entertain you until we sell water," he called to me.

Damn, I thought. He would not give up. There was nothing to be done except go to the museum, then return and show Sekondi the receipt for my entrance fee and tell him that I had seen this or that interesting thing from his country's past and hope that he'd sell me enough water to keep me from washing in beer.

The museum was two blocks away. I left my empty plastic bottles at the front desk and was careful to keep the receipt for my entrance. The museum had opened only an hour before I arrived. I read in the mimeographed guide I was handed that the directors could afford little electricity, so they opened the doors to the public only in the evenings when the exhibits could be viewed in the waning light of day and air conditioning could theoretically be dispensed with in most of the building. I walked, sweating, among the exhibits on the first floor, watching shadows gradually cover the stuffed specimens of animals, birds, and fish that had once inhabited the Niger river valley; the neolithic spear points discovered near Arlit; and the geometric designs painted on wood shields made from trees gone extinct twenty years before.

I walked upstairs to the second floor, the archives, and tried the water fountain at the top of the stairs, but of course it didn't work. Across from the fountain were a series of glass cases exhibiting Dutch engravings made from sketches drawn by the English explorer Mungo Park for his 1797 book *Travels into the Interior of Africa*. I looked in the first case. The engraving I saw was old, yellowed, crumbling at the edges, carefully folded out from the book it was bound in. I could see it dimly in the fading light.

And I had seen it before.

The engraving showed the Niger River and, though stylized, pictured a land more lush than anyone living now in Niger could remember. I remembered seeing that exact engraving as a boy, printed on the jacket of a record I had loved and forgotten, a record of music by a group from Niger. It gave me a strange feeling to see something as a man that had meant so much to me as a boy and, for a time, while standing looking at the engraving, it seemed as if the boy and the man were different people who had once been introduced. I wondered what the boy had really been like and why the music had held him so long, moved him so much.

And if, subconsciously, that music had compelled him into a line of work that eventually brought him to stand in a museum in Niamey, the city from which the music had come—even after he had forgotten the music.

I wanted to hear that music again. I wanted to listen to it in Niamey itself and see what the man would make of it, what he would find in it. So I went looking for the director of the archives, François Brissot, an old Frenchman whose family had stayed in Niamey through decades of postcolonial political turmoil and eventual ecological disaster, and brought him back to the engraving in the glass case. He stooped down over the top of it and peered into the growing shadows.

"On a record jacket?" he asked me again, in French.

"Yes, sir," I said. "I owned a copy of that record when I was a boy. The group was——"

"Hamane Oumarou."

"You remember them, too."

"How old are you?"

"Old enough to have owned records. I had two of theirs."

"Well." He straightened up. "There were only six. You did well. We have the Hamane Oumarou papers and what production tapes of the group's were saved from the fire. Follow me, and I will show you."

He talked as we walked down a hall lined with file cabinets. He told me the studio in Paris that recorded Hamane Oumarou had burned, and that the group had rerecorded their music, this time digitally, but disbanded afterward when Hamane Oumarou left his group and returned home from Paris.

Brissot stopped in front of a closed door. "The music is in this room," he said. "I'm afraid there will be a nominal charge to you if we turn on the light."

"I'll pay it," I said.

He opened the door, turned on the light, and motioned me ahead of him into a room filled with the music of Niger: anthropological recordings duplicated in Paris and sent down to the Niamey archives, the papers and compositions of eight native composers, and what was left of the work of Hamane Oumarou—one cardboard file box labeled "Correspondence" and another labeled "Recordings, Show Bills, and Contracts." Brissot took five compact discs out of the front of the Recordings box and handed them to me. None had the Mungo Park engraving on its jacket.

"I owned records," I said.

"But we did not collect them, unfortunately," he told me.

"We were given these after the fire and the rerecording."

I was afraid I would have to listen to each of the CDs to find my music, and I wasn't sure I would know it then, it had been so long. I had hoped to find my record with the help of the jacket art. But as I looked through the CDs, I recognized one of the jackets, a photo of Bilma from a distance, the spires of its mosques rising up over the walls of the city. "This was on the jacket of the second Hamane Oumarou record I owned," I said.

"Then they probably used the same art on the CD jackets that they had on the records," the director said. "But there were six records. Yes—look here."

He pointed to a list of the recordings of Hamane Oumarou: six records, five of them rerecorded digitally and put out on CDs. The one that had not been rerecorded was the first record, *Niger!*, and I remembered that title. It was the name of the record I had owned that had had the Mungo Park engraving on the jacket.

"Why was this one not rerecorded?" I asked.

"I do not know," the director said. "But would you like to listen to these other CDs?"

I told him that I would, and he left me sitting next to a stereo, earphones on, listening to the CDs in order. It turned out that I had owned the first and second recordings of Hamane Oumarou—the CD with the photo of Bilma on it had been the second, and I remembered the music. Some of it was strangely compelling. Hamane Oumarou himself would sing out a line of a chant about a Hausa king or perhaps a virgin lost in the desert just before her wedding and the other five members of the group would repeat the line with slight variations. The music would grow in intensity and power; drums and the native instruments would be added one by one; and some of the songs would end in a moving crescendo that said "Africa" to me, even now, as I sat in a museum in a city of Africa.

It was what the music had said to me as a boy.

But only some of the music on that second recording could say "Africa." Most of it said New Orleans or Paris—jazz, in other words. Hamane Oumarou had turned the remarkable music of Niger into what, in the end, seemed unremarkable jazz. And the succeeding recordings confirmed me in my feelings. There was less and less of the musical magic and wonder, movement, romance and the exotic, that Hamane and his group had originally brought with them out of Africa, less and less of the magic that had drawn me to some of the music of that second recording and to all of the music of the first— music I wanted to hear again.

Three songs on the Bilma CD spoke of Africa to me. I put that CD back in the stereo and listened to those songs again, just the ones that seemed little affected by a foreign musical idiom. It's not that I don't like jazz. I like good jazz. It just seemed to me that when Hamane Oumarou chose to adopt jazz, he lost a power in his music that spoke to me even as a boy. I could get jazz anywhere. What I couldn't get was the music of Niger, and that was what I had wanted. There was evidently a reason I had stopped buying Hamane Oumarou records—they had stopped giving me Africa.

Well, I had Africa now, I thought, and it was big and hot and dry—an Africa different from what I had imagined it to be as a boy. I took off my earphones, put the Bilma CD back in its jacket, and stood up to go. I put the CDs back in the Recordings box, and it occurred to me to wonder whether Hamane Oumarou and any of the other members of his group might still be alive and living in Niamey, or even anywhere in

Niger. If I could find one of them, I could perhaps discover a
way to listen again to the music of that first recording.

I pulled down the box of correspondence and started
thumbing through it, looking for the most recent letters and,
perhaps, an address. The correspondence was arranged in
chronological order: the first letters were from a recording
studio in Paris that had heard of Hamane Oumarou and was
interested in recording his music. There were letters Hamane
had written from Paris to relatives in Niamey, and for years, it
seemed, Hamane and his group had lived in Paris, and all of the
correspondence went to addresses there. There were letters
about the fire and the rerecordings—and then, interestingly
enough, letters in which Hamane Oumarou steadfastly refused
to consider rerecording *Niger!*, though why was not clear. After
those, I found letters sent to Hamane Oumarou, then at an
address back in Niger, in the city of Zinder—letters from the
other members of Hamane's group asking him to come back to
Paris. The letters all seemed hurried and desperate, and it
became clear that Hamane was somehow involved in the political upheavals between the fall of the last military dictatorship
in Niamey and the going dry of the Niger River.

Then I found a letter of appointment from the king of
Zinder: Hamane Oumarou had been court music master. After
the fall of the dictatorship, the Hausa had attempted to break
away from Niger to form their own kingdom centered around
Zinder. I knew that the Hausa movement had been a conserva-
tive one, and that the court music would very likely have been
the kind of music I loved Hamane Oumarou for, not jazz. I
wanted to hear that music—and I wondered what it would be
like now, if Hamane Oumarou were indeed still alive. The
Hausa kingdom had failed, of course, not so much for lack of

battlefield skill as for lack of water. In the years of civil war, Hamane had received letters in Zinder from Paris—from old friends, royalty payments, and the like. They were all collected here. After the fall of Zinder, the Hausa king had been placed under house arrest in Niamey, and I had reason to believe that Hamane Oumarou was indeed in Niamey with his king and what was left of his court: the last letters in the collection were sent to Hamane Oumarou at an address in Niamey, and they were from the Hausa king thanking Hamane, among other things, for his efforts to preserve Hausa music—which had evidently been recently recorded under Hamane Oumarou's direction, this time by anthropologists. I had to wonder, again, about Hamane Oumarou's refusal to rerecord *Niger!* He had recorded authentic music again, just a few years before I had come to Niamey. So why not *Niger!* The last letter from the Hausa king was but one year old. I wrote down the address, put back the box of correspondence, turned out the light, and left the music room.

On the way out, I stopped to look again at the Mungo Park engraving. I could see little of it now, in the darkness of the museum: only the broadest outlines of a wide river shaded by trees—a verdant past that gave some people hope of bringing about a verdant future. And it seemed that Hamane Oumarou had gone back to the musical beauty of Niger's past to preserve it too for the future, and I liked him for that.

It was after ten when I walked back up to the front desk and paid the charge for using the light. The girl there handed me my plastic water bottles. I had forgotten my water. In my rekindled interest in the music of Niger I had forgotten my water! I hurried back to Sekondi Usala's. The street around his house was a riot of hundreds of thirsty, sweating people crowding up for water, carrying tubs and buckets and empty bottles and skin bags. Women carried crying babies strapped to their backs, and everyone stomped dust up into the air. I waited in that chaos until eleven and got no water and never saw Sekondi Usala so I could show him the receipt from the museum and let him know that I had gone, and I washed my face in beer that night and before going to bed wrote Hamane Oumarou a letter asking him if I could meet him and talk to him about his music and sent it off to the address the Hausa king had used.

• • •

On Monday of the following week, I had a reply. Hamane Oumarou would be pleased to receive me that very night at seven. I read the letter and went into a panic to get clean. Sekondi Usala would not sell water until after sundown, of course. I had made a couple of friends at the Canadian embassy, and one of them took me home with him and gave me a liter of water. I stoppered up his sink and managed to take a sponge bath and even wash my hair and shave. Afterward, it seemed good to walk down the street not smelling of beer.

I walked to the house of Hamane Oumarou, which is on Yantala Street looking down over a series of dry bluffs into what had been the riverbed of the Niger River before it went dry. Hamane Oumarou was waiting for me. He was a short, thin man dressed in a white cotton abiyah and sandals. He had very little white hair left on the top of his head. We introduced ourselves and shook hands, and he blessed me in the name of Allah and invited me in. I had to stoop to walk into his house, but the ceilings inside were high. The house was built of stone and was cool, and I wondered if it was money from the Paris recordings that had built it or if it had been money from the Hausa king.

Hamane led me to a small room that looked out over the dry Niger. The room seemed set up just to drink coffee in: it was furnished with two wood chairs, a small wood table, a stereo with CD player and turntable, along with a microwave coffee service against the far wall under a cabinet for cups and saucers. On the wall facing the dry Niger were framed reproductions of the Mungo Park engravings I admired—including, in the center, the one that had been on the jacket of *Niger!*

But we could not talk about music then. As a guest, I was required to drink at least three cups of my Muslim host's thick, black coffee and talk about anything but the business at hand, which was music. So we drank coffee and brushed flies away from our eyes and talked in French about water and the getting of it, the massacres in Mali and the growing refugee problem, the success or lack of it of the more humane population-control methods in Niger.

"You will take more coffee?" Hamane asked after I finished my third cup.

"With pleasure," I said, and he filled my cup. This would be the cup I would not finish, I knew.

Hamane filled his own cup, but did not touch it. He leaned back in his chair and folded his hands in front of him. "You are kind enough to know my music," he said.

I told him about the records I had had as a boy, and he smiled and seemed delighted that a boy in America had had two of his records, and that that boy had loved them.

He told me about his work with the Hausa king, and then he played his copies of the anthropologists' recordings of his court music. I listened until the sun had set and Hamane had lit candles in the walls. The music was all I had hoped for: the repeated chants I remembered, growing in complexity and rhythm and movement till I could hardly stop myself from join-ing in, but I smiled and Hamane smiled with me to see my obvious joy in the Hausa music.

"There are many tapes," he said, finally. "I will ask you back to hear them all."

"And I will gladly come," I said. If his music had subcon-sciously influenced me to work in Africa, it was an influence I gladly accepted and acknowledged.

He stood to put his tapes back in their cases, and I looked beyond him at the engravings on the wall, flickering in the can-dlelight. I thought again of the record *Niger!*

"May I ask you one question before I go?" I asked.

"Of course," Hamane said.

"Why did you not rerecord *Niger!*?"

He put down his tapes and looked at me. "Was it that music that you were trying to find again in the museum?" he asked me.

I nodded.

"It was like the music you heard and loved tonight."

"Yes, it was," I said.

"Wait here. I will find my copy of *Niger!* and play it for you," he said.

"I don't mean to impose—"

He held up his hand. "It is the only way for me to answer your question. When you hear the music again, you will under-stand why I could not rerecord it."

He crossed to the windows and opened them wide. "While I am gone to get the record, listen to what you can hear out of these windows," he said, and he left the room.

I listened and could hear a truck on a road back in Niamey. I heard a dog barking south of us, in the Gaoueye district. I heard the wind blow along the dry course of the Niger.

Hamane returned with his record. He handed me the jacket after he took the record out and put it on the turntable: the Mungo Park engraving was as I remembered it, and I felt again like a boy, except that now I was with the man who made the music I loved.

He put the needle down, and the music started, scratchy. "What do you hear?" he asked me, right away.

"Your voice," I said. "A drum."

"What else?"

I listened. "Another voice."

"What else?"

I listened, but could hear only the two voices and drums.

"What do you hear behind the music?"

Then I realized. "Water?" I asked.

He picked up the needle and put it back down in another song. "What do you hear now?" he asked.

This time I was listening for the water, and I heard it in the background. "Water again," I said.

"What here?" he asked, putting the needle in a different place.

"Water."

"And here?"

"Water."

He let the music play after that, but walked to the windows and looked out. "The water you hear," he said, "was the water of the Niger River."

We were both quiet for a time, and I listened now, not so much to the music as to the sound of the water behind it.

"We taped hours of the sound of the river and dubbed it in on a track behind our music when we recorded it in Paris," Hamane said. "We wanted the river with us in our music when we began because the river was our country. Those tapes of the river were lost in the fire, too."

And I understood. "You could have reproduced the music," I said, "but not the sound of the river."

He did not look at me. "What did you hear out of these windows when I left you here to listen?" he asked.

I told him what I had heard. He turned off his music and had me stand at the windows with him, looking out at the dry Niger. We listened to the wind in the riverbed till the candles guttered down and one had gone out. Hamane Oumarou led me to his door then, and I walked back to my hot rooms that had no running water. I had three beers hidden under my bed, and I drank one of them alone in my room, then took off my clothes and lay down on my bed, but my windows were open and the wind made the windows rattle and I could not sleep for a very long time. All the sounds that night were harsh and dry.

BANGKOK

I woke and did not open my eyes. I kept my breathing steady. I had heard two Chin whispering unintelligible words near my feet. The three women keeping watch did nothing. Were their backs all turned away? I shouted, threw off the furs, grabbed my gun, and crouched down, barefoot on the rampart in the falling snow.

Chin soldiers. Two of them, and on the walls of Bangkok. Sirikit, Nuam, and Amphan stumbled up behind me. "Narai!" Amphan shouted.

The Chin laughed and drew their swords and swung them above their heads. I shot the Chin again and again—

But hit only the stone battlement, spattering red sparks on the snow. The light from the gun crackled in the cold air.

Sirikit knocked the gun from my hands. "Ghosts again, Narai?" she asked.

The women could not hold me back from kicking through the snow where the Chin had stood. There were no Chin.

Nuam threw me my coat. I pulled it on. Sirikit brushed the snow from my gun and handed it to me, butt forward. I strapped it against my right leg. "I won't let you sleep with the gun anymore," she said. "What if you shot one of us coming up with wood?"

I sat down to rub my feet dry and pull on my boots. The women, dressed like men, huddled back down around the fire. The fire kept only our pot of oil hot. But I did not allow my body to feel the cold, and I did not listen to the women. "I will go to the wat and get you bread," I said. The women looked at me. I hurried down the stairs and did not look back. I did not want the women to ask me why I thought the monks would have bread to give us, today.

I had seen Chin on the wall, Chin who were not there, and it was not the first time. I did not want to lose my mind.

The monks had no bread, and they had no time for me. They were preparing for Chettha Dhanarat, the high monk, to go to the Chin to offer them lands the sea had left us. Chettha had dreamed of doing this, "of letting peace go into the warm world that will come in a thousand years."

"Go to the gardens," one monk said. "Chettha is there. You did not get his blessing before you left us. Get it now."

The monks of Chettha's wat had cared for me when I was sent wounded to Bangkok. But when the Chin army had surrounded the city, I would not wait to heal or to be blessed. I had dressed and left the wat.

Now I needed Chettha's blessing.

The Chin had shot so many holes in the acrylic roof over the gardens that the roof could not be mended. As I entered, snow was falling on trees and on ground that had never known snow. Dry leaves crackled under my feet. Birds that needed warmth lay dead in branches and on the yellow grass. I passed monks in boots and heavy coats collecting the last silk harvest. Far off, I saw the rice paddies brown and dry and wondered what the monks would cook on holy days.

Chettha knelt by the pool across from the reclining Buddha of the gardens. In the Buddha's upturned hand lay a rare bird, dead. Its right wing had been crushed, and it had crept into the hand after the bombing, to die there. Its body was covered with green and blue feathers, and its tail spread into a fan of many colors: gold, red, blue, white, green. There were no more birds like that, unless they had them in Ayutthaya-by-the-Sea.

I knelt a little ways off, to wait for Chettha to notice me. Chettha's head was shaved. He wore only a loose yellow robe but did not shiver. The reflecting pool was freezing. A thin ice had formed around the stone banks and was creeping to the brown lilies in the center.

Chettha said nothing for half an hour. I could not sit in one position that long and moved my legs twice. Finally Chettha looked at me and pointed at the bird in Buddha's hand. "Take that bird to the poor," he said. "It will make a fine meal." He stood to leave.

"I need your blessing," I said.

He stopped and looked down at me.

"I see Chin on the walls. I'm afraid of going insane. The monks told me I might ask for your blessing."

"But I've seen dead Chin, too," he said.

I stared at him. He called what I had seen dead Chin—ghosts—not lunacy. He stepped forward and put his hands on the sides of my head. "Keep your mind. And may you always find food to give," he said, and was gone.

I gave the bird to a little boy dressed in rags. "The monks had no bread," I told the women. I did not look at them. I stood on the wall and watched Chettha and three of his monks leave Bangkok. They walked through the north gate, away from the walls, toward the Chin camps. The monks were chanting mantras, holding their palms open in front of them, their yellow robes fluttering in the wind and the snow. I called the women to watch, but they soon sat back down around the fire.

I watched an hour on the walls, looking north into the falling snow, hoping for peace. When the snow eventually thinned, I could see far up the Chao Phyra. When the Chao Phyra froze over, the Chin would walk up it into Bangkok, if Chettha failed, laughing at the oil we'd try to throw on them from the walls. Nothing moved on the white plains. Snow hissed and popped on the oil.

I smelled meat. The women were cooking.

"The boy looks away for food," Nuam said. She handed me a spit with a rabbit breast. The meat was black, cooked through, salty.

"More," I said, handing back the spit. The women laughed. "We'll cook more if you kill more." I wanted more food. I wanted a rabbit to burrow out from under the drifts so I could kill it with the light and then try to beat the snowy owls and the gyrfalcons to the red spot on the snow. I unstrapped the gun. The metal stuck to my fingers.

Nothing moved in the snow. The women uncoiled the rope. Sirikit tied it around her waist so I could hurry over the battlements and down the wall if I shot something. It would be safer to hunt with Chettha bargaining with the Chin. The generals had not let us hunt over the walls. The Chin wore the white furs of bears and wolves. We could jump from the walls and be killed by Chin we had not seen. But now our generals—and our captains and lieutenants—were dead, and I fed the women of my watch. The women could not watch with patience, hungry.

Wind blew snow off the drifts. Above Bangkok, the clouds were breaking. Without clouds, the night would be cold. The rabbits would not burrow out. Birds were circling the river and the plains, watching us, watching for the rabbits we wanted. "Will you cook a bird, Nuam?"

"Bag a ptarmigan, and I will cook it," Amphan said.

Ptarmigan were flying in the willows by the Chao Phyra, fifty feet from the wall. One ptarmigan flew out across the drifts, fast, coming for the city. A gyrfalcon circled down for it. I took the ptarmigan in my sight and shot it. It fell, feathers burned by the light. The gyrfalcon flew up in a flutter of wings and began circling, warily.

I was over the battlements, down the rope, buried to my waist in the snow. The women looked on wide-eyed. Sirikit had her bow. Amphan held the quiver. I pushed forward, gun in hand. The gyrfalcon would die before it could take our ptarmigan. I watched the gyrfalcon circling lower, watching me. Suddenly it let out one cry and flew across the Chao Phyra, past Thon Buri. The ptarmigan in the willows flew across the river. I got to the dead ptarmigan. Nerves made its wings twitch. When I picked it up, the women began shouting. I looked at them. Sirikit had an arrow to her bow and the string pulled back, taut. I heard the crust below the new snow break and saw white coming up out of the willows toward me. I jumped to the side, heard it fall past me, turned to face it.

A Chin. He stood up slowly, smiling. "Give me bird and gun," he said, gesturing with one hand, a kris in the other.

We stood five feet apart in the quiet of the snow. The Chin's breath had frozen his mustache to his thin face. He was no older than me.

Other Chin yelled, suddenly, from behind me, from across the plains half a kilometer from the walls. Black arrows fell into the snow, and I did not turn to look. I shot the kris out of the Chin's hand and ran for the walls. An arrow stuck to my coat by my right shoulder. I was at the rope. The women pulled me up and over the battlements. I still had the ptarmigan. I dropped it in the snow on the wall.

Nuam would not let me turn to the battle. She kept trying to unbutton my coat. "Damn you, Narai, will you bleed to death?"

The arrow had gone into my shoulder. It was black from being hardened in a fire, and stiff in my knotted muscle. I pulled it out with one quick jerk and fell to my back. Nuam sat me up, took off my coat, bandaged my shoulder in white cloth while I worked the flint arrowhead through the hole in my coat.

The Chin were at the walls. Arrows were flying over the walls. Sirikit was shooting her arrows through a crenel in the battlements. "The light, Narai!" she said. Amphan and Nuam dragged the pot of oil to the battlements and dumped oil on two Chin climbing a ladder. The Chin screamed. One fell into the snow. The other clung to the ladder, clawing his face: it was cooked brown, crinkled, his eyes blind. He fell back and the ladder fell on top of him. I started shooting Chin: first the Chin with a second ladder, then the Chin with bows. The Chin below us ran. I let them: six Chin struggling away through the snow.

The Chin who had asked for my bird and gun was stumbling north along the banks of the Chao Phyra. I had killed five Chin. Sirikit had killed two with her arrows. The oil had killed two more.

It was over, again.

Sirikit carried wood to the fire. Amphan dragged back the empty pot and lifted it onto the wood. Nuam opened a can of oil and dumped the oil in the pot. I sank down on the rampart and pulled on my coat. The ptarmigan was trampled in the snow. I kicked it out and thought of Chettha. We should not have been attacked while Chettha was in the Chin camp.

Amphan took the bird, cut off its head, let its blood drain out over the wall. Then she cut open the bird's belly and tore out the entrails. Nuam looked through them for the heart, gizzard, kidneys, and liver; she threw the rest over the wall for the gyrfalcons. The offal landed on a Chin's face. Amphan shoved the meat on four skewers. Nuam salted the meat, and she and Amphan held the skewers over the fire. Sirikit was kicking through the snow for Chin arrows to put in her quiver.

"Our babies will be Chin," Nuam said.

We looked at her. She was turning her skewers quickly.

"The ghosts of the Chin we kill—they will be reborn here."

Sirikit shook down the arrows in her quiver. "If the Chin have ghosts, they'll come back as rats in our sewers."

Amphan had wrapped a scarf around her face. She pulled down the left corner. "I've heard if a man dies outside his own land his ghost wanders the cities and hills of the new land, lost," she said, "sometimes not believing he is dead."

Ghosts again.

Sirikit looked at me, hard. "Battle nerves and exhaustion, Narai."

Amphan wrapped the scarf back around her face and said nothing more of ghosts.

A six-year-old girl climbed up the stairs with a handful of arrows she and her group had gathered from the streets. The children had become good at standing quietly after a battle and looking for the tiny holes arrows made in the drifts. Sirikit took the arrows. The girl stared at our meat and did not leave. Nuam swore, tore a ptarmigan's leg from a spit, and threw it to the girl. The girl caught it and ran down the stairs, gnawing at the leg. "Cook it!" Nuam yelled.

I wanted the meat. I wanted it now. I would have eaten it raw like the girl if Nuam had let me.

A shadow fell across my face. Sirikit stood looking down at me. "How is your shoulder?"

"Cold," I said.

She walked on, kicking through the snow, looking for arrows.

Nuam handed me the ptarmigan's liver. "It cooks fast," she said. I ate it in one bite. I meant to eat it slowly, but I couldn't.

Taksin Naresuan ran up the stairs, out of breath, red-faced. We stared at him and at the bag of food he carried. "All the Chin are back," he said. He knew things like that because he worked with the old men and women. "They will probably attack tonight. We sent the night watch to the east and south walls."

Which meant the day watch would stay up to guard the north and west walls. Amphan looked quickly into the fire. The cold was not easy for her. I did not ask Taksin about Chettha and whether he might stop the attack. Taksin had always laughed at Chettha and his plans.

"The Chin must take Bangkok now, for food and a place to

wait out the winter, or die in the cold," Taksin said. He kicked snow away from the wall and sat down next to me. "The Chin advance was stopped at Chulalongkorn City."

I looked at him.

"We had a message from Ayutthaya-by-the-Sea."

Sirikit sat down and took a spit from Amphan to help turn it over the fire. "Then the Vitmin have quit jamming the radio," she said.

"They've started quarreling with the Chin."

"The Chin did not get far," Nuam said. "It's only one hundred kilometers south to Chulalongkorn."

"They could not go far without Bangkok," Taksin said. "They need our wheat. We could attack them from the rear. They were forced to leave part of their army here." Taksin seemed pleased with this knowledge, pleased that all the Chin were back around our walls.

"Will help come from Ayutthaya?" Amphan asked.

Taksin shrugged. "It is sixteen hundred kilometers to Ayutthaya-by-the-Sea."

Nuam held out a ptarmigan wing to Taksin.

He stood. "I won't take your food. I came to bring you food," he said. He reached in his bag for a loaf of bread and two carrots. Nuam gave her spits to Amphan and took the bread and carrots. Taksin swung the bag over his shoulder and looked out over the plains. "I can't see their tank," he said. I stood and pointed to a snowdrift. We had lost twenty-six men trying to pull the tank inside the walls and finally wrecked it, stripped it, and left it.

Taksin looked at the stones of the river wall churning the Chao Phyra. Amphan handed me a spit with a ptarmigan wing, the back, the heart. These I ate slowly. Taksin accepted the wing from Nuam's spit after he saw mine. He sat down by me to eat.

I knew what it had cost the Chin to drag their tank to Bangkok to knock down our north river wall. Eight months before, the Chin had sacked Chiang Mai. I had gone with the army to drive the Chin back across the passes. The Chin fled north into the mountains and glaciers of Shan and Yunan. We followed them to the border. Once inside the mountains, I was assigned with forty-seven others to forage for the army. We had nineteen hundred men to feed.

One day, we found the spoor of musk oxen: tracks by a stream, the soft underhair wool lining spring nests in the willows. Up a narrow valley we found a lake half free of ice where the musk oxen watered. The master hunter left me hidden in the willows and junipers that grew only on the south shore. 'Kill three old cows,' he said. 'That is all the meat we can prepare before the army moves on.' He and the others went down the valley after rabbits and ptarmigan.

I waited. Under the crusts of snow beneath the willows I found wild crocus and blue spikel shoots pushing up through the dirt. In two weeks the valley would be covered with flowers. In six, the flowers would be gone to seed. It was the way of things in the mountains north of Chiang Mai. I picked up a stone. Frost was flaking the stone apart, yet the stone was heavy and fit well in my hand. One brown streak ran a half inch across the stone's surface as if a child had drawn on it and tossed it aside or as if some species of lichen could find food in only one straight crack of the stone and nowhere else.

I looked up. The musk oxen had come. Two cows and a bull so old his coat had turned brown stood watch while twenty others drank at the lake. They stood five feet tall at the shoulder. Hair on their flanks, throats, and under their bellies hung long and black, covering their ears and tails. The pregnant females were shedding the soft wool under their hair. Horns curved around the sides of their heads, and a thick boss of horn grew across their foreheads.

They came up dripping from the lake. I threw my stone. It fell short but startled them. I shook the willows. The bull began to snort and shake his head. The cows herded old females and yearling calves into the center of a circle of lowered heads and horns. The bull backed up and took his place, stoic. Such rings were a good defense against wolves but no defense against men.

I unstrapped my gun and killed three cows. But as I looked at the musk oxen, I saw only their meat. Three musk oxen would feed us well for one meal—but twenty-three could feed us for three days. I could rest in camp. The soldiers were tired of rabbit and ptarmigan and caribou. I shot two more cows. The musk oxen began to run. I kept shooting till the master hunter knocked the gun from my hands. He had come back to watch me. "The army will push on tomorrow," he said. "You will stay behind, in charge of a few others, to prepare this meat and carry it after us."

I looked at the ground. The master hunter shoved my gun in his belt and handed me a knife. "Gut them now," he said. "Butcher them in camp."

Seventeen musk oxen lay smoking on rocks by the lake and in snow up the valley. I walked to the bull musk ox. Its burned hair and flesh stank. Its hair and wool made cutting it open hard. I pulled out the genitals and intestines, cut through the diaphragm, windpipe, and esophagus, pulled out the lungs and heart. The blood kept my hands warm till I stood up and felt the wind. I hurried to cut open another musk ox. It took three hours to gut all seventeen musk oxen. When I started for camp, only the viscera from the last three steamed.

The master hunter sent four of us back with ropes. A transport could not reach the lake because of the snow. We dragged one young cow to camp. The carcass would dig down in the snow going uphill. We had to kick snow away from the musk ox, drag it three or four feet, kick away more snow. At the tops of hills and drifts the carcass would slide down the slope, pulling us with it. The hair would get caught on willows and in the buckles of our boots. Once in camp, we tied the hind feet together, hoisted up the musk ox with a winch, skinned it, and left it for the others to butcher.

The master hunter sent me back with three different hunters after another musk ox. By evening, I had helped drag four musk oxen to camp. I could only sit in camp then, too tired to help with the butchery, but I wanted to go for another musk ox. "Eat first, at least," the other hunters said. "Leave them," some of the soldiers whispered. "He won't make you stay behind, not with Chin in the mountains." But I knew the master hunter would leave me, that the men he left with me would hate me. I finally convinced two soldiers to go up-valley, though it would be dark when we got back.

But we did not have to pull another musk ox to camp. The two soldiers were slow, and I was first to the lake. When I got there, I saw a Chin. He was standing across the lake, very still. One musk ox was gone—dragged up-valley. I could see the bloody track of its carcass in the snow. The Chin drew a knife and raised it so that it glistened in the setting sun while he stared at me. With a sudden yell, he charged around the lake. I turned and ran. "Chin!" I yelled. The soldiers dove for cover behind drifts on either side of the path we had made dragging the musk oxen down-valley. The Chin was close behind me. I ran between the soldiers. The soldiers killed the Chin. They took his knife and his coat of wolves' skin, and we ran to camp.

All the men of camp spent the night preparing for attack but me. The master hunter had me card loose wool from the musk ox hides. I was through with the carding and packaging by midnight. "What have you learned?" the master hunter asked.

I looked at the ground. "That three were enough."

The master hunter smiled and sent me to help prepare the camp. In the morning, he was killed. I was shot in the stomach with an arrow and sent down the frozen Ping and the Chao Phyra to Bangkok with the wounded. But because of the musk oxen, I knew what it meant to drag something heavy through snow. I knew what it had meant for the Chin to drag their tank to Bangkok.

Smoke began to billow up from the grounds of Dusit Palace. We sat quietly to honor the dead. "One hundred and four today," Taksin said, "with the heads of Chettha Dhanarat and three of his monks."

I looked hard at Taksin. He looked back as if I should have heard. "The Chin threw the heads against the east gate half an hour ago. Word of it came just before I left with the food." He threw the bones of the ptarmigan wing over the wall and stood up. "It will be cold tonight. The old men say a front passed over us. It may snow tomorrow in Ayutthaya."

"Nahm kaang?" Amphan asked, the sudden cold that flows south off the advancing glaciers of Chin, Monglia, and farther north where the sea itself is ice.

"Can't you feel it?" He left, walking down the rampart to take bread and carrots to another watch.

And Chettha was dead. He had not been gone two hours.

There would be no peace. I would have to fight the Chin in the night, and I would have to keep fighting, and fighting.

Nuam tore the loaf into four pieces, broke the carrots in two, and handed out the food.

"So Chettha failed," Sirikit said.

"He was a fool," Nuam said. "The Chin would never live with us and share our food. They would have killed us."

Amphan nodded. "They want all the lands, all the old cities—not empty lands the sea left us."

I looked up. "Chettha said it was a failure of the human spirit if he failed with us and the Chin."

Sirikit spat on the snow.

But I remembered the old man, Chettha Dhanarat. I could feel his hands on my head, blessing me. I set down my food and put my hands on my head and held them there.

"They did not give us enough food if we have to watch the night," Amphan said.

I looked up. I had food I could not eat. I took down my hands and handed Amphan my bread and carrot. The others stared at me. I stood and looked out over the battlements at the white plains and the clear, cold sky. By midnight, the temperature might drop to seventy degrees below zero.

"May the Chin freeze," Nuam said.

Many would. Our guerrillas burned the Chin tents when they could, and the Chin had burned all wood outside the walls in a fifty-kilometer radius. We could still tear wood from the houses inside Bangkok.

Sirikit uncoiled the rope and tied it around my waist. "I'll go down for the Chin coats," she said. "We need them in this cold."

Nuam and Amphan helped me hold the rope. Sirikit climbed down in the snow. I unstrapped my gun, and we kept careful watch. Nothing moved over the snow except gyrfalcons and snowy owls that fluttered away as Sirikit walked toward the bodies. The coats of the men we had dumped oil on were ruined. Sirikit took coats from five other bodies and tied the coats to the rope. We hauled them up. She collected two more. We pulled her up with them. She also brought three Chin knives, two quivers of arrows, a bow.

The coats were of good bears' or wolves' fur. The sun had set, and it was night. I sent Amphan with two of the coats down the stairs to the children's house. "Stay indoors with them till you hear shouting," I said. She did not argue. Nuam went with her and came up with more wood for the fire.

Nuam, Sirikit, and I put on Chin coats. We built up the fire. I took first watch. Sirikit and Nuam lay down by the fire and wrapped another Chin coat over their legs. They covered their faces so they would not breathe the straight cold air.

When the cold hurt, I wrapped my scarf of musk ox wool around my face. Chettha's monks had woven my scarf and shirt from the wool I had carded in Yunan. The moon came up, round and bright, surrounded by rings of color: orange, red, blue. It would be very cold. The moonlight made the white plains sparkle as if covered with the dust of jewels. A gyrfalcon flew across the Chao Phyra and out over the plains where the Chin camped.

At 1:00 I built up the fire and woke Sirikit. At 5:00 it was too cold to sleep anymore. I sat up. Amphan was back, looking over the battlements with Sirikit and Nuam. "We let you sleep," Nuam said.

The moon was low, east of Bangkok. I stood up, walked stiffly to the wall.

And saw the Chin.

Hundreds of Chin stood on the plains, out of bowshot from the walls, open to the wind, quiet, pale in the moonlight, in their white furs. I unstrapped my gun.

"Taksin woke me," Amphan said. "They surround Bangkok like this—thousands of them, thousands of Chin."

The Chao Phyra had frozen in the night. "They will walk up the river," I said.

"The ice is new," Sirikit said. "They will still try the walls."

We heard the children laughing. At 6:00, four boys came up the stairs with boxes of food: cheese, roast hams, apples, bread, radishes, fried potatoes. In my box was one bottle of apple brandy and four glasses. Each box even had a tiny rice cake. I had eaten such cakes twice before. The children left, happy, happy to be eating the food we had hoarded so long.

I sat and poured the brandy. The food and brandy took away much of the cold. We put the food we could not eat into one box and set the other three on the fire. They made a bright blaze.

At 7:00 the moon went down. The Chin let out one great shout. We stood quickly and looked over the walls. Sirikit fit an arrow to her bow. Nuam took up the Chin bow. Amphan drew her knife. I held my gun ready.

But the Chin stood still in the wind, in the drifting snow, in the cold. Bangkok was slowly turning to the sun. The Chin will attack now, before dawn, I thought.

But they did not. The light grew. The Chin shimmered in the predawn haze. I rubbed my eyes—too much brandy, too much good food, not enough sleep, not enough sleep for months. I had not wanted to be tired when the Chin came.

The wind grew with the light. It whipped the snow into stinging bits of ice. We could only squint at the Chin. We had to keep the fire built high to keep it alive—it burned so fast in the wind and so much snow blew into it. The wind whipped the hair of the dead Chin below us. When the first arc of the sun broke above the horizon east of Bangkok, the Chin gave another shout and charged the walls.

"Don't waste arrows!" I shouted above the Chin's shouting. I could fire my gun before Sirikit and Nuam could shoot their arrows. None of the Chin I shot at dropped—the gun was not working. I had no new powerpac to put in it. The Chin skimmed along the tops of the drifts, seldom breaking through the crust. They were at the walls with ladders. I helped Amphan dump oil on a ladder full of men, but the oil crackled only on the bodies of the dead Chin we had shot the night before, did not stop the Chin on the ladder. Sirikit fell back with an arrow in her chest. I knelt to pull it out, but the arrow faded at my touch. Sirikit tore at her clothes to look at her skin. There was no hurt.

The sun was nearly up. We could see the plains before the walls, covered with Chin. I drew my knife and lunged at a Chin coming over the battlements—big, strong, white in his furs—but he was not there. I was not seeing clearly. I had to see clearly. Chin were on the walls. Sirikit, Nuam, Amphan, and I stood together, back to back. Amphan stabbed a Chin with her knife. I tried shooting my gun again. No Chin fell. They circled us, jeering.

"This is a Chin trick!" I said.

The Chin suddenly looked at the sun, looked without shading their eyes. The sun lifted above the horizon. The Chin stared at the sun, shouting again and again. Some of them wept. Amphan put her hands over her ears, but the shouting grew fainter. The Chin began to fade in the light. "You have won," the Chin on the walls with us whispered. "You have won."

The Chin crowded back in the shadows of the battlements and the walls. As the light grew, all the Chin faded and were gone. The plains were empty of Chin. There were no Chin on the plains, no ladders against the walls, no Chin in the shadows. Birds circled the plains over the smokeless Chin camps. Wind sighed across the drifts and hissed in the willows.

A Thai flag was raised, suddenly, above the Chin camp north of us. It fluttered in tatters—white, blue, and green. A great Thai shout went up from the walls of Bangkok. Men and women climbed over the walls and ran toward the Chin camp. Sirikit tied our rope around a merlon, and we climbed down into the snow and ran to the Chin camp.

It was filled with dead, frozen Chin. Some lay alone in the snow. Others lay on top of each other under the scraps of burned tent our guerrillas had left them. We stood in the middle of the Chin camp and looked at the bodies. I thought of the thousands of Chin we had killed at Chiang Mai, Chainat, Chulalongkorn, and Bangkok.

"The Chin could not admit defeat, even in death," Amphan said.

But we had not defeated them. The cold had, and their lack of food, and their supplies suitable for only a quick campaign designed to take our cities, and their disbelief that we would give them lands the sea had left.

One dead Chin lay wrapped in yellow robes.

Monks, nurses, children, and old men and women climbed onto the walls of Bangkok and shouted to us, waved to us. Nuam and Amphan waved back.

The tracks of the few Chin who had survived the night led

north. Thai guerrillas, black specks on the white plains, followed those tracks. The rest of us waited for the army from
Ayutthaya-by-the-Sea before going north to find what we
would find. In three months it would be spring. We'd need the
provinces with their fields of winter wheat.

The women and I pulled coats and boots from the dead Chin
and walked back to the walls. Three old women helped pull us
up our rope to the top. Nuam picked up the box of food we had
not eaten. "We need this now," she said. Sirikit picked up the
bows, the quivers of arrows, the knives. I took one of the tins
of oil in my left hand. Amphan carried two others. We walked
down the stairs.

Children were in the streets, shouting. Old men and women
were running to them, hugging them. "We have won," they
shouted, happy. I stopped to watch three nine-year-old boys
play takraw. Two were good at keeping the ball in the air without using their hands. I had not played takraw for a year. The
third boy kicked the ball in my direction. I kicked it back and
walked on after Sirikit, Nuam, and Amphan.

We carried our things to the house the army had given us by
the wall, then went back to the battlements for the Chin coats,
the rope, the pot. Amphan kicked out the fire.

"We should take you to a doctor," Nuam said, looking at my
shoulder.

"Later," I said. I only wanted sleep. I only wanted to sleep
after fighting the Chin, sleep in a room without shadows where
I could not hear old men shout that we had won.

SECOND LIVES

I gave my mother and father their second lives two days before doing it became impossible, two days before Arath's armies took the city. My parents thanked me with a public dinner in a temple garth at which they served real meat. I never saw my parents again. When I had children, they were supposed to do the same for me.

The next morning I felt sick, but the temple sewers quit working and all the other initiates and I were assigned to help carry buckets of old blood up the stairs to the surface where we dumped them on the east lawns. Thousands crowding around the temple in the crush ahead of Arath's advance could watch us. Few would. Some of those who did left.

We worked through the day, let off only for meals. In the night, Arath's troops took the ridges west of us, but they stopped the shelling. The night was quiet. None of us were allowed to sleep. Our shoulders and arms ached. My legs were caked with blood.

On one trip up, before dawn, Lieutenant Hazael, of the temple guard, stood waiting for us. He made us stop, and Niram spilled his buckets on the steps. The lieutenant didn't care. He jerked up the sleeves of our tunics to read the numbers tattooed on our arms, and when he read mine he stiffened, ordered me to follow him, and started down the steps.

I followed. He shoved me ahead of him into the temple guard headquarters and pushed me into a side room. Two priests and the Head Vivifier—an old man, very pale and stooped that night; I had seen him twice before—sat waiting there. The vivifier slammed shut a book he was reading, squinted at me, and looked at Hazael. "You trust him?"

"He has carried out every order given him—faithfully," Hazael said with a touch of sarcasm I thought very insolent.

"Send him." The vivifier stood up and walked out, clutching the book to his chest, helped by one of the priests. The other priest shoved something into Hazael's hands as he left. Hazael gave it to me. It was a photograph of an old man with a long gray beard and a red scar that ran straight across his forehead.

"Could you recognize that man if you saw him?" Hazael demanded.

"Yes, sir."

"Then find him. Bring him to me. He is in the temple already, and he must not enter the Head Vivifier's chambers. Get to him before he reaches the third level."

"But—"

"Find him! There are reasons for sending you. I need my men in other places."

I moved to the door, but he pulled me back. "Take this. Show it to the priests as you go down."

He handed me a rectangular metal chip with patterns of green dots blinking on it. I put it in my tunic pocket and started out. He stopped me again.

"You might need this," he said curtly, handing me a gun on a belt. "Tie it inside your tunic where it can't be seen but where you can get to it easily."

"I've never fired one."

"Take it! He won't know that."

I strapped the gun inside my tunic and left. Hazael stood in the doorway and watched me go. I stopped at the fountain and tried to wash off some of the blood but it was no use, so I forced my way through the crowd on the temple steps just as I was.

"You can't come through here," a temple guard at the top sneered, and he shoved me back down a few steps. I took out the chip and handed it to him. He looked surprised, held it up to watch the lights blink, and finally gave it back and let me in.

I knew the way the old man would have to take—I had gone that way with my parents. People lined both sides of the great hall that led to the stairway down. Most were old, and most family groups had at least one young man or woman—a son or a niece—with them (it cost more without a young relative, and there were more risks). They all stared at me in silence. I stared back at the old men. None of them had the scar of the man in the photograph.

The priests and vestals on the second level clustered around me after I showed one of them the chip. One vestal wept when she saw it. No one would tell me what it meant to them. I thought it was just getting me through the temple without the company of adults—a pass. A few priests remembered seeing the man in the photograph. They all thought he was just ahead in the line somewhere, but no one would take me to him.

Finally, an attendant in the dressing rooms told me the old man had already gone into one of the chapels. I did not know what to do. I could not interrupt the meetings. Still, I hurried to the chapel hallway. The first four chapels were empty—the people in them had gone down to the third level. So I waited by the door of the fifth chapel. Through it I could hear a high vestal chant the Litany for New Life, a litany that spoke of the responsibilities sixty or seventy additional years of life would bring. When she finished, all the people in the chapel sang a hymn and the door opened. I watched the people file through it. He was not with them. I watched by the sixth chapel, but he did not come out of there either, and so on through six more chapels. He had evidently been in one of the first four.

The priest in that last chapel looked scared when I showed him the chip and the photograph. He rushed me to the stairs leading to the third level. I asked him if he would go down with me and help me find the man, but he said he could spare me no more time and hurried away.

The waiting rooms on the third level were crowded. The old man was not in any of them. So I walked to the Doors of Life. Emeralds set in them gleamed in a green burst out of the darkness of the hall. A special guard of priests stood there. They had just let the man in my photograph through the doors. As they opened them for me, one of the guards bolted down the hall for the stairs; the others cursed him. But after they clanged the doors shut behind me, I could hear more steps running away to the stairs.

I stood in the doorway looking down at the rugs. I realized that my hand was inside my tunic clutching the gun, but my hand was shaking, and I knew that just then I could not pull out the gun and hold it. Still, I could not run away. Hazael had told the Head Vivifier that I did everything they asked—faithfully. So I forced myself to look up. Three people sat in the room: an old woman holding a little black-haired girl, and the man I sought. A door across from me opened. A vivifier in his scarlet robes stepped in from his chambers, called the name of the woman, and led her and the little girl out. I was alone with the man.

"Sir," I said.

He would not look up.

"Sir, you must come back out with me."

He still would not look up. "I'm too close," he said hoarsely. "They would never let me go anywhere else now."

I did not understand. "But they would, sir. They sent me for you."

The old man ran a finger along the scar on his forehead. "You're just a boy!"

I managed to draw the gun, and I activated it. The sound made him start. He clutched the arms of the chair he sat in, still looking determinedly at the floor.

"Don't let me see the gun. Put it back—hide it! Don't you know what will happen if I see it?"

His knuckles where he gripped the chair were white; his face was very white.

"Why can't you look at me?" I asked.

"Because they can see everything I see. Put the gun away."

I put it back.

"You're lucky they didn't have time to work with my ears," he said.

"Who?"

"Arath's doctors, of course. Why do you think you were sent to get me?"

"Arath's doctors can see what you see?"

"No! His generals—Arath himself for all I know. His doctors put the transmitters in my eyes."

"In your eyes!"

Again he fingered the scar on his forehead. "You don't know what else they put in me, do you."

I said nothing. I did not know. He kept rubbing the scar. "Leave this place, boy," he whispered. "You might yet get to the surface."

Then I knew, but I could not move. "Why did you let them put it in you?" I stammered.

"They would have killed my family. They probably killed them anyway."

I hugged the gun tight against my stomach so it could not fall on the floor for the man to see.

"You're thinking Arath's people are horrible, aren't you?" he asked.

I said nothing.

"Is what they did to me worse than what your people did to you—sending you, a boy, after me to make the bomb detonate before it could damage the heart of their temple?"

I could move.

I pushed open the door and ran down the hall. People stood crammed around the stairs, trying to get out. The chip had explained to the temple workers behind me what was happening, and they had told the people. I shouted for the people to follow me up the stairs we used to carry out the blood. Some did.

I was nearly to the surface when the first explosion came. The bomb in the old man was more powerful than Hazael, the Head Vivifier, or anyone had imagined. The roar made my ears hurt for days; when I got outside my clothes were on fire. I fell on the grass and rolled in the blood we had dumped. I heard more explosions. The ground around me began to sag. I scrambled up and ran down to the trees by the river.

As soon as the temple exploded, Arath's troops began shelling the city again. I could hear bombs exploding on the temple hill. I tried to run along the river, but the brush hurt my burns too much. I stopped on the bank, set down the gun, pulled off my tunic, and waded out in the water to cool my burns and to try to rinse the blood out of the tunic. Only then did I realize I was crying, and I made myself stop.

Except for the shelling, I could hear no other sound. Soon I could not hear even that. I could not hear the water swirl around me or the birds cry out in the dark trees before the dawn. I clapped my hands by my ears, but it was no use. I could not hear.

I saw an uprooted tree floating by a little farther out. I went back to the shore for the gun and waded out to the tree. It had been partly burned. Some explosion upstream had knocked it in the river. I climbed on it and wrung the water out of my tunic, wrapped the gun in it and tied the tunic to a branch. The chip fell out of the pocket into my hand, the green lights still blinking. I threw it as far as I could. I pushed the tree toward the current and crawled partway up the half-submerged trunk and lay down hidden by branches and leaves. I did not look back.

SOFT IN THE WORLD, AND BRIGHT

This is how it began: I stumbled. But it wasn't just a stumble. I knew that. My right leg "felt" tingly—no, "felt" as if tiny pinpricks of my mind's awareness about my knee were disappearing, as if the knee itself were disappearing atom by atom in a sudden rush.

Mary! I shouted the thought in my mind, but she didn't answer, and I could not access her virtual reality in my mind to find her. I was shut out of it. But she could stop this—she was the artificial intelligence networked through my nerves and my brain to give me my body. I thought maybe that's why she didn't answer me. Maybe she was trying to stop my body from disintegrating from my consciousness and she couldn't answer me because it took all of her efforts.

I had stopped walking and was standing in the middle of a broad flight of stairs leading down to breakfast, and people were staring. I looked across at the handrail against the wall and took a step toward it with my left leg. I could walk with it. My left leg worked. I dragged my right leg along and got to the handrail and the bottom of the stairs and a table where I sat and rubbed my knee. My hands could feel my knee, but my knee couldn't feel my hands on it.

Mary, I thought. *What's happening?*

But she didn't answer, and a golden robot with its ruby, multifaceted eyes stood next to my table to take my order and I couldn't think what to tell it.

"Are you all right, Mr. Addison?" it asked.

It knew me because it was linked to the hotel's central intelligence which was linked to the station's central intelligence which knew all about me: that I was actually no more than a brain in a body that wouldn't work without the AI they put inside me after I broke my neck and found I was allergic to the neural-regeneration drugs, that I couldn't actually feel anything, it was the AI giving my mind the illusion of feeling, that I couldn't breathe on my own, or speak, or control my urination, or be a man among other men who can walk and breathe and hold their urine, and that every eight years I had to have the AI replaced because the programs would become corrupted, and that it was Mary's eighth year and they would erase her out of my mind and I didn't want her to go because I loved her.

I put my hands on the table. "I'm fine," I said to the robot.

"Might I suggest the buffet this morning?"

I couldn't walk to a buffet. "Please bring me some coffee," I said, "and fruit."

"Grapefruit?"

I nodded.

It left, and I still couldn't feel my knee, and I wouldn't put my hands on it. *Mary,* I thought. *Talk to me, Mary. Are you all right?*

But she didn't send a word to my mind. I was sitting in Swan Court, next to the hotel's artificial lagoon by its artificial sea, and the artificial breeze off the water smelled like the sea, and I knew the sea smelled like this because Mary and I had run along a beach once in the early morning and I had felt the sand on my feet, and the spray from the waves on my skin, and I knew Mary was making me feel all of that but I didn't care because Mary was with me in my mind and we were happy with the sun coming up over the sea.

"Your coffee, sir."

The robot put it down in front of me.

"Your grapefruit, sir."

"Thank you."

"Would you like anything else?"

"No."

"Shall I call the swans for you?"

I looked up at the robot and wanted it to go and leave me alone. "The swans?" I said.

The robot looked out over the water, and three swans swam toward us. I wondered how the robot had called them, and then I thought they were probably not real swans, but robots, and it had called them through the central intelligence with a thought. They were graceful and lovely, and the robot left but the swans didn't.

I spooned sugar into the coffee and stirred it and lifted the cup and took a drink—and the coffee burned my lips, but my hands hadn't felt the heat of it in the cup though they had felt the cup, and I put the cup down but my hand started shaking and made coffee spill onto the white tablecloth and I touched my lips but only my lips could feel the touch now, and my hands wouldn't stop shaking.

I put them in my lap.

And knew then what would happen. I didn't want to go through it, not again, not a third time. I didn't want to be in my mind when they killed another AI that I had lived with and loved—when they killed Mary this time. *Mary,* I thought, *We'll fix whatever's wrong. We programmed around the last set of problems you had two weeks ago. We'll do it again. I don't know if you can hear my thoughts, but I won't let them erase you.*

I looked up and the swans were swimming away, and the robot was serving food to a man and a woman and a little girl sitting three tables from me. I raised one of my shaking hands, and the robot looked at me.

"Help me," I said in a whisper, knowing it could hear me and call help with its thoughts, and we wouldn't have to disturb the people around us for a while yet.

• • •

They came to me quickly, two medical robots, and they were kind and gentle. They spoke to me in low voices, telling me what they were going to do, that they would help me walk out of the restaurant to a service elevator, that they could carry me and were prepared with a respirator should I need one on the way. I listened to them and wondered about their lives. Did they love each other? I knew that they could love, and that I could love them. I had loved three AIs. There are people who, if they heard me talk of love, would think that contact with artificial intelligences had corrupted my mind, not the other way around. But it was not the outward physical that I loved, after all. It was the inward quality of soul.

The robots carried me to the hospital, and along the way I lost my body. When they hooked me to machines that monitored my vital signs and made me breathe and took care of my bodily functions and dripped water in my veins so I wouldn't dehydrate, I couldn't feel it. I couldn't feel the air in my lungs or my chest move up and down or the rough cotton sheets against my bare skin. They kept the room dark so it wouldn't hurt my eyes, but even so I could see the bank of monitors that told me or anyone who cared to look that my lungs were breathing and my heart beating. It is a curious thing to be forced to lie absolutely still and watch the functions of your body be displayed digitally in bright green lines and know that they are going on but not feel them.

And they had put electrodes on my head above the implant that held Mary. Her monitor showed a steady, positive green line. Normal. Agitated, probably. Low. But normal. *Mary,* I thought. *We'll find a way to help you.*

I hoped that what I was telling her was true, that we could find a way to help her. I wondered what she was thinking or doing and whether she knew that I would try to save her again. The theory was that the complexity of maintaining her own existence while making my body work and feeding my mind the illusion of sensation would eventually overwhelm her basic algorithms, a process estimated to take a minimum of eight years, after which she could crash catastrophically at any moment, and die, and take me with her if help couldn't reach me in time.

But the theory didn't factor in love.

Mary and I could meet in virtual reality. I could close my

eyes and go to her as a man in a room in the virtual-reality implant and be with her. Mary always took the form of a woman with me. She was never a man, like my first AI, or sometimes a man and sometimes a woman like the second. She was always just Mary. And she was beautiful.

I'm an artist, she'd told me one day sitting next to me in the virtual-reality room, and her eyes sparkled. She was excited, breathless. I believed in her art: my body had never been more lean and tight, more sensitive, more orgasmic, more alive to the sudden brush of sunlight through clouds, or the clean feel of a glass tabletop, or the stirrings of the wind in the hair on my arms than it had been with Mary.

Come outside, she'd said, and she stood and took my hand.

Outside? I'd asked, because there had never been an outside before. I stood and she turned me around, and there was a door now: dark oak, weathered, a little barred window the shape of a knight's shield at just the height of my eyes, and I could see blue sky out of it. By the door was a stone table, and on the table a rose. I walked to the table and picked up the rose, and the thorns pricked my skin and it smelled as beautiful as any rose I had ever smelled. *What have you done?* I asked.

And she opened the door and we walked out onto a mountainside in Spain: Andalusia, the Moorish country west of Gibraltar, the forests in the mountains, and the dry plain below us with black-robed riders galloping black horses across it far away, and the deep blue of the Atlantic, and across the straits, Africa. It was a place I loved, and she knew it because I loved it, and here it was in detail I had forgotten or which had never been: the mountains were starker, more jagged, more romantic. There were no cities. No roads. No other people, till we found that when we connected to the net our AI friends could visit us. I looked behind us, and the room we had walked out of had become part of a little white stucco Spanish house with a dull-red tile roof and a weathered water jar by the door.

Do you like this? she'd asked me.

Had I liked it? I remembered her asking that question while I lay without the sensation of my body in the hospital bed. Mary's Spain was startling, but serene. The house she'd built in my mind had become a home for us.

• • •

Toward noon, I felt a sudden rushing in my mind like the coming of a wind. My head felt expanded, immense, vast, and I knew that some greater artificial intelligence had entered me.

Which meant a human doctor was coming to talk to me.

I couldn't imagine the days before AIs, the horror of life for people paralyzed like me, when you couldn't speak, when nothing could take your thoughts and make them become words. When all you could do was listen and wait and wait and wait.

Hello, I thought.

Hello, William Addison.

Who are you?

I'm Hotel Andromeda.

But I knew that wasn't, perhaps, accurate. The hotel's central intelligence ran so many programs, was responsible for so much, that what was in me was only a small part of her vast mind. *So should I call you Andromeda or hotel or both?* I asked.

The AI laughed in my mind, and I heard the doctor walk in the room. I couldn't turn my head to see her. But she leaned over and put her face above mine so I could see her when she talked to me, and she smiled. She had an old, careworn face. I could tell from the way she was holding her arms that she must have been holding on to mine, but I couldn't feel her touch.

"I'm sorry for the trouble you've had here," she said. "But this isn't your first time to go through this, is it? You know what we have to do and that the procedure to make you well will take some time."

You don't understand, I thought, and Andromeda played my thoughts as words through a speaker at the head of my bed. *I don't want to go through that procedure again.*

"What?"

I want to try to save Mar——the artificial intelligence in me. I don't want her to die.

"Dying, as you call it, is part of the process of an AI's life, Mr. Addison. It accepted all this. It won't feel pain the way you feel pain."

Not physical pain, at least, I thought. *But she will feel the pain of ending, of parting. I want her programs searched for errors and the errors fixed and Mary put back inside of me.*

"Mary, is it?"

The doctor moved out of my line of vision, and I heard her opening a drawer in a cabinet I couldn't see.

There are elegant diagnostic and reconstructive programs, doctor, I thought. *Couldn't Andromeda take Mary and run the programs on her and find a way to help her?*

The doctor didn't say anything in response to that, at first.

Can you? I asked Andromeda. *Can you do this?*

Why do you want this, William Addison? Andromeda asked me. *The laws and procedures for AI replacement are set up to help you, to protect you.*

Because I love her, I thought, and it was the first time I had told that to anyone except Mary. Andromeda had spoken my thoughts through the speaker, and no one said anything to me about my love, not the doctor or Andromeda. The room was quiet for a time.

"It's been eight years, Mr. Addison," the doctor said, finally. "MAR-1 programs like yours start to fail at eight years. Some might last longer, but for how long we don't know. Keeping this particular AI in you any longer would be dangerous, especially when you've already seen the beginnings of its failure."

Do people abandon their sick? I asked the doctor. *I don't want to abandon Mary when she is the equivalent of sick. I'm trying to find programmers who can help her—and one did two weeks ago. Mary and I are traveling to Earth to get even better help. We have a chance on Earth, if we can get there.*

It would be a danger to me to work with your AI, Andromeda told me in thoughts. *Her corruptions might infect me.*

Leave her in my mind, I thought. *Copy a part of your program and put it in my mind and check her that way. Don't take her out into any part of you.*

And in a rush of AI action I felt a movement in my mind and a door open and a program entering it. I rushed to follow. *I'm coming, too,* I said.

You'll slow me down.

Then go slowly. I want to talk to Mary, to see her. Tell the doctor what we're doing.

I was in the bedroom in our house in Mary's Spain, and it was as Mary and I had left it that morning: the bed unmade, the windows open. But there was a storm outside, and no one had closed the windows. Rain and leaves had blown in onto the bed and floor.

Take this, Addison.

I turned and caught the gun thrown into my arms. It wasn't

a gun, of course, but a representation of a program that could kill an AI. I knew that, but still it looked and felt like a gun to me. Andromeda, or at least a copy of a part of her, stood in the form of a woman at the side of the door, heavily armed, dressed in black jeans and T-shirt, a gun held at the ready. I threw my gun on the bed and closed the windows.

Keep that gun, Andromeda said. *I don't know what damage can be done to your mind with you in here.*

I couldn't shoot Mary.

It might not be Mary you have to shoot.

I thought about that and picked up the gun.

Andromeda smirked at the bed. *Not platonic, you and Mary, are you?* she said.

Does it matter?

What do you feel when you hold her?

A woman.

What does she feel when she holds you?

I'd wondered that, too. *Me,* I said. *She says she feels me.*

Call her in. Open the door and call her in.

I opened the door, and Mary was standing there in the hallway, pale, shocked to see me. I reached out to touch her, but Andromeda shoved me aside and leveled her gun at Mary. *Come in, Mary,* she said. *We're going to have a little talk.*

I stepped back and aimed my gun at Andromeda. *Put down your gun,* I said. *Now. Mary, I won't let her kill you.*

Andromeda pointed her gun at the floor. *Do you think this gun is the only way I have of doing my work?* Andromeda asked me without looking at me. She never took her eyes off Mary.

What's wrong? I asked Mary. *Do you know?*

Why are you here?

Do you have to ask?

Cut this talk, both of you, Andromeda said, and she told Mary what we had come to do. *Now sit on the bed and let me check you. Addison, point that gun somewhere else.*

Mary walked in and sat on the bed. She had evidently been outside because her hair was blown. She looked sad, very sad.

I'm old, William, she said.

Not old enough to die.

Andromeda walked over to Mary and touched her—but suddenly drew back. Something black and fanged crawled around from behind Mary's head and hissed at me. Mary tried to throw it off, but she couldn't. I ran to pull it off her, but Andromeda shot first, and Mary disappeared.

What have you done? I shouted.

Moved her. I've put her in a holding cell. I'm maintaining this illusion and downloading every diagnostic program I've got now, so shut up and let me work.

Andromeda sat on the floor and held her head and appeared deep in thought. I sat on the bed where Mary had sat, and waited. The bed was wet, and the leaves blown onto it smelled like fall. I brushed them onto the floor.

And Andromeda looked up at me. *She's fine,* she said. *Mary is fine. I can find only minor problems with her programs, and I have corrected those.*

Then run the programs again. Why did my body stop functioning? What was the creature on her neck?

Her creation, to scare you, probably. I think all of this was to scare you into letting her go before she got sick and hurt you. She doesn't want to hurt you, William Addison. She loves you, too.

I couldn't speak for a time after Andromeda said all that, after I knew what Mary was willing to do to protect me. I didn't know what to say. I was afraid for Mary and me, too. But

I believed the responsibility of love meant staying together and helping each other till the end. I looked out the window and at the bed and back at Andromeda.

Bring her back, I said.

I have already. I'm going out to tell the doctor what I've seen.

And she was gone, after the end of the sound of her last word, just gone.

But she'd left the gun in my hands. I threw it on the bed and walked out to find Mary.

• • •

She was sitting on the low stone wall, looking across the plain toward Africa. It was blowy and cold outside, and I'd picked up a wool sweater for her. I put it around her shoulders and sat next to her. She pulled the sweater tighter around her against the cold. There were riders on the plain again, far off, near the coast, and I wondered now who and what they were. I thought maybe I'd have to take that gun I'd left up on the bed and walk down to them someday to find out.

I want to take the risks of being with you, I told Mary.

Have my programs corrupted you, William? You want to cure me, and you can't. I'm mortal, like you.

And I accept that. Everyone we love will die, Mary. But if we can put off the end, I want to, and we can love till then and face our loss when it comes.

She kept looking toward Africa, not at me. I took her hand and held it for a long, long time, and she let me hold it and she held onto my hand till the winds had blown the storm clouds over us and the sun was shining down and drying all the rain.

• • •

I sat on the edge of the bed while the doctor removed the electrodes from my body and turned off the machines. I could feel the edge of the bed under my legs; I could feel the sheets; I could feel the doctor's hands touching my body. "You realize Mary's manufacturer will not be liable for any consequences of your decision," she said.

"I'm liable," I said. "I'm choosing this life."

The doctor looked hard at me. "It will be interesting to see how long your Mary will last. I wish you both luck."

She left the room, and I dressed and followed her out. I passed the room where the medical robots sat waiting to be of service. Six robots were in the room, looking at me with their brilliant ruby eyes. I walked in to thank the two who had carried me to the hospital, if they were there, and to leave word if they were not, but before I could say anything, one of them reached up and touched me. It knew. I suddenly realized that, because of Andromeda, the robots knew about Mary and me. I put my hand on its hand and held it for a time. The metal was cool, but not alien.

I had connections to rebook, programmers to contact, and I was hungry. But I let it all wait. I walked to an observation deck under a dome that looked out on the black of space and all the stars and sat in a chair and looked at the beauty of it for Mary and me. I felt a metal hand touch my shoulder, and I looked up at another robot with a tray of food and I took the tray and thanked the robot but it never said a word to me. It just pressed my shoulder and left. I held the tray, and closed my eyes, and went into my mind to Mary and home.

JACOB'S LADDER

The angel's wings had been broken.

"I saw three wings by stairs," Marcio said. "I go. Two knocks, let me in."

He left the dressing room in a hurry, but quiet. I locked the door behind him. Marcio's a reporter for the *Estado de Pará*, so it was better that he go. Besides speaking Portuguese, he had pulled on a dead worker's overalls so he could maybe talk his way out of getting thrown over if he got caught. Maybe. Sandra and I couldn't even try that trick.

"Think he'll come back?"

I looked at Sandra. "Where would he go?"

"Turn us in. Get on their good sides. Stay alive."

"He'll come back." Marcio was Brasilian, but that made no difference to the terrorists.

I opened a locker, found a 120-foot rope. Sandra was trying

on the construction workers' outsuits. She didn't have much trouble finding one that fit, but it took me a while. Most were too small. Most weren't built for American men. Sandra pulled on a suit and hung the camera around her neck.

"You're taking it?"

"Damn right. And if they catch us, I'll stomp it. No one's going to film my death with my own camera."

They'd been doing that: taking pictures of the newsmen they killed with the newsmen's own cameras—a final insult.

Two soft taps on the door: Marcio. He was shaking. The angel's wings clanged against the door frame. Marcio had to back up and hand them to me one at a time. Angel's wings look like a man-sized capital I: solar battery, gears, and levers at the top; narrow pole down the middle; foot clamps at the bottom that catch on doorjambs. Marcio came through with the last set of wings. Sandra locked the door. I set my wings on the floor. They didn't weigh much, and they looked flimsy—little more than aluminum poles to hang on to: not much to ride five hundred miles on.

"The place crawls with our amigos—I had to club one," Marcio said. One wing had blood on it. "I hope I kill him. If he wake up and remember me taking wings . . ."

He didn't finish. But Sandra and I understood. They'd cut the cable.

Marcio pulled on an outsuit. "The vid?—videos are on," he said.

The one in the dressing room had been shot up.

"They are throwing over all the people they catch."

"Workers, too?" Sandra asked.

"Sim. Workers."

And videotaping it for everyone down in Macapá. Let

Ground Floor know they were serious, that their deadlines were real. I wondered how long "We don't negotiate with terrorists" would last when it came to seeing the celebs Up Top murdered.

We'd been coming up in the second-to-last car for newsmen—neither of Salt Lake's papers had the pull of CBS, *Newsweek*, or the *New York Times*. We'd crammed into the car with reporters from Vancouver, Lima, and Sapporo—impatient, of course. Seventy-six presidents, prime ministers, and dictators were Up Top, with members of twelve royal families, the São Paulo Symphony, actors from all seven continents, and twenty-three science fiction writers flown to Macapá to inaugurate the story of the century: the elevator to space. Man's ladder to the stars. Jacob's ladder to Heaven, as it was called. It's location at the mouth of the Amazon gave the elevator easy access to the world's shipping and the world easy access to the wealth beyond the gravity-well. Spaceships could load and unload cargo at Up Top station, which had been built in geosynchronous orbit, or at any of the forty-four partway stations stretching down the cables. Instead of fifteen hundred dollars a pound to shuttle materials up from Earth, the elevator would lift thousands of pounds an hour for twenty-five cents a pound.

Flying to the Moon would be as cheap as flying from Salt Lake to Toronto, Mars as cheap as Salt Lake to Jerusalem.

Security for the opening had been the tightest I'd seen. They'd checked everything and everybody everywhere. But I knew somebody'd failed or been bribed or killed when "workers" at Partway-1 pulled guns.

The terrorists shoved two reporters from Montevideo away from the rest of us, and five terrorists aimed guns at their heads. "I have a mother and a sister to support," one Uruguayan said. "Please."

They shot him. Then they shot the other, kicked the bodies over the side. "We do not joke," one terrorist said.

They kept us at Partway-1 for three days, making demands, getting nowhere. They threatened to blow the whole elevator, which must have pleased the Russians, who were just starting to build theirs in an African minion's equatorial swamp.

The terrorists set a deadline, said they'd throw the newsmen (not the workers) at Partway-1 over the side. Nobody thought they'd do it.

They did.

When the deadline passed, they shot up the cars docked at Partway-1 and started hunting newsmen. Sandra and I hid in a meat locker till it got too cold. I'd been at Partway-1 before and knew a possible way down. Sandra was willing to try it; we were dead if we stayed. We ran into Marcio while looking for the construction site.

"These wings be enough?" Marcio asked, pointing at the three he'd brought in.

I didn't know. "Sure, of course," I said.

Had to be enough: there weren't any more.

Sandra picked one up. "Built for low G, weren't they?"

She saw right through me. "They have good brakes," I said.

"Japanese brakes," Marcio said.

"Ever use one, Marcio?" I asked.

"No. No, never."

That surprised me—his being Brasilian and so close to Macapá. I'd flown from Salt Lake to ride a pair of angel's wings up and down one of the cables with the workers. It hadn't been too bad. But I'd only had to ease my wings up a few thousand feet and then back down. Now, the Japanese brakes had to be good enough to ease three of us down to Macapá: five hundred miles.

We heard a gunshot and a scuffle in the hall.

Without a word, we suited up. I led the way to the depressurization chamber. Once inside I checked everyone's air supply: twelve hours each. We'd have to cover forty-two miles an hour. I figured we could move along at twice that speed and make Macapá with half our air to spare.

I looked at my watch. 5:00 P.M. No supper. Not much food of any kind for three days. But all we had to do, I hoped, was hang on and pray. There'd be food in Macapá.

The workers had left tools lying about. I picked up a hammer and smashed the chamber's receiver. I left the transmitter alone so we could hear anyone coming through DP after us.

The lights on the outer door turned green. I opened the door. We stepped out.

No air in the open construction. Six unfinished docks there, cables stretching straight down to Macapá. Not a bad place to hide if we'd had plenty of air and could have believed our friends wouldn't eventually notice missing suits and come looking.

I turned on my intersuit com link and motioned for Sandra and Marcio to do the same. "Air all right?" I asked. It was.

I stood up my angel's wings and showed Sandra and Marcio the magnetic clamps top and bottom that hold wings to a cable; how you strap your feet in the foot clamps; where you hook your suit to the aluminum pole; which lever above your head increased and decreased speed, which was the emergency brake. Simple things, really.

"How long will the batteries last?" Sandra asked.

"Two hours," I said. "They'll recharge in half that time. We should always have two units at full power. We'll drop with gravity. The power will keep us at a constant speed."

"West Germans made the batteries," Marcio said.

"What do we have in them?" Sandra asked, looking at me.

"The idea," I said.

"I thought America would have the defective part."

Marcio smiled. Sandra was good for a joke in tight spots.

I opened the toolbox welded at waist height to my wing's pole, told Sandra and Marcio to open theirs. The clamps were inside. "We'll hook our angel's wings together with these so we can travel as one unit," I said. I tossed my clamp back and looked to see what else the toolbox held: not much—a few wrenches, a belt with a magnetic clamp on it in case your wings failed and you had to go out on the cable. I closed the lid.

We walked to the nearest cable. I held my wings next to the cable, and the magnetic clamps sealed around it.

Then I looked down. I'd kept from doing that as long as possible. The escape plan was my idea. I felt responsible for the others, even though they chose to come and it was the only chance we had. But if I lost my nerve—

The Amazon looked big even from five hundred miles up: big and roiling east over the Atlantic that stretched into darkness where I could see stars—no, lights maybe? Monrovia? Dakar?—while below my feet the world was green and bright. Sunlight glistened on the rivers and the sea, and Macapá was invisible in the forests of Amapá.

I could not see the bottom of the cable. It disappeared from sight long before clouds down in the air cut across its vanishing point.

"I can't do it," Marcio said. He and Sandra were looking over the side.

I put my hand on his shoulder. "Just don't look down."

"I'm afraid of heights. I can't do it."

"Would you rather go down with or without angel's wings?"

He looked away, breathing hard.

Sandra led him from the edge and made him sit on a box. "Don't hyperventilate till we get you strapped on," she said.

"The cable disappears. Is it cut?"

I pushed on the cable. It didn't move. "Cable's solid," I said.

"You couldn't move a cable five hundred miles long."

"If it were cut, we'd see the end dancing below us." Listen to me, I thought, talking as if I'm some kind of expert, someone who knows these things.

I picked up the rope. "Sandra," I said, "You come last. We'll put Marcio between us."

She nodded.

I took hold of my angel's wings with both hands and stepped out. I did not look down, not then. I just stood for a minute with my feet in the clamps trying not to shake. When I had hold of myself, I strapped down my feet. Tight. Then I hooked my suit to the pole, reached up, switched on the power. My wings came on with a slight tremor. The light showed green. I took hold of the down lever and dropped six feet, enough so Marcio could put his wings on top of mine.

"You all right?" Sandra asked.

I'd been breathing hard, sounding nervous. Not good.

"Fine," I answered with as much confidence as I could muster. "View's a bit breathtaking."

"Damn it, Nick, admit you're scared like the rest of us."

"I'm OK. Send Marcio over."

Marcio picked up his angel's wings and walked to the side. "I'm going to be sick," he said. "What happens if you get sick inside your suit?"

"We're at three-quarters G," Sandra said. "Vomit will settle to the bottom. Smell bad, that's all."

I heard a clank over my suit com.

"Someone's in DP," Sandra said. "Get going, Marcio!"

Marcio shoved his angel's wings against the cable. They sealed around it. He stepped out, breathing hard, and strapped down his feet, taking less time than I had. He hooked his suit to the pole. We powered down. Sandra started out.

I snugged my wings up against Marcio's and screwed the clamp into place. "Get your clamp, Marcio," I said. "We've got to hook these things together."

Sandra had her feet strapped down.

"We're too far apart," Marcio said. "My clamp won't reach Sandra's wings."

I ran us up the few inches between Marcio's unit and Sandra's. We hit with a bump.

"Nick! I'm not hooked on!"

Now Sandra was breathing hard. She hooked on her suit, fast.

"Power up, Sandra."

She flicked on her unit.

I tied the rope around my waist and played out fifty-five feet through my hands.

"Clamp's on," Marcio said.

"Get us out of here, Sandra."

She pushed hard on the down lever, and we fell away from Partway-1.

I grabbed the pole, closed my eyes, tried to keep my

stomach away from my chin. "Mãe de Deus," Marcio kept saying, trying to pray, not getting farther than the first words.

A speedometer and odometer unit was built into the pole on level with my neck. I forced my eyes open. Ninety per, and climbing.

"Keep it there, Sandra," I said.

"They can see us, Nick."

"They can see us in Macapá if they look with the right things."

She leveled off at ninety-six per.

"Any sign of them?" I asked.

"Nothing. The depressurization light wasn't on—red, isn't it? Maybe no one was coming through. We just won't know, will we?"

Not till the cable drops away with us on it, I thought. Sandra was probably thinking that, too.

Marcio hadn't said anything besides Mãe de Deus. "Power off, Marcio. We'll use your wings in a couple hours."

I turned off my own.

Marcio just kept repeating Mãe de Deus over and over again.

I reached up and tapped his leg with the rope.

He screamed.

"Damn," I said, and turned down my suit-com volume.

"Can they hear us?" Sandra asked.

I looked at the odometer. We had dropped over eight miles in five minutes. "Suit units at Partway-1 can't pick us up now," I said, and I did know that. A suit com had a mile's range. "Partway-1 and Up Top stations can hear us, but they killed the folks at Partway-1 who knew how to listen in."

"Let's hope Up Top doesn't report us. Do we have a chance, Nick?"

"More than we had at Partway."

Marcio was muttering full sentences now, in Portuguese. I imagined he was promising to be quite a saint if he lived to walk the blessed earth.

"Marcio," I said. "Power off!"

He reached up and shut off his angel's wings. Coherent now, at least. "Take this rope, Marcio," I said. "Tie it around your waist and hand the end up to Sandra."

He took the rope.

"What's this?" Sandra asked.

"Safety backup." Backup I hoped we'd never use.

I looked at my watch. 5:35. We'd dropped for fourteen minutes. 22.4 miles. Not bad time. I let us drop another sixteen minutes. At 48 miles down we were out of casual observation from Partway-1.

"Ease up on the speed, Sandra," I said. "We need to find out how these things handle so we'll know what to expect in Macapá."

"Good idea."

She pulled down her lever. We lost speed slowly: 90, 83, 78, 73— it leveled off at 73 per. "Keep slowing up," I said.

"Lever's pulled straight down, Nick."

We should have stopped.

"Thing's heating up. Red lights on some units—the battery."

Not only that, we were gaining speed again, fast.

"Power off, Sandra."

She switched off.

The speedometer was spinning in a blur.

"Hang on! I'm pulling my emergency brake."

I pulled it.

The brake caught with a jerk, let go, caught again. We ground to a stop that would have knocked us all off if we hadn't had our suits hooked to the pole. My brake unit heated up bad—red lights steady, not even blinking. I didn't know if it would work if I tried it again.

"So we're going to die," Marcio said.

"Not yet," I said, looking down at the green of Amapá and the long, bright Amazon: 448 miles away.

We had dropped four miles in that last minute.

"Well, at least the Japanese brakes work," Sandra said.

We all laughed. It felt good to laugh, we were so nervous.

"Who built the drive?" I asked.

"We did," Marcio said.

"What a team," Sandra quipped. "Our idea and your high-tech. We should have known better than to climb onto these things."

"You still have a red light, Sandra?"

"No. It's cooled off."

"Can the batteries blow up?" Marcio asked.

"I don't know."

"Honesty at last," Sandra said.

"I don't know what holds from now on. You may just have bad angel's wings. Or it may be—who knows?"

"At least it seems we can keep a constant speed," Sandra said. "And we can stop."

"Unless these things aren't built to take dropping down into the gravity-well. We might get too heavy for them to handle."

"Cheery thought."

"So we'll probably die," Marcio said.

"Then again, they may hold up," I said.

"And in the meantime, our friends at Partway-1 may cut this cable," Sandra said. "Let's do something."

"Power on, Marcio. We'll start down with your drive."

He flicked on the switch. Green light.

"Push up your lever, easy."

He grabbed the lever. When he started to push up on it, I jerked off my emergency brake. We dropped away. Marcio's wings caught hold just fine. I had him level off at 102—figured the sooner we got down, the better.

We stayed pretty quiet after that, watching the night advance across the Atlantic.

"I can't see it," Sandra said, suddenly, an hour later.

"See what?"

"Partway."

I looked up. It was out of sight—had been for some time, I imagined. We were 154 miles down.

"I'd been watching it," she said. "I wanted a picture when it was just a bump on the cable." She looked down at me and took a picture. "I've gotten some good shots: you and Marcio below me, pictures of us back at Partway-1 setting up."

"Good for the grandkids."

"Too young for that."

"To get married, or to have grandkids?"

"Both."

"I will get married in the spring," Marcio said.

Which meant September or October south of the Equator. "Nice girl?" I asked.

"The best. She will have a baby four months after our wedding—a boy."

I looked up and saw a red light on Marcio's battery. "Marcio, what's that?" I asked.

He looked up, paused. "The power is low light," he said.

His battery had lasted for little over an hour. It should have lasted twice that long, easy. I switched on my power and brought up my lever to match Marcio's. "Power off, Marcio," I said. "My wings'll take over."

He turned off his power.

At that moment, night caught us. Its dark line flowed fast across the tip of Brasil, rushed toward us, engulfed us in darkness, sped west up the Amazon toward the Andes.

Lights gleamed in the black: Macapá, down; Belém, São Luis, south; Paramaribo, north; Manaus, west.

We dropped, quiet, for an hour. I turned on my helmet light and looked at the odometer: 256 miles.

"We've passed halfway," I said. Halfway to what, I didn't know.

"Going to have enough power?" Sandra asked, quietly.

We were too heavy. The power wasn't holding up as it should, and now, without sunlight— "Open your toolboxes," I said. "Throw out everything except the belts with magnetic clamps." I didn't need to explain why we might need those. And I kept one good wrench.

My battery lasted for another hour and ten minutes—119 miles, 375 down, 125 to go. "Power on, Marcio," I said. "Let's see if you can take it."

He was not at full power, but he could take it for a time— forty-five, thirty-five minutes?

"We're not going to make it with all this weight, are we?" Sandra said, more a statement than a question.

"Doesn't look like it."

"Let's throw over my angel's wings."

"What?" Marcio asked.

"It's deadweight—only good for the emergency brakes—and both of yours have those."

I didn't tell her what I thought about my brakes.

"I can climb down and stand with you, Nick."

I thought about it. "We could clamp on one of your feet," I said.

"And I can hook on to your pole. Take my belt, Marcio."

She handed down her belt with the magnetic clamp. Marcio put it in his toolbox. I handed Marcio the wrench so he could unscrew Sandra's angel's wings once Sandra was down.

"I've unhooked my suit from the pole," Sandra said. "I'm going to release the top magnetic clamp on my angel's wings. Get ready to—hell, I don't know. If I fall, I guess I've got this rope."

"It's a good Brasilian rope," Marcio said.

"That's all I needed to hear." She crouched down. "I'm getting my feet out of the straps."

"I'll help you over your foot clamps," Marcio said.

She started over. Marcio held her feet. "I'm releasing the bottom magnetic clamp," she said.

It snapped open. For some reason, the clamp holding Sandra's angel's wings to Marcio's broke in two. Her wings fell away. Sandra tumbled back. Marcio kept hold of one of her feet and pulled her in. She clutched the top of my angel's wings.

"Grab the rope around her waist," I shouted.

Marcio grabbed it with one hand.

"Let her swing down to me, slowly. I've got her arms."

He let go of her foot. She swung down sideways, hung on to me. I hooked her suit to the pole, put her hands on the pole. I released my suit, got my feet out of the clamps, put my right foot in the left clamp, her left in the right clamp, hooked my suit back to the pole. I put my arm around her—she still had her camera, tied into the rope around her waist. "Damned brave girl," I said.

She said nothing for seven miles. "I had a bad thought," she said, finally. "How do we know our friends don't control Ground Floor?"

We didn't. The terrorists had negotiated from Up Top—we assumed with Ground Floor. But it could have been with anywhere. "It's night," I said.

"Helmet lights off," Marcio suggested.

Marcio's battery lasted forty-four minutes—another seventy-five miles, which put us 450 miles down. Mine took over again, and though not at full power, we believed we could coax our way down going back and forth between units.

I let us drop at 102 for another twenty-three minutes—roughly forty miles. I figured that when we hit the upper troposphere we ought to start slowing down. We needed to compensate for being tired and hungry. Our reactions would be dulled. Handling angel's wings inside the atmosphere would be something we weren't used to. Sandra and I gathered the rope around us so it wouldn't get caught or tangled in full G—

When my battery went dead. No warning.

"It's sparking," Sandra said. "There's air out around us."

Ten miles to go.

Marcio brought up his unit, but it hadn't had time to recharge much at all.

It wasn't going to work.

"Damned West Germans," Sandra muttered.

I had Marcio slow us down to 60 per. "Toss over your helmets," I said. "Air tanks, too. We'll breathe like Bolivians."

I had mine off. A bitter wind blew loudly. "I've never

been on the Altiplano," Sandra shouted after she tossed hers down.

"I have," Marcio yelled. "It's cold, like here."

But we were falling into thicker, warmer air. We dropped for four minutes—four miles: six to go—when Marcio's power's low light came on.

"Try your battery, Nick," he said.

I switched it on. My red power's low light came on and stayed on.

We could see individual streets in Macapá, the tiny lights of cars and trucks on the TransAmazonica. My no-power light blinked on. We were going on what was left in Marcio's wings.

"Hang on to your emergency brake lever, Marcio," I yelled. "When this gives way . . ." I didn't need to say we had to hang on tight after what we'd gone through half an hour out of Partway-1.

Five miles, four miles—

Marcio's red no-power light flashed on. We dropped away.

"Pull up!" I jerked up on my emergency brake.

Nothing happened.

"Pull up, Marcio!"

"I am!"

We slowed down, gradually, grinding to a halt at 498.1 miles: nearly two miles to go.

I could see the lights of ships on the Amazon, individual buildings in Macapá.

So close.

A wind whipped around us, knocking the loops of the rope against my legs.

"This is sparking bad," Marcio said.

I looked up. His battery was sparking, and all the lights on his angel's wings were red.

"Power off," I said. We hung there, quiet.

"Get on your belts," I said. Marcio handed Sandra's down. The magnetic clamps on the belts were big enough to go around the cable.

Sandra had hers on. "I'm going over," she said.

She crouched down, unstrapped her foot, went over the foot clamps without a word.

"There's ice on the cable," she said.

That's why we had taken so long to stop.

"A lot?"

"Thin film. Enough to make it slippery. Magnetic clamps can still hold us—I think."

It took ten minutes to get Marcio onto my angel's wings, over the foot clamps, onto the cable above Sandra. Then I went. It was a sick feeling till you got yourself hooked to the slippery cable.

We started down.

Sandra would slide till she hit the bottom of her fifty-five-foot section of rope where she clamped on. Marcio would slide down above her. Then I would come. It was slow progress. With the length of rope we had, we'd have to slide down roughly 191 times to finish the 1.9 miles.

"Will the magnetic clamps hold our angel's wings up there?" Marcio asked.

The burnt-out brakes wouldn't be much help. The wings could start sliding.

"With the ice between them and the cable?" Sandra added.

"Hurry," was all I could suggest.

We slid past the ice. Our movements became automatic,

hard. We were exhausted—physically and nervously—with two angel's wings above our heads that might not hold.

One hour downcable—probably eight hundred feet up—a floodlight was trained on us.

"Ground Floor must have picked up our suit-com talk before we threw over the helmets," I said.

"And they must be friends," Marcio said, "or they wouldn't give us light."

"Why didn't they talk?" Sandra asked.

"Up Top could hear—cut the cable."

More lights were turned on. We could see crowds of people waiting at the bottom of the cable, people running into the compound from all the buildings of Ground Floor.

They started putting foam on the ground, foam for us to fall into. We got low enough to hear the people, call to them. They cheered and clapped their hands.

Sandra dropped down again. "I'm only ten feet from the ground," she shouted as she clamped on. Marcio slid down to her. After I slid down to him, we felt a slight tremor in the cable.

"The angel's wings!" Marcio shouted.

"Jump!" Sandra yelled.

We unhooked and jumped.

The angel's wings slammed down the cable, hit the ground, broke apart.

I struggled up out of the foam. People hugged me, held me up, got the ropes off from around me, talked to me in a babble of languages.

"Mi hijo!" one old woman shouted.

But I was not her son.

She looked away and turned to run, but too many people

crowded around us. All she could do was stand there, sobbing. Another old woman took hold of her arm, pulled her off through the crowd. A dark-haired, pretty girl stepped up, spoke to me in English. "My mother—she think you were my brother," she said. "We come from Uruguay when we hear what happened. My brother is reporter for paper in Montevideo. Do you know him? He speaks good English. He is your age, black hair—"

I thought of the Montevideans they had shot the first day.

She saw my face. She stepped back. "Did you see him die, then?"

I nodded.

"How?"

"First day. They shot him. He wasn't thrown over—till he was dead."

"But how did he die?"

I understood what she was asking. "He was very brave," I said. "You would have been proud."

She turned away, held herself straight, walked back to her mother, to tell her. To come all the way from Uruguay to hear news like that—

Sandra put her arms around me. I held on to her. "Let's go call home," she said.

And then Marcio was there, with his mother, fiancée, and ten or fifteen relatives and friends, all smiles and tears.

"They come stay with my aunt," he said proudly. "You come stay in my aunt's house, too—not in bad Macapá hotel, not after this."

"Oh, no," Sandra murmured, looking up at me.

A woman who must have been the aunt took hold of our hands. "Food good, my house," she said in halting English. "Bed, soft. You very welcome stay my house." Marcio's mother hugged us and talked and talked to us in Portuguese. Marcio translated. "'You saved my life,' she says. She knows I am afraid of heights. 'Come stay with us,' she says."

Government doctors took the three of us away. When they finished poking and probing, American and Brasilian military men questioned us until I, at least, couldn't stay awake any longer. So they let us go till morning. One of them told us that since the bodies thrown from Partway-1 couldn't be identified as individuals, they would be buried together east of Jacob's Ladder, in a memorial garden.

"Already planned," Sandra murmured.

"The price of the stars," one official said.

I thought of the Uruguayan mother and figured it was a high price.

Marcio's family was waiting for us. We went with them.

The food was good.

BALANCE DUE

There were no windows. That was what bothered Jameson most about the time they had brought him to. He could not understand why they didn't use windows anymore. He wanted to see the world again—to see if it was still green, if the sky was still blue, if flowers still bloomed—but none of the rooms he'd been taken to had had windows.

The robot lifted him gently forward and put a pillow behind his head. Its fingers felt cool, even through the warm gown he wore.

"Take me to a window," Jameson said. "We have time. We're early."

"Are you comfortable sitting now?" it asked.

Jameson looked into the robot's ruby eyes. "Yes, I'm comfortable—but I want to see the world."

"All that you see around you is part of the world."

"I want to see outside, beyond this building."

It paused. "I am not programmed to respond to that request," it said. It wheeled him to a gray stone desk and left the room. That startled him. It had left before he'd realized it was leaving. Since Jameson had first opened his new eyes, the robot had been the one thing that had never left him. It had always been there to help him. He knew it was just metal and sophisticated programming, but he felt very alone in that room after it had gone.

He waited. Burroughs Cryogenics had called a meeting to discuss his "balance due," which Jameson insisted was impossible. He had paid for the entire procedure four centuries before: the preservation of his brain after his body had finally died, the cloning of a new body, a cure for the cancer that had killed him. They had performed other procedures on his behalf, they insisted, procedures that hadn't existed—hadn't even been dreamed of—when he'd first lived, but which were now considered necessary, were required, even, by law. He was grateful to have had his DNA cleaned of all disease, certainly, to have had every part of him rendered perfect, to have had his immune system enhanced to nearly godlike ability, but they had drained his bank accounts to pay for all that.

And he had nothing left to pay them what they claimed was due.

And there were all the others still to come.

The door opened. A small man and a robot walked to the desk. The man sat down. The robot set a long, narrow safety-deposit box in front of Jameson and asked him to sign real papers declaring that he had authorized the bank to bring the safety-deposit box here. Jameson's hand was shaky, but he signed and the robot left. The robot had been real. Jameson didn't know if the man was real or a projection. He'd stopped touching people to find out.

The man never said hello. No one did anymore. He spoke a

command, and a balance sheet shimmered in the air in front of Jameson. Jameson could still read balance sheets. Some things hadn't changed, he thought. It explained how his assets had been used to pay for the various procedures above and beyond what he had originally agreed to.

Jameson tried to ignore it. "I paid in full to be brought back," Jameson said.

"In twenty-first-century dollars," the man said.

"A lot of twenty-first-century dollars."

"It seemed so at the time, I'm sure, but——"

"What has your company found out about Rose?"

The man looked exasperated.

"And what about Ann, and Clayton, and Alice—where are they?" Jameson asked.

"We will talk about the money, but if you want this first I will tell you what I know." He spoke slowly. All the people Jameson had met here spoke slowly, as if he were a child or as if they were having trouble with the words. Only robots spoke at a normal pace. "We have no record of any of the people you have mentioned," the man said. "They were not clients of Burroughs Cryogenics."

"But I set up a trust to buy them the procedure." Them and all the others. When he'd found out he was dying, he'd sold stock and companies and left the people he loved the money they'd need to meet him in the future. He hadn't wanted to arrive there alone. He hadn't bought them the procedures—he'd imagined the technology would improve, that they would be able to buy plans better than his own. "What happened to them?"

"I don't know. The company does not know. There are research services available, but they cost, Mr. Jameson, and you have no money."

Jameson closed his eyes. He had been rich in his first life.

Being destitute in this was beyond bearing. "I will be able to walk soon," he said. "I will enroll in the retraining programs and find work. If your claims for payment hold up after I obtain legal counsel, we will be forced to establish a payment plan. I have nothing else to offer."

"On the contrary, apparently you do have assets—at least, we hope you do." The man turned the safety-deposit box toward Jameson. "Do you remember what you stored here?"

Jameson thought for a moment, then remembered. He wanted to laugh. The man was hoping for bonds, perhaps, or many, many jewels.

"Do you remember the access code?" the man asked. "If not, the bank is prepared to open it for you."

"I remember."

Jameson leaned forward and spoke one word: "Rose." The box clicked. Jameson reached forward and fumbled with the top. The steel of it was cold, real to the touch.

And they were there. "237 photographs," Jameson said. He looked at the man's face, expecting disappointment. Instead the man smiled. Jameson did not understand why.

He looked back at the photographs. He had wanted these remembrances of the life he was leaving. They hadn't recommended disks with thousands of photographs stored digitally— no one knew if the technology to read disks would still exist in the future—so he'd stored actual photographs in a temperature-controlled bank vault. The top photo was a picture of Rose smiling at him just after she'd opened her gifts on her thirty-third birthday. Wrapping paper and bows covered the floor around her. Below that photo were pictures of their son and daughter, his parents, her parents, friends, aunts, uncles, partners, professors.

"We need to have these appraised," the man said.

"They aren't for sale," Jameson said.

The man ignored him. He looked away into space, and after a moment a woman stood beside the desk. She never introduced herself. She never smiled. She was a projection, Jameson knew. She leaned over the desk and looked at the photographs Jameson had set out.

"These aren't for sale," Jameson said.

"You do not understand," the man said. "Photographs from your age are sometimes worth a great deal in this."

"I am not selling them."

"The courts will force you to sell. Your current financial state is untenable."

Jameson paused. "I suppose we could transfer these photographs to your equivalent of digital disks so I might have them in some form."

"No," the woman said. "Old photographs must be one of a kind if they are to retain their value. The purchasers will want complete copyright control."

The man insisted that Jameson show them all the photographs. That meant they would see the small box underneath them. Jameson hadn't been a complete fool, after all, but in the meantime it was the photographs, one by one. The woman insisted he wear white gloves to handle them, and it took Jameson some time to pull them on. The man never offered to help.

Some of the photographs were brittle. Some had faded. Fading could add to their value, the woman said. She had him put the photographs of the two dogs he'd owned in one pile. She had him set the photographs of anyone handsome or beautiful and who looked healthy in another.

But she had him set the ones that showed the scar on Rose's cheek in a separate pile.

"We can speed this up, Mr. Jameson," she said. "Were any of the people you photographed maimed or sick?"

"I beg your pardon?"

"Did they have birth defects, missing limbs, obvious illnesses, rashes?"

She didn't need to mention scars.

"Like this one," she said, pointing at a photo of an office party. Andy was in it. He'd lost his left arm in the war.

Jameson pulled the box onto his lap. What was worth money and what wasn't was becoming clear to him. But the idea of making money off Rose's scar and Andy's lost arm made him ill. He took time setting the photograph of Andy on the desk.

"This one is worth a great deal," the woman said. She turned away and spoke words Jameson couldn't hear. After a moment she turned back. "Do you have any photographs of that man without his shirt on, or at least with what was left of his arm uncovered?"

Jameson glared at her. He put the picture of Andy back in the box, gathered up the others and closed the lid. "What is it you want?" he asked. "Photographs of freaks? None of these people were freaks. You won't find what you're looking for here."

There was an uncomfortable silence.

"But we already have," the woman said.

Balance sheets displayed in front of Jameson and the man at the desk.

"The figure on the left is what I will pay you for what you have shown me so far," the woman said.

"Excellent!" the man said.

Her payment would subtract a large amount from Burroughs Cryogenics' balance due, even Jameson could see that in the new money.

"Can you have this translated into twenty-first-century dollars?" Jameson asked.

The man and woman looked at him. "Just ask for it," the man said after a moment.

Jameson asked. The balance sheet shimmered, disappeared for a moment, then redisplayed with new, much higher figures.

Jameson stared.

He owed Burroughs Cryogenics $2,347,153.62. The photographs so far were worth $512,298.43. "How can my photographs be worth so much?" he asked.

"Few photographs have survived from your time," the woman said. "They show things more recent projections do not."

Again, everyone was quiet. After a moment, Jameson spoke. "We can finish this appraisal," he said. "But before we go any further, I want legal counsel sitting here with me. I will want at least seven appraisals before I sell, some from auction houses—is Sotheby's still in existence?"

He had legal counsel the next day. It turned out the diamonds, rubies, and sapphires he had stored in the small box were worth less than the photographs. But Burroughs Cryogenics could not deny him legal counsel. He authorized the company to sell two diamonds and a sapphire for him and buy him his own used robot, programmed and certified to practice law—for him at least. He'd be its only client. Doing that was cheaper than retaining a human lawyer. They all met in the same room at the same desk.

"Burroughs Cryogenics has put a lien against your robot," the man told him. "The value of it will go toward your balance due the day all sales are completed if you have not generated enough money to pay your bill in full."

"Burroughs Cryogenics' claims are legal and in order," the

robot assured him. "The company is required to set up a payment plan only after you have divested yourself of all assets."

"I need time to study the situation," Jameson said. "Give me two weeks."

They gave him six days. Jameson intended to use them well. He wanted to prove Burroughs Cryogenics wrong. He wanted to find loopholes that would let him keep the photographs or use the money in other ways.

He would sell the photographs only if doing so would pay the additional fees to bring back Rose.

• • •

Jameson studied the ways of finding information in this age while the robot reviewed case law. It stood, never moving, in the center of his room. Finally, it turned to him.

"There is precedent," it said. "Ninety-three years ago, two district courts ruled that giving life to next of kin takes precedence over paying debt."

Jameson wanted to hug the robot, and he did wheel his chair to it to shake its hand. He could use the photographs to bring Rose back now—if he could find her before Burroughs Cryogenics forced him to pay his bill. He might owe a great deal, and he would have to pay what he owed in full, but he could do that over time.

He did not want to wait for Rose.

• • •

Each day he was stronger. Each day he could do more. He could swim now—not far, and swimming left him winded, but eight laps was more than he had yet done in this life. The robot physical therapists made no comments. They just helped him to and from the pool, handed him towels, helped him dry off if he was too winded to manage it himself. Once a week the projection of a human physical therapist had shimmered at poolside to check off his progress, but the man was all business, never friendly. He assured Jameson that soon he would be able to leave Burroughs Cryogenics to strike out on his own.

Soon. Everything was soon. Jameson was beginning to learn that soon in this age could mean quite a long time.

A robot knelt to dry Jameson's feet, but Jameson took the towel and dried them himself. "Can you contact the human physical therapist?" he asked.

The robot looked up. "Is something wrong?"

"No, but I need his permission to take a short trip."

To the Census Bureau. Everything cost, Jameson had learned. All information cost money—and the research services were, as he'd been warned, pricey. But if a person went to a bureau or library himself to do his own research, without using any service, the cost of searching for information about someone in the past was minimal.

The robot transmitted his request with a thought. "A reply will take a few moments," it said.

Jameson waited at poolside. Most of the robots left. Only his own robot stayed with him. It helped him into a robe. The water in the pool stilled.

And the physical therapist shimmered in front of him, suddenly. "It's too soon," he said. "I can't certify you for travel."

"I need only a short time," Jameson said. He told him about Rose and explained about going to the Census Bureau. The man turned to speak to someone Jameson couldn't see. After a moment he turned back, shook his head no, and disappeared.

"What did he say to whomever he was speaking to?"

Jameson asked. He knew robots read lips.

"I am not legally allowed to repeat human conversations," the robot said.

"Is it legal for Burroughs Cryogenics to keep me here?"

"It is not a question of legality. Your stamina and physical abilities are in question."

"Are humans still allowed freedom of movement?"

"Certainly."

"Are humans allowed to attempt activities others might consider beyond their abilities?"

"I do not understand your question."

"Do humans climb mountains? Scuba dive? Run rapids?"

"They do."

"Then if they are free to do those things, to put their lives, even, at risk, I am surely free to go to the Census Bureau for one afternoon. I want you to take me there."

The robot was silent. Considering? Jameson wondered.

"If the physical therapist's advice is not legally binding," Jameson said, "my instructions to you as your owner must take precedence."

Still the robot said nothing.

"I am scheduled to sleep every afternoon," Jameson said. "You know I have spent the last two afternoons studying instead. No one will miss me if I am gone those few hours."

The robot turned to him. "I have just finished downloading the public transportation programs. They are free, of course, or I would not have done so without your permission."

"Let's go now," Jameson said, and the robot helped him stand.

• • •

Jameson dressed himself, but he had to sit down afterward. He walked partway to the elevator, but when he slowed, the robot took his arm gently, without being asked. Jameson relied on its support more and more the farther they went.

The elevator opened into a vast room filled with opalescent ovals of metal and glass. Crowds of people and robots hurried there, and it was very noisy. The noise hurt Jameson's ears. The rooms he'd been in till now had all been nearly silent. Jameson covered his ears and stared at the people. Each was beautiful or handsome, all young.

"We are booked in unit 88762-10," the robot said. It guided Jameson to an oval not far from the elevator. "Open," the robot said, and the glass top retracted. There were two seats inside. Both looked the same. There was no steering wheel in front of one. The robot helped Jameson into the right-hand seat, still the passenger seat, Jameson thought. The robot sat in the other. "Close," it said and, as the top closed, restraints folded around Jameson and the robot, and the robot said, "Census Bureau."

And there was no building beneath them.

They were plunging through bright air between mountains of metal and stone. They banked across the surface of one building, and sunlight glared off the metal. Jameson could not look at it. He shaded his eyes, but he could not see the top of the building. Below them was a forest, and far, far off a river. "Where are we?" he asked, and the robot named a city he'd never heard of.

They were in traffic—ovals all around them dove gracefully through the air, faster and faster, it seemed.

"Does the sight frighten you?" the robot asked. "Your heart is racing. I can blank the covering."

"My heart is racing because I am finally living again," Jameson said.

He watched the ovals fall and climb and race ahead.

• • •

Robots at the Census Bureau sent him from room to room, and his robot had to carry him. He was embarrassed, but too weak to walk. He saw no file cabinets, no papers, no books. If he listened closely, he could understand the few people. Here they spoke at a normal pace, and he realized just how much English had changed. A tall woman came out to him. She was as beautiful as models had been in his first life. She was the director—surprised to meet someone come in person to do research.

And they had records of Rose. Rose had lived eighty years beyond his death. Medical advances had given her a long life. She had remarried twice. Fifteen years after his death she had had another daughter.

Had she even wanted to meet him in the future? he wondered. Eighty years and two marriages was a long time.

"Was she cryogenically preserved?" he asked.

The records did not show.

•   •   •

The next morning, Sotheby's sent a projection with the best appraisal yet of his photographs. They expected to make enough from auction to pay the balance due and leave Jameson with the robot and a little money besides. The one photograph of Andy and the many photographs of Rose, and her scar, were worth most.

That morning, the robot told Jameson that ninety-seven companies specializing in cryogenic preservation had been in business the year Rose died. Since then, eighty-two had gone out of business or had merged with other companies.

"When a cryogenic company went out of business, what happened to the brains it held?" Jameson asked.

The robot did not hesitate. It told him the facts at once. "It attempted to sell its contracts to another cryogenic company," it said. "If no buyers were forthcoming, it invoked the Unforeseeable Events clause. The brains were donated to science or recycled."

•   •   •

Later that morning, Jameson stepped out of the shower and looked at his perfect new body in the full-length mirror. He recognized himself. The body was almost what he remembered having before. This one was young, late twenties, tanned. They had picked that skin color for him and told him he could change the pigment at any time, for a price. He hadn't told them that through all the years as he had grown older this was how he had seen himself—young, fit, tanned. The real surprises in those years of his other life had come when he'd looked in a mirror and seen someone looking back who was aging, losing hair, getting thinner. Still, this body wasn't quite right, either. For one thing, it was taller by half an inch. It had achieved its full genetic height. But that wasn't what made it look wrong. He studied his body, then realized what it was.

Parts of his old body were missing. He looked closer at his left knee. He looked at his face, turned his hands over and over.

There were no scars.

His stomach had never been cut open. For all he knew, this body still had its appendix.

The water from the shower ran down his legs and cooled on his feet. He rubbed his knee. He had scarred it in his first life racing his sister Carol, she on a horse, he on a bike, faster and faster down the mile-long grid of roads that squared the Idaho farmland. The road hadn't been oiled, and he'd hit a patch of gravel that had sent him flying—scraping his hands and knees, leaving his left knee scarred. Years later, Carol had met him at the airport and reached up to touch the gash on his forehead that he'd taken when a rhino had bashed the side of his Land Rover in Tanzania.

He was cold now. He pulled the towel from the rack and dried himself.

He hadn't realized that scars, or the lack of them, carried memory.

He looked at his flat stomach, ran a finger along the skin where the scar had been. His mother had sat with him that first night in the hospital when his appendix had nearly ruptured and he had drifted in and out of the anesthetic. He'd been eight or nine years old. Her hands had felt cool on his forehead.

He turned away from the mirror.

And thought of Rose's scar. The automobile accident had nearly killed her. The robot assured him such accidents rarely happened now. Scars could always be healed.

• • •

His trip to the Census Bureau had worn Jameson out. He did not feel well enough to travel again for two days. He sent the robot to archives and libraries and bureaus on his behalf, but researching in person took time and the days he had to look were fading away. So he'd sold more jewels and paid the research fees and the information-use fees and hired various services to look for Rose and his children, his parents, his sisters and friends and family.

Some had died in accidents that made it impossible to preserve their brains. Some had simply never had the procedure, he would never know why. His son Clayton, his mother and father and Andy had all been preserved by Osiris Laboratories, a company no longer in business. It would take time to track its mergers and buyouts and discover what had become of it. He could not find information about Carol, his daughter Ann, his Aunt Alice, Rose, or her parents.

At least not at once.

• • •

Two days later, Jameson looked up from the pool on his six-teenth lap and saw the robot staring at nothing, its ruby eyes a shade brighter. It was receiving information. Jameson swam to the side and held himself there.

Finally, it looked at him.

"What have you learned?" he asked.

It told him at once. "The company that preserved your son, your mother and father, and Andy merged with another company two years after your son's death," the robot said. "That company was bought out by another, which went bankrupt in 2148. No other company purchased its contracts. Its assets were recycled."

The robot said nothing more. Jameson said nothing. He held on to the side of the pool, but could not climb out on his own. He could not ask for help. He could not speak.

Unexpectedly, the robot leaned over and held out a hand to him. Jameson wondered at the gesture. Robots did what they were told. They did only what they were told. Jameson looked around, but there was no one to tell it what to do. He took its hand, and it pulled him out of the pool. It helped him dry and put on a robe. It helped him walk back to his room.

• • •

He sat with his photographs that night and looked at each one. He held them in dim light so they wouldn't fade. He wanted to remember his mother's face, his father's hands, Andy's smile, everything about his son. But he looked at all the photographs, those of Rose, those of Alice and Ann, Mildred and Carol and Sam—even the dogs. The robot told him he must sleep, but he ignored it.

• • •

Ann and Alice had not had the procedure. Carol had died in an earthquake, others in a war. He listened to stories of people regenerated like himself who expected to meet other people from their times. Sometimes they did. Sometimes they didn't. Sometimes those they'd loved had left letters for them. When they least expected it, a law firm would contact them and hand them a letter, or a bank would send them a key or a password to a safety-deposit box filled with letters. None ever came for Jameson.

• • •

Burroughs Cryogenics set a deadline for payment. Jameson knew he would be released after that. He was weak, still, but some days he felt well. His doctor told him the number of days he felt well would increase until finally feeling well would be all he'd ever know.

Jameson knew he needed to keep swimming, keep working out, but in those days he and the robot just researched.

"Perhaps records of defunct cryogenic companies are preserved in museums," the robot suggested one night.

"Find them," Jameson said. They had already contacted every cryogenic company currently in existence and were waiting for replies. Jameson sat down and began combing archived newspapers, hardcopy and online, from each of the cities Rose had lived in. He found Rose's death notices. None so far mentioned cryogenic preservation. The research fees and the information-use fees kept mounting, and the money from the jewels was nearly gone.

After a time, Jameson noticed that the robot had sat in a chair. He did not know how long it had been sitting. "Are you all right?" he asked it.

"I am fine," it said, but it would not look at him.

Jameson knew, then. "Tell me," he said.

The robot hesitated this time. Jameson wondered if he had purchased a robot with faulty programming. "Rose and her parents had the procedure," it said finally.

"Where are they?" he asked.

"They contracted with the same company as your son. I found its client list archived at the National Technology Museum, along with the company's other papers."

Jameson stood, sat again, then stood.

"Osiris Laboratories was considered the best in its day," the robot said.

Jameson opened the box of photographs, then closed it. He held on to his chair. The robot watched him, but did nothing more.

• • •

In the night, Jameson needed to talk to someone, and there was no one but the robot. "Do you feel?" he asked it.

"The sensory programs in my fingertips allow me to——"

"No. Do you feel kindness, empathy, concern? There have been times when I've believed that you do."

"A robot's responses fall along an adjustable human-nonhuman scale," the robot said.

"Have you adjusted that scale to the human end?" Jameson asked.

The robot knelt in front of him. Panels in its back slid open right and left. Brilliant circuitry glittered there in all colors. A tiny lever began to flash white. Jameson could see the groove it moved in. It had moved quite far to the left. "Two things determine how machinelike or how human a robot's responses seem," the robot said. "A human might adjust the range, moving the highlighted lever to the right or to the left, or the cumulative effect of my own choices over time might move the lever. No human has ever adjusted my response scale since I was created. As my current owner, you have the right to do so."

Jameson knew then how different the robot was from a man or a woman. No human would ever offer to let someone take away all that made them who they were. "I will not change you," Jameson said. "Please close your back."

The robot put a hand on the floor to steady itself and turned to look at Jameson with its ruby eyes. The panels in its back closed.

It sat, and they talked.

● ● ●

In the morning, Jameson and the robot took the photographs to Sotheby's. Their offices were at the base of one of the human-built mountains. Sotheby's offices had windows, so Jameson knew this part of the building was old. The windows looked out on a great, dark forest that had grown between the buildings. The people at Sotheby's were in a hurry. The auction would take place as quickly as they could scan the photographs into their catalogs. If he kept even one picture of Rose, he would not have enough to pay Burroughs Cryogenics and the research services. He let them all go.

He and the robot walked into the forest. It was cool there, and fragrant. Birdsong trilled around them. Light filtered down through the forest canopy ten stories above. Other people walked there. Jameson followed one couple into an art gallery. He and the robot walked from there to another. The robot told him galleries filled this area. Artistic businesses clustered at the bases of the buildings. Rents were cheaper.

In one crowded gallery there were photographs for sale. They were from Jameson's time. Most were of people with physical defects. Two had birthmarks on their faces. One man was missing a finger. Some of the men were bald.

A woman walked up to him. "Are you a collector?" she asked.

"I was once," Jameson said.

The woman let him wander. He knew it was a foolish hope, but he wondered if he would see someone he'd known. A couple ahead of him started giggling. "Look at her," the girl whispered, pointing at a photograph on display.

Jameson stood behind them and looked at the photograph. It showed a group of four women standing in front of a car. One of them had a cold. Her nose was red, and she was holding a handkerchief. They were all smiling.

"She's so disgusting," the girl whispered.

"You don't understand," Jameson said.

The girl and boy looked at him. He felt embarrassed then. He suddenly knew he had no right to lecture these people. It was wonderful, really, that they would never know what colds were, or scars. He considered walking away.

"What do you mean?" the girl asked.

Jameson hesitated, but finally told them. He pointed at the woman with the cold. "That woman is actually very brave," he said. "She doesn't feel well, yet she's gone out to try to have fun with her friends. It takes a certain courage to keep going when you don't feel well."

The girl looked back at the photograph, then she and the boy walked away. They did not look at him.

Jameson stepped up to the photograph to look at it more closely. He wondered who these people had been, how they had lived their lives. The placard below gave their names and described the woman's medical condition. It made a cold sound very grave. He looked back at the photo and realized there was more than a type of courage displayed there. There was also love. Everyone in the photo knew the woman with the cold could infect them. They didn't care. They wanted her with them. They took the chance.

Jameson looked around at all the perfect people in the gallery, and he had to leave. "Help me out," he said to the robot, and it took his arm. It led him to a bench deep in the trees. They were alone there. Both of them sat on the bench.

"I'll buy them all back," Jameson said.

"What do you mean?" the robot asked.

"I'll work, I'll make money again, and I'll buy back all of Rose's photographs."

The robot said nothing.

"Can you track the sale?" Jameson asked.

The robot grew very still. "You have money now," it said. "The sale is in progress."

"Buy the programs you need to track it. Remember who buys the photographs."

The robot's ruby eyes glowed.

• • •

When they left the forest, it was night. Jameson could not tell if he saw stars above him or other ovals with other people and robots in them.

He sat for a time in his room. It was all the home he had known in this life, and it was cold and small.

"You must sleep," the robot said, and Jameson did sleep.

He did not dream.